CRIME & CRIMINI

A Loire Château Mystery

by Eugénie D. West

THE SAMOTHRACE PRESS

This is a work of fiction. Names, places, events, motives, persons, characters and descriptions in this book are products of the author's imagination and/or are used fictitiously. Any other interpretation is beyond the intent of the author.

This book is dedicated to the owner of the
magnificent château de Reignac in
France's Loire Valley,
Erick Charrier,
and to Françoise and Thierry, his
principal staff.
Without the fortunate inspiration brought
by my visit to their splendid property,
this book would not exist.

About the Author

The author of 'Crime & Crimini,' Eugénie D. West, was a reporter for a weekly newspaper for more than 15 years. Many of the events in her 'Reporting is Murder!'© series, of which 'Crime & Crimini' is the tenth book, are drawn from actual cases the author encountered during her time on the news beat, and from crimes that occurred in the surrounding area. The treatments given these cases in West's books are fictional, with motives, details and outcomes that are not the same as the actual ones.

While most of the series' books are set in small towns in and around Pittsfield in Western Massachusetts, 'Crime & Crimini' is one of a handful set in foreign locales where West has had the good fortune to travel, and be inspired.

In this book, set in the historic Château de Reignac in the beautiful River Loire Valley in France, West's protagonist, sleuthing journalist Gracie Barufaldi, is attending a week long Cordon Bleu intensive food and wine pairing course, something she's always dreamt of doing.

In lieu of the customary group of local characters, residents and friends who feature in the books set in Massachusetts, West provides readers with an equally intriguing ensemble cast in 'Crime & Crimini,' including culinary students from throughout Europe, an intimidating and exacting Chef, and the gracious and conscientious owners of the historic Château de Reignac where the course is held. Each character brings her or his own history, prejudices and temperament to the course and the story; this results in vibrant interactions and a lengthy list of suspects when one of the students is found dead.

West is inspired by people she has known and places she has been, but the characters in her books are fictional: amalgams of qualities, characteristics and traits from scores of acquaintances, strangers and other personalities. They are created to fit with and further the story.

West holds a Ph.D. in English and enjoys history, languages, music, science and travel. Like Gracie, she lives in a rural part of the northeastern United States, travels often and widely, and is an accomplished cook. West writes her novels under a *nom de plume* borrowed from a paternal great great great grandmother.

Visit West on her Amazon Author Page, and find her on Twitter, Facebook, Pinterest, Goodreads and on her blog, ThebooksofEugnieDWest.blogspot.com.

Important Facts About 'Crime & Crimini'

This book is inspired by and set at the stunning, historic, immaculately kept Château de Reignac in the Loire Valley in France. I had the good fortune to stay there for several days recently, choosing the property because it had once belonged to the Marquis de Lafayette. Lafayette had helped the Colonists a great deal during the American Revolution; having completed much of my genealogy, I knew that one of my ancestors had also rendered aid and supplies to Colonial troops during that same War. While I have no way of ascertaining whether or not the two Frenchmen knew each other, I like to suppose they might have. Since I was in France to visit the towns where some of my ancestors were from, the Château de Reignac seemed a good choice to use as a 'home base.'

It was perfect. The Château is centrally located in Reignac, on the River Indre in the Loire Valley, right in the middle of everything anyone might wish to see: other historic Châteaux, quaint villages, mediaeval fortresses, historic churches and museums, gorgeous scenery, and some of the best food and wine on the planet. Coupled with this, the warm and inviting welcome from Erick Charrier, owner of the Château de Reignac, as well as his staff, made me feel at home instantly.

I was also fortunate that Erick did not tire of my endless questions about his Château and its history, and I was delighted that he was so willing to show me every nook and cranny: hidden windows, concealed doorways and other intriguing features. Please allow me to say here that while the real Château de Reignac is very much as I have presented it in 'Crime & Crimini,' I have, of course, changed a few things. I expanded the professional kitchen, re-arranged some of the guest rooms, and a few of the more unusual features of the fictionalized Château are purely products of my imagination. However, the beauty and history of the place is in no way embellished!

U.S. readers will note that I use the European method for numbering floors: what we call the first floor in the U.S. is called the 'ground floor' in Europe and most of the rest of the world. What we call the second floor is therefore called the 'first floor.' I hope U.S. readers will bear this in mind as they digest my descriptions of the Château and the movements of the people within, and not find it too unwieldy.

The Associated Press (AP) style guide for punctuation is used. French readers will notice some differences, therefore, particularly with regard to the way quotations are marked. I hope this won't be too confusing.

Some readers may feel that the book contains rather a lot of detail about food and various recipes. While this may be true, if readers are not interested, they can skim over these portions and still absorb the flavor (*sic*) of the book. Readers of the rest of my 'Reporting is Murder'© series will know that recipes, cooking and discussions of food are a regular feature in all the books: like me, Gracie is a 'foodie,' although undoubtedly more skilled in the kitchen than I.

I have made my Château's fictitious owner, Claude, a descendant of Louis de Barberin, the man who re-constructed the real Château in the early eighteenth century. I did this as a testimony to the actual, current owner of the Château, Erick Charrier's, devotion to his Château and its history, even though he is not related to Louis de Barberin. When I asked permission to use the Château as a setting for one of my books, and to use one of my photographs of the property as a book cover image, Erick happily agreed. I hope he is not disappointed.

A big thanks to my proofreaders as well, and to my friend Carroll who helped me brainstorm for the final title of this book.

(Should anyone not know, 'crimini' is a type of mushroom, basically a small portobello, *agaricus bisporus*, used widely in various kinds of cooking. It's also known as the brown or chestnut mushroom.)

Anyone inspired to visit the Château de Reignac after reading this book is encouraged to do so. I am certain that the beauty and history of the property and the surrounding area will delight you, and the warmth of the people will cheer you.

~EDW

Also in the
'Reporting is Murder!'© Series
by Eugénie D. West:
Baby's Breath
Coercion
Black Card
Where There's Smoke, There's Murder
Spin
Tide's Reach
Natural Causes
Precipice
Counter Measures
coming later in 2016:
Apple of My Eye, Nearly Departed
§
And as
Deborah L. Courville
(historical fact-based fiction):
A River In Time
Treachery in Time
A Christmas in Time
§
Raphael's Story

CRIME &

CRIMINI

chapter One

The view from Gracie's tower room at the Château de Reignac in France was of a swath of green parkland: even in mid March, the grounds at the Château were lush, with graveled walkways and extensive bridle paths bordered by daffodils, all winding through gently undulating meadows. The trees were hazy with plump buds, and the mid afternoon sun made the droplets left by that morning's rain sparkle, it seemed, with delight.

She sighed. It had always been a dream of hers to take a course at the famous Cordon Bleu school of cookery. This week-long intensive seminar hosted by the Château and run by the Cordon Bleu was a 'specialty' course, designed for 'skilled' students: those who had considerable cooking experience. It would focus not only on inventive, cutting-edge and creative cuisine and presentation, but specifically on food and wine pairings. The location, smack in the middle of the Loire Valley with its châteaux and famous vineyards, could not be more perfect.

Because Gracie was a news journalist, not a chef, or a sous chef, or anything remotely connected to the food industry, she had needed to ask her close friends, restaurateurs Joey and Tyler, to send a letter of recommendation to the Cordon Bleu on her behalf when she applied. The Cordon Bleu was quite strict about prospective students' qualifications.

Joey and Tyler ran the prestigious two-Michelin-starred *Mange Tout* in Boston's Copley Square, and knew only too well what an accomplished home chef Gracie—Joey's buddy since kindergarten—was. Their letter, along with Gracie's honest and informed answers to the 'skill level assessment' questions on the application, had garnered her admission to the exclusive seminar.

Now, it hadn't even been twenty-four hours since Gracie had left her long haired orange tabby cat, Pumpkin, at Joey and Tyler's Brookline condo, where the feline would be well looked after while Gracie was in France. Then Gracie had boarded the plane at Logan Airport, slept most of the seven hour flight to Charles deGaulle Airport, collected her hire car and driven the three hours down to Reignac, a small town just east of Tours.

Fortunately, most of the journey had been on one of France's wonderful autoroutes, the A-10: although pricey, with tolls averaging a dollar per mile, the autoroutes were a dream to drive. Well constructed, smooth, multi-lane roadways, they featured beautifully maintained rest stops, called 'aires,' complete with real restaurants as well as the gastronomically superior French version of 'fast food,' every twenty or so miles. And since the speed limit was 85 miles per hour, Gracie had made good time, even though she'd treated herself to lunch at one of the larger establishments when she had just passed Blois and less than an hour remained of her journey.

She had kept her slightly jet-lagged brain sharp by converting the kilometers per hour on her rented Renault Elf's speedometer into miles per hour, and by calculating the distances she saw posted along the roadway from kilometers to miles as well.

However, there was no doubt that she had been glad to arrive at the Château de Reignac. Perched, as many châteaux were, on a hill just above the town, the Château was an eighteenth century construction on the site of a former fifteenth century château. As such, the views over the surrounding countryside and the River Indre were stunning, and changed with each direction one faced. Complete with acres of manicured grounds, fairy-tale turrets and graceful balconies, the present day Château de Reignac was a four star hotel with an impressive wine cellar and a highly regarded restaurant. This would be the site of the Cordon Bleu course, and the students would not only have command of the huge professional kitchen that occupied most of the Château's basement level, they would also have the run of the Château, as their numbers meant it was fully booked, and thus closed to outside guests.

The Château was owned and run by a descendant of the man who had re-built it in the early 1700's: Louis de Barberin. Claude Barberin—the 'de' had disappeared during the French Revolution—had very cleverly realized that the huge Château was far too large to continue as a simple family home, so he'd decided to renovate the property and open it as an hotel and conference center. After considerable training in hospitality and hotel management, Claude had begun to oversee the extensive remodel on the Château itself. This included the installation of a professional kitchen with catering capabilities, the addition of numerous conveniences like automatic lighting and an elevator, and the restoration of the interior furnishings to their gracious eighteenth century palettes and styles.

Claude fashioned a comfortable apartment for himself on the top floor of the Château and re-configured existing rooms into spacious guest rooms with en suite facilities. Each room was decorated differently to honor various historic personages connected with the Château, and the appointments were all period correct, usually antiques, and priceless.

With his small team consisting of Managers Monique Lubin and Michel Turcotte, as well as a few local people employed part-time as needed as maids and wait staff, Claude had managed to create a destination hotel in small, rural Reignac, and drew a sophisticated clientele from all over the globe.

The Cordon Bleu course would begin on Monday morning. Sunday evening, there was a reception and a dinner—cooked by Claude and Monique—for the students and their instructor, the famous chef, Martin Pernod. Known for both his temper and his talent, Pernod was renowned for his swiftness, his skill and his lofty standards, to which he held not only himself, but his students. Pernod's approach to teaching was that students either had the knack for cooking or they did not: there was no middle ground, and he swiftly winnowed out anyone who could not keep up with his lightning-fast directives in the kitchen classroom.

Although the course regulations did not specifically say that students found wanting could be dismissed, Gracie privately thought that the week of classes and judging might very well be rather like the television series 'Chopped.' She had briefly wondered if she had bitten off more than she could chew (pun intended), signing up for this course with this instructor. However, she reassured herself that if the admissions committee had judged her unqualified based on her application, they would not have allowed her to participate.

So she had decided to do her best, but above all, to have fun. If she hated it, or if Chef Pernod threw her out, she was, after all, in the Loire Valley: she doubted she'd lack for things to do and enjoy!

Now, Gracie stood in front of the armoire in the dressing area that linked her bedroom and bath, and regarded the clothing she had brought with her. She needed to choose an outfit for that evening's reception and dinner; as it was very likely the only time all week she would not be in one of her chef's white tunics and patterned trousers, Gracie thought it would be good to make an effort to look somewhat stylish.

She was fingering a multi colored silk chiffon bat wing jacket she could easily pair with black dress trousers and a black camisole when her iPhone sounded its ringtone: to celebrate her trip to France, this was currently the first few bars of Edith Piaf's 'Je Ne Regrette Rien.'

It was Jack.

"Bon soirée," Gracie answered happily, grinning.

"Well, hello to you too," Jack answered, chuckling. "I got your email," he continued. Gracie had sent an email to him once she had landed in Paris. "How's the car, and how was your trip to the Château?' Jack asked, fast. "What's your room like?"

Gracie filled him in on the delights of the French Autoroute system, as well as the amazing mileage of her diesel car. "It's phenomenal—the fuel gauge needle hardly moved, and I drove almost 200 miles today!" she enthused. As for the Château, her description of it and her delight in it were infectious, and Jack found himself thinking that perhaps the two of them could return to the Château de Reignac some time, together.

Then Gracie asked if Jack had any interesting cases: as Chief Detective in Berkshire County, Massachusetts, where they both lived, Jack dealt with most of the major crimes that occurred in their area. Since Gracie was a news reporter for an area paper, their paths had crossed several years before; despite the fact that they had to be careful about the ethics and propriety of sharing information on cases Jack investigated and Gracie reported on, they had managed to carve out a relationship. It had grown from an immediate mutual liking and respect, to a friendship, to something rather more than a friendship. Although neither was completely certain what, exactly, their relationship was at the moment, or where it would ultimately lead, they were both happy to be in it.

Jack answered that the crime front had been quiet, as it had been most of the winter. "I blame the weather: it's too damn cold for anything, including crime," he groused.

Gracie agreed. "But spring has arrived here in France, and it's such a treat!" she commented, glancing again at the greenery outside the window. Vines that looked to her like a mix of grapes and some kind of flowering climber that no doubt would be both verdant and fragrant come summer, snaked their way up the tower's curvature and around the windows of her room. Gracie's room was the 'Marquis de Dupleix,' honoring the former Governor General of France's Compagnie des Indes; it was decorated in soft greens and burgundies, and was said to be the most peaceful room in the Château.

"Don't rub it in," Jack replied, "we're expecting more snow tonight," he informed her.

Gracie made sympathetic noises, decided on the silk jacket, and walked back into her bedroom while Jack asked her if she'd seen any of the other students.

"Not yet," she replied, "although while I've been up in my room, I have heard some distant conversations and banging of suitcases," she offered. "So I expect they are arriving. We have a reception tonight."

"Oho, sort of a meet and greet?" Jack asked.

Gracie concurred. "Exactly. When I got here, I was early, and the first one to arrive, so the Château owner, Claude, gave me a wonderful, thorough tour of the place," she went on happily. "There are mediaeval towers, and a hidden window, and a bunch of secret staircases—well, not really secret, they used to be servants' staircases, but no one uses them now and they're hard to find—and there's this huge, huge kitchen, and a wine cellar, and even a chapel on one end!" she exclaimed.

They chatted about the course and the Château and about what Gracie might do for the few days after the course ended, during which she was staying on at the Château to sightsee. Then after a few more remarks, they disconnected. Gracie wanted to have a short nap to further combat the jet lag, and then a nice, hot shower before the excitement of that evening.

With a last look out her windows at the verdant countryside, she fastened the antique shutters and drew the burgundy brocaded draperies, plunging her room into soft shadows. Then she sank down onto the comfy half-canopy bed, pulled up the fleecy, cream colored blanket, and fell instantly asleep.

chapter Two

The central part of the ground floor of the Château de Reignac contained its 'salons' or reception rooms, as well as a few guest rooms, a library with floor to ceiling books on every subject imaginable, and the dining room. The welcome packet Gracie had been handed upon her arrival had contained a course outline, a short history of the Château and a map of the grounds, a brief biography of the instructor Chef Martin Pernod, and a list of the students. There had also been a note requesting that the students assemble in the 'grand salon,' the larger of the two, at seven o'clock Sunday evening. Dinner would be served at eight o'clock in the dining room.

As she ran lightly down the wide marble staircase of the Château, Gracie heard doors opening and closing and the sound of voices from both above and below her: it was a happy, cheerful babble, full of expectation. She turned right, heard the ornate casement clock in the hallway strike seven o'clock and walked quickly through the reception alcove where Monique and Michel handled guests' arrivals, departures and requests. The alcove was bookended with double glass doors: the front entryway to the Château and doors which led to the terrace and gardens in the rear. It was an airy, bright space with a large oak reception/concierge desk, a couple of chairs and a padded love seat, a computer and printer, file cabinets and a telephone. The floor was made of large square tiles in alternating black and white and the walls were blushed a creamy pink. Landscapes hung in gilt frames from slender metal chains that were anchored near the ceiling.

With a smile at the nearest landscape—it looked like a Watteau to her—Gracie crossed the marble threshold and found herself in the first, smaller salon.

Several well-upholstered chairs and sofas in pastel shades offered spots to sit, and portraits of benign-looking nobles graced the shadow striped cream and beige walls. Large floor to ceiling double glass doors, softened by cream fabric draperies with a delicate fuchsia and forest green print, looked out over the gardens and terrace. A tasteful display of maps and brochures on area sights and activities was tucked into one corner and table lamps emitted a warm glow.

The room was deserted, so Gracie glanced beyond, into the 'grand' salon, and saw several people standing around, talking in anticipatory tones and looking excited. She walked through the large archway that connected the two salons, her feet passing from Aubusson rugs to parquet floors and then onto a huge Tabriz that centered the floorspace of the larger salon.

This room was, indeed, 'grand' in all senses of the word, but it was also quite inviting. A fire crackled cheerily in the cavernous, deep grey marble fireplace that dominated the far end of the large room, and gold-embellished columns supported the imposing archway she had just traversed. More tall windows dressed in sheer striped silk panels in soft green, cream and cherry offered views of the Château's gardens on one side, and its forecourt on the other, with the town of Reignac in the distance. The high plaster ceiling featured elaborate medallions with beautifully proportioned gold and crystal chandeliers hanging from the center of each. These gave a flattering but ample light that fell on armchairs and sofas done in coordinating tones, and tables in luscious dark woods. These were grouped throughout and created a generous space for people to gather and visit, read, or just relax.

"Bon soirée," Gracie said to her fellow students as she entered the grand salon, and she smiled and nodded cheerfully.

They greeted her in the same way. Because there were only fourteen students in the course, and because the welcome packets had contained everyone's names, Gracie hoped it would not be too difficult to figure out who was who. Thank goodness they had not adopted the U.S. habit of name tags, something Gracie despised. Never mind ruining the look of one's outfit, a name tag disallowed the pleasant discovery of other people's personalities along with their names. Maybe, at some kind of huge event with hundreds of attendees, name tags would be useful, but not with a small group like this one.

A rather squat woman in a hideously violet suit done in a nubby material, her crimped grey hair much resembling a pad of steel wool, checked the pamphlet from the welcome packet as though confirming Gracie's identity, then came dashing over to her and stuck her hand out forthrightly.

"You must be the American journalist!" she declared cheerily in English, her Scottish brogue unmistakable.

Gracie nodded and admitted that she was.

A young girl in a white button down blouse and tailored black trousers silently offered a silver tray of filled champagne flutes to Gracie, who smiled, said, 'merci,' and took a glass.

"Elspeth Hume," the violet woman informed Gracie, still in English, shaking the hand that did not hold the champagne flute. "From Edinburgh, Scotland," she added.

Gracie smiled: the woman's accent was unmistakable. "How did you know I was American?" she asked, succumbing to English and wondering if her French accent was so bad that her single 'bon soirée' had betrayed her.

Elspeth looked satisfied by Gracie's confusion. "Well, you saw that handy list of all the students? There were only four single women, myself included. I've met the other two, so by process of elimination, you had to be you!" she explained cheerfully. "And besides," she went on, dropping her voice, "I heard one of the blokes talking about you," she revealed, sipping at her own champagne. She very nearly smacked her lips as she regarded Gracie with her lively grey eyes. "Nice stuff," she said of the drink.

"Talking about <u>me</u>?" Gracie pushed, delaying her own sip of champagne until she had her answer from this almost overwhelmingly ebullient woman.

"Aye," came Elspeth's reply. "He was apparently offended you'd been admitted to the course, because you're not a chef," she whispered. "In a restaurant, that is," she clarified.

"So?" Gracie could not help a defensive tone.

"Oh, 'tis no matter to me, my dear," Elspeth reassured her, "and likely not to most others taking this course," she mused, with a quick glance around at the other students: more had arrived in the salon, and it appeared as though everyone was there. "We'll all have enough to do just getting through it, never mind criticizing each other," she proclaimed. "I've learnt that's a good rule to follow, no matter what the situation," she added, just a touch preachily, and nodded her head. She took another mouthful of champagne.

Gracie nodded and felt the flush that had heightened her color subside. "Who said that—about me, and whom was he talking to?" she asked her informant.

"Bob Kress—to Chef Pernod!" came Elspeth's quick reply, still *sotto voce*. But she shifted her eyes towards a group of people to her left, and Gracie risked a quick look.

A tall, very skinny man in what looked like formal evening wear from the early twentieth century stood chatting with a very sophisticated-looking woman and man who were clearly a couple: the woman had her arm possessively around the man's waist. She looked quite effortlessly elegant in the way that French women have, in a mulberry colored wrap silk top and matching wide legged trousers. A large, square silk scarf in tones of berry, white and black that Gracie identified as an Hermès —though she couldn't be sure of the pattern—was tossed over her shoulders and perfectly knotted. She was turned away from Gracie, but her dark auburn hair was plaited into a French braid and tucked in at the nape of her neck. She wore stylish beige patent leather pumps with very high, spindly heels. Her husband—who appeared several inches shorter than his wife— was dressed in grey trousers and sports jacket, and a grey silk turtleneck. Gracie thought he looked as though he would fade into the background next to his wife.

"That's him, with the Bernards," sniffed Elspeth as she clocked Gracie's look. "They're from Rouen," she added, making it sound almost like a crime.

"What did Chef say when Mr. Kress said that?" Gracie whispered, curious.

"Chef Pernod told him—in rather halting English, by the way, as I expect he mostly speaks French but apparently Robert Kress does not, speak French that is, or not much—that your credentials had gained you entry to the course and that you were very welcome." Elspeth replied in rapid, convoluted syntax. She paused, and looked at Gracie directly, cocking her head to one side like an intrigued parrot. "What credentials, if I may be so bold as to inquire?" she asked.

Gracie explained about Joey and Tyler, their restaurant *Mange Tout*, and their letter of recommendation to the Cordon Bleu on her behalf. She finally allowed herself a sip of her champagne. Delicious!

"Two Michelin stars? That's quite an achievement, especially for an American restaurant," Elspeth agreed happily, apparently unaware of the back-handed compliment.

"And it's only been open for a little less than ten years," Gracie continued, smiling.

They were about to continue their conversation, and Gracie was going to ask Elspeth to please speak French, when Claude Barberin, the Château's owner whom Gracie had met earlier, entered the salon. He was attired in dark trousers and a white chef's tunic, but the latter was partially unbuttoned and a red and white pinstriped dress shirt peeked out beneath. His dark hair, liberally shot with silver, was carefully coiffed, and his smile lit the room. Of course, Gracie recalled, Claude was doing the cooking for tonight's dinner, along with Monique. She sent him an answering smile.

Claude was accompanied by a tall, well-muscled man in a navy silk suit that seemed to strain at the seams. The man's dark blond hair was slicked back with some kind of pomade, yet one or two sheaves of it still fell over a broad forehead marked with lines. Piercing blue eyes surveyed the little group of students as though already deciding the fate of each. His nose looked as though it might have been broken in the past and not properly set, and Gracie thought it gave him quite a pugilistic air.

Chef Pernod, of course, Gracie thought. She had seen him on the Food Network occasionally, and he sometimes was a guest on what passed for the network morning 'news' shows. If his reputation were true, he might have, indeed, got a broken nose once. Probably in a bar fight, Gracie laughed to herself.

Claude clapped his large, well-manicured hands for attention, graciously welcomed everyone, and beamed at them as though hosting the Cordon Bleu seminar was the most wonderful thing in the world.

Well, perhaps to him, it was, Gracie thought to herself. He had seemed to her a most genial host, and since he had studied at the prestigious school before opening the Château as an hotel, and was largely responsible for creating the menus at the Château de Reignac, his interest in cooking was obvious.

As Claude spoke, Gracie furtively glanced around at the other students, and wondered who everyone was, besides the Bernards, Elspeth and Mr. Kress. She spotted two men, very sharply dressed and very tanned with extremely white smiles and thought they must be the couple from California she had noted in the Course Students list.

Claude introduced Chef Pernod, who accepted the smattering of applause as his due. Then it was time for everyone to introduce themselves so that people could finally get to know each other and match the names in the pamphlet with the faces in the room. Gracie paid attention.

There were: Brigitte and Gilles Bernard from Rouen, Bob Kress from Southampton England, Sam Lewis and Peter Fontaine from San Francisco, Elspeth Hume from Edinburgh Scotland, Philippe Zafran from nearby Bléré, Henri Schilde from Antwerp Belgium, Gary Jerome from Brisbane Australia, Angelique Rochambeau from Toulouse near the south of France, Anna Guteknecht from Differdange Luxembourg, Roberto Narcissi from Genoa Italy, Jean Soules from Paris and Gracie from Massachusetts in the United States.

Quite a mixed group. Fluency, or at least competence, in French had also been a requirement of the course, since Chef Pernod taught in French. Elspeth had indicated, however, that Chef Pernod could make himself understood in English, and quite possibly a couple of other languages as well. Clearly, the 'requirement' was open to a lot of interpretation.

Gracie eyed everyone as they introduced themselves, and as the man from Southampton spoke his name, Elspeth, who still stood next to Gracie, discreetly elbowed her in the ribs. "There's your *nàmh*,"Elspeth whispered, though it sounded like, 'there's yer neeyami,' to Gracie's ears. "Your enemy," Elspeth clarified, and Gracie gave a hard look to the lean, sharp featured Kress. She still couldn't figure out his formal evening wear: no one else was dressed so elegantly, and it seemed to her a bit over the top.

Maybe she could ask him: anyone dressed like that would probably welcome others' curiosity, even hers! And doing that might get them into a conversation, and maybe she could find out why Kress had objected to her presence.

While Gracie was ruminating, Claude invited them all to come down the main hall and into the dining room, and be seated at the several small tables scattered across the beautiful tiled floor. This one was done in shades of burgundy, black, green and cream with an elaborate scrolling pattern. An equally beautiful coffered ceiling bracketed the room, which had the ubiquitous tall windows, this time overlooking the Château's gardens.

Gracie loved all the windows in the Château, and realized that when it had been built, electric lights had not yet been invented. Day could be prolonged by the use of candles, of course, and later oil lamps, but capturing as much natural light as possible through many tall windows allowed people living back then to enjoy as much daylight as possible. Additionally, the use of so much glass, which was expensive to make and to transport, was an easy way to advertise ones wealth.

Claude explained that place cards had been set at each table, and that these were to be everyone's permanent dinner places for the week. During breakfast and lunch, the students could sit where they liked and mingle a bit more.

"We tried to mix native French speakers with those whose first language is something other than French," Claude explained. "We encourage you to speak French as much as possible, since your classes will be conducted in that language," he added in an avuncular tone. "Some of you are fluent in several tongues," he added, with a quick, admiring glance for Gracie, who, he had learned, was fluent in six. "So you may find your table to be quite cosmopolitan!" Claude declared with a smile, and invited everyone to be seated in anticipation of the first course.

All the tables were dressed with white cloths and napkins, a small votive in a frosted cup adding a warm ambience. Gracie found herself joined at her table by three men: Henri Schilde, Gary Jerome and Roberto Narcissi. Henri was a bit chubby and had a round, almost cherubic face crowned by thinning brown hair; he wore black framed glasses and sported a small mustache. Gary was as slender and tanned as the guys from California, but more outspoken and flashy-looking: his white dress shirt was unbuttoned to the third button, showing a thick gold chain and some pukka beads against a smooth brown chest. His hair was spiked, and reminded Gracie of Rod Stewart's hair style. Roberto, thin and dark, seemed very nervous, and kept biting his fingernails—not a good habit for a chef, Gracie thought. He was immaculately dressed, however, in leather trousers and a dark red silk shirt, his curly hair clipped close to his well shaped skull.

"Oh, 'tis too bad we're not together," Elspeth commented with a downturned attitude as she found her seat.

"Well, you're at the very next table," Gracie reassured her with a grin. "I'm sure we'll manage." Secretly, she was grateful: Elspeth seemed nice enough, but a bit overwhelming, and Gracie wanted to have the opportunity to get to know the rest of her fellow students.

Gracie's table companions all fumbled over each other to pull her chair out for her, which she found charming. Then everyone sat down.

Elspeth was seated with the two Californians, and Gracie soon overheard their joyful discovery that they had adjacent rooms. "We're neighbors!" she heard one of the men exclaim excitedly, with a flash of that very white smile. The two men looked almost like mirror images of each other with their closely-cropped dark brown hair, blue eyes and tailored black silk shirts and trousers. The man from nearby Bléré, Philippe Zafran, was also at Elspeth's table. He had a nice face just starting to get jowly, light brown hair cut in a basic style, and rather surprisingly attractive green eyes that elevated his appearance beyond the ordinary.

Gracie looked around to see where Robert Kress had ended up: he was at a table with Angelique Rochambeau from Toulouse, the quiet man Jean Soules from Paris, and the motherly-looking Anna Guteknecht from Luxembourg. Anna was probably about the same age as Gracie, but her strawberry blonde hair was jumbled up in a slightly disheveled bun, and she wore what Gracie thought of as matronly clothes: a plain short sleeved cotton top in pale pink and a flowing, flower-printed longish skirt in matching shades of pink, yellow and brown. Jean Soules was dressed all in beige, his rather longish face topped by dull brown hair cut neither too long nor too short. Even his eyes were medium brown: he was the type of person people would describe as 'average looking,' and be correct. Angelique's back was to Gracie, but she recalled the French woman was blue-eyed, with thick, wavy, sun-streaked blonde hair. Tonight she was wearing a blue silk blouse and a charcoal grey pencil skirt. She seemed uneasy, though, and fidgeted in her chair.

Chef Pernod was sitting with the couple from Rouen, and the wife—Brigitte— looked as though it were their right; the empty chair at their table would be filled by Claude, when he wasn't cooking. Brigitte Bernard's nose wasn't really in the air, but her body language broadcast loud and clear that she felt herself to be several cuts above the rest. Her husband was nearly invisible, his demeanor was so self-effacing.

With soft jazz playing in the background, everyone began to talk with their table mates about themselves and their reasons for taking the Cordon Bleu seminar. Gracie learned that Henri was a sous chef in a rather well known restaurant in Antwerp who was taking this course in the hope that it would catapult him into a promotion. Gary revealed that he was only a lowly sous-sous chef—'one step above a skivvie, yeah?' he joked—at a Michelin starred restaurant in Brisbane, but had plans to open his own establishment in the city's trendy West End, featuring native Australian foods cooked in haute cuisine style. Roberto spoke briefly about his family's *trattoria* in Genoa, where he had learned, as he said, the trade: how to cook, how to serve, how to order provisions, and how to hire and fire staff. It would be a dream come true, he said, if he could use what he learned in this course to help his father and uncle expand their family business.

Moments later, Monique and Michel sent up the first course, which two young men in black and white serving attire brought to each person.

"Bon Appétit!" Claude said jovially, raising his champagne glass.

Everyone began to eat.

chapter Three

Early Monday morning, the course began. All the students wore traditional heavy white cotton chefs' tunics with their own personal choice of trousers. Gracie wore black and white checked trousers, Gary's were purple and white striped and —surprise, surprise, Gracie thought—Jean Soules' trousers were beige.

Although all the students had once again gathered in the grand salon after dinner the evening before with coffee and brandies, and although Jean Soules had been among them, Gracie had yet to hear the man utter a single word to anyone.

She had attempted to engage him in conversation, but had learned only that he was a sous chef, as most of the students were, and worked in a restaurant in Paris: he didn't give the name. He said he hoped this course would help him move up. Duh. Well, maybe he was shy, Gracie thought to herself now.

She had been much more successful using her charms on Bob Kress: as she'd planned, she had gone over to him after dinner, introduced herself and asked about his formal tuxedo. She'd learned that he was taking the course because he would very soon open his own restaurant in his home town of Southampton, England. His vision was to have a three-level Titanic themed restaurant in a three story industrial building he had just purchased on the quayside. The tuxedo, he said, was authentic Edwardian 'white tie and tails' evening attire, and he wore it because it connected him with the grand era in which the Titanic was built.

Gracie had been fascinated, since the Titanic was a subject both she and her friend Susan Ellen Payne enjoyed—they had even visited Southampton and the pier from which the ill-starred liner had sailed—so connected with Kress by asking informed questions and displaying her enthusiasm for the subject. Kress had taken the opportunity to tell her more about his scheme.   The ground floor would be the steerage class restaurant with a pub theme and as much nautical bric-a-brac as he could collect from car boot sales and jumbles, he had explained. The first floor would be Second Class, decorated in a way that copied what was known of the Titanic's Second Class Dining Room as exactly as possible. And the top floor would be First Class, with replicas of the table settings, flatware, china and room furnishings. He was trying to acquire original furnishings from Titanic's sister ship, the Olympus, to add to the authenticity, but they were scarce. All the menus, he had enthusiastically told Gracie, would be drawn from actual menus on the Titanic, and on other great steamers of the time.

Gracie had told him that his plans sounded wonderful, and she wished him the best of luck. 'Email me when it's open, if you would,' she had asked, handing him her card. 'I'd love to try it the next time I'm in England.'

Although she had not had an opening in which to ask him about his initial disapproval of her, Gracie felt that she had made great strides in changing Bob Kress' attitude and opinion where she was concerned. She hoped that once the classes began, her efforts in the kitchen would do away with any lingering prejudice against her he might have.

Now, Gracie noticed that the Bernards and Henri Schilde, the chubby sous chef from Belgium, had tunics with their names emblazoned on the breast. Everyone else's tunics, including Gracie's, were plain. And she couldn't help noticing that Brigitte Bernard's tunic appeared to have been custom made for her, fitting her trim figure like a glove. Not for her the usual boxy, utilitarian shape! This morning, Brigitte's dark auburn hair had been swept up into a perfect—of course—chignon, and was topped with the small white cap they all wore. Not the Chef's toque, but a smaller version that sous chefs usually sported. Every student had been issued one, and every student had one on even if it made them look a bit silly; but for some reason, Brigitte's looked like a fashion statement.

Gracie had braided her shoulder length, espresso-colored curls and wound the braid into a bun at the nape of her neck: even at home, she was conscious of stray hairs getting into food, and intended to be particularly careful here. Although it wasn't any kind of beauty contest, Gracie felt dowdy compared to the soignée Brigitte, and was happy when the woman from Rouen positioned herself far away from Gracie in the Château's huge basement kitchen. It didn't escape her, however, that Brigitte had snagged the center spot in the front row.

Roberto slid into the work station to the right of Gracie, who was imagining all the work that had had to have been done to retro-fit the kitchen for fourteen student chefs. Four rows of long portable tables marched down the center of the kitchen's open space; each table had four work stations built in. The students would share the kitchen's two six burner range tops and three double ovens as well as the other stationary appliances, but the work stations contained individual small sinks, cutting boards and tiny *mis en place* areas, and were individual to each student. Small locking drawers were also fitted under each work space, and students could use these to store any implements or specific culinary tools they might have brought with them. They were responsible for the key to secure the drawer, and

Gracie tucked hers into the small drawstring bag that held her iPhone, in a trouser pocket.

During his introductory remarks, Chef Pernod cautioned that if the students found the arrangement crowded, they should use it as a learning experience, because working in professional kitchens usually meant working in tight quarters. "Be sure you've washed, and don't be stingy with the deodorant," he quipped as though he were addressing five year olds.

Everyone nodded and looked around as though they thought the set up was splendid. No one surreptitiously sniffed their collars or underarms.

To Roberto's right was Jean Soules, and to Gracie's left was Anna.

Originally, Elspeth had attached herself to Gracie at the third table down from the head of the class where Chef Pernod stood. However, this had changed as the class had just been beginning, when Angelique had arrived—very nearly late—and had looked dismayed at the vacant spot remaining for her in the second row.

'Oh, no,' she'd murmured; then, noting Elspeth in the row behind, Angelique had whispered in that lady's ear and Gracie, next to Elspeth had overheard.

'I can't be this close to the front,' Angelique had told Elspeth pleadingly. 'Will you switch with me, please?'

Elspeth had at first appeared to not wish to do this—she wanted to be next to Gracie. But then she'd realized that moving up a row would put her closer to Chef Pernod, and right behind her new friends and neighbors Sam and Peter, who were in the front row next to the Bernards. So she had agreed.

Angelique had stood next to Gracie, then, who'd smiled and said good morning, but the blonde woman had still looked ill-at-ease, and had frowned to herself and fidgeted with her cap.

Chef Pernod had begun class then; Philippe, who was immediately in front of Gracie in the second row, had turned and given Angelique an odd look, as though he were wondering why she had wanted to change her work station. Or maybe he'd been wondering why she had been late. Then everyone's attention had shifted to their instructor.

The Chef had barely begun barking out his 'rules' for the class—"You will call me, 'Chef,' not 'Mr. Pernod,'— when Anna, who had taken the spot directly behind Gracie, had appeared at Angelique's side, and with a tiny motion of her head and a sweet smile, had indicated that the apparently shy Angelique should switch places with her. This had put Angelique in the last row, directly behind Gracie, and next to Robert Kress. Henri and Gary finished out the second row now, along with Philippe and Elspeth.

Angelique had shot Anna a grateful smile and moved, and Anna had slipped in next to Gracie.

"And have we all finished playing musical chairs?" bellowed Chef Pernod, his brows drawing together in a frown and his sharp gaze directed at Elspeth, Anna and Angelique. "Your places at this moment," he continued, emphasizing the adverbial phrase, "are where you will cook for the duration of the course. No more changing!" he ordered. "You don't like it? Too bad: you will find yourselves, in the professional kitchen, very often working next to someone you'd never dream of seeing socially. Deal with it."

Again, everyone looked around, innocently bland expressions on their faces, as though everything were perfectly great, no complaints, thank you!

After the introduction to Chef's 'rules,' the morning was spent orienting the class to where supplies were kept, and reviewing the overall course goals. Chef Pernod's delivery was very rapid, and he moved his arms a great deal as he spoke. He also made numerous side comments of a generally disparaging nature that Gracie realized were meant to be humorous: Chef Pernod clearly felt that if he hadn't made it as a chef, he could have succeeded as a stand up comedian. After a few sentences, his quickly-gabbled French became easier for Gracie to understand, and she was completely absorbed in his directives.

There were no 'do-overs,' said the Chef: you made your dish and, bad or good, you would be judged on it. "In a restaurant, the customer does not wait while the chef says, 'oh, let me try that again, I'll get it right the next time!' " he declared sarcastically.

"If you don't have time to do it right, you surely don't have time to do it over," Gracie muttered to herself, agreeing, but wondering how successful she'd be.

Chef Pernod also explained the judging system, an element of the course Gracie had read about in the literature, but not really focused on.

At each dinner, the students' dishes would be served to someone other than themselves: it might be Claude, or Monique, or Michel, or one of the other students, or even Chef himself. Each diner would have a score card on which they would make any pertinent remarks and grade the dish set before them on presentation, originality and taste, on a scale of one to four.

After dinner each night, Chef and Claude would tabulate the scores and the next morning the large scoreboard at the entrance to the dining room would list how everyone had done. Additionally, a running tally would be kept, so everyone could see who was ahead and who was falling behind.

"I shall just be very happy to finish," Roberto murmured feelingly as Chef finished explaining the judging, and Gracie shot him a fast grin.

"Me, too," she commiserated.

Gracie was happy to hear that in addition to visiting local Markets during the week-long seminar, they would also visit at least one winery. Chef Pernod explained that they already had reserved a tour and tasting for the entire class at nearby Château Moncontour in Vouvray, and hoped to add another vineyard trip to the class as well.

Château de Reignac produced a small number of bottles of wine each year from its own vineyards, and in addition, was renowned for a very fine—and very large—wine cellar, or 'cave.' That had been one of the reasons it had been chosen as the location for this particular course. The cave took up most of the lower basement, Chef Pernod told his flock, and he assured them they would be given a tour of the wine cellar just before lunch that morning.

In the kitchen, there was an alphabetized spice cabinet that Gracie found herself envying. It was about five feet across and equally tall, and divided into sections: sweet spices, savory spices and seeds/nuts. Although Gracie thought her own spice collection was quite extensive, this kitchen stocked things she had barely heard of, like vadouvan and cassia buds.

There was also a good sized greenhouse window that faced south—a big brother to the one in Gracie's own kitchen at home—in which a variety of fresh herbs such as basil, parsley and tarragon grew. A cold larder off the main kitchen was where smoked meats and fish were stored, with five huge refrigerators and several freezers housing more items that needed temperature control. A shelved pantry was connected to the kitchen by a tiny hallway: here one could find any type of dry or tinned item one might need.

The kitchen itself was equipped with every sort of cooking utensil and machine, although gadgets for their own sake were not in evidence. Bowls, mixers, blenders, wire whips, mashers, cutting boards, tongs, spoons and measuring devices were arrayed along the counters against two tiled walls; on the other wall sat the ranges and ovens, with shelves over them for larger equipment storage. The fourth wall at the front of the kitchen housed the windows. Brilliant white industrial light fixtures hung from the ceiling and illuminated every corner.

Each day a breakfast and a lunch buffet would be provided to the students in the dining room on the ground floor. Each morning's class session would consist of theory, discussion, or Market/Vineyard day, plus prep work as needed; each afternoon's session would see the creation by the students of the dishes that would make up that evening's three course dinner: starter, main course and dessert. The students' offerings would be what everyone ate for dinner each evening: no ordering out or getting pizza! So the incentive to do well was strong.

The application had demanded that the students already have 'considerable skill,' and part of the application process had been to indicate how familiar one was with various cooking techniques. Chef Pernod dispensed, therefore, with most of the basics on Monday: he knew that everyone already should be able to choose proteins, de-bone a chicken, make a reduction, make a roux, dice vegetables, and perform many other operations essential to the professional chef. Woe betide them if they were not really as competent as they had claimed! Gracie was pretty confident of her skills and hoped that she would be able to keep up adequately.

She took quite a few notes in the looseleaf notebook she'd brought along, and noticed that several others did as well.

Chef Pernod also firmly believed that excellent knife skills were the foundation for being a good chef, and that without them, one could never hope to excel in the kitchen. Because knife skills were difficult to determine through a written questionnaire, all the students were put through their paces with their knives on Monday morning, so Chef could spot any weak areas immediately, and assess their general skill levels. Each student had been asked to bring her or his own set of knives; since most chefs had a treasured set that they used all the time, this had been no problem.

Gracie had wrapped the Korin set she used in a specially-made pocketed leather pouch, and tucked it in her checked baggage. Now, it was a touch of home to feel the familiar handles in her grasp.

Gracie julienned carrots, minced shallots and made a chiffonade of a bunch of parsley with almost no issues, and almost as well, she thought, as everyone else. She shot a glance over to Henri, who was in the row in front of her and to one side, and noticed his chopping was lightning fast and his cubes and slices incredibly precise. Wow: was he part machine, to cut with such accuracy?

When the students were asked to prepare a turnip, a carrot and a potato as they would if the root veggies would be used in a fricassee, Gracie first 'topped and tailed' them, then used the 'tournée' method to make the rounded shapes flat-edged cubes and oblongs. Then she diced them as evenly as she could into smaller pieces. It wasn't as fast or as neat a result as Henri's, but her efforts were, apparently, quite satisfactory: she was rewarded with a nod of approbation—and a little surprise, she thought— from Chef Pernod.

"You did well," Roberto murmured to Gracie as the Chef moved off. "Most non-professionals don't know how to do that: they try to cut round things while they're round, and it can get very messy," he noted. Since learning that Gracie's father had been Italian, and that she could speak the language a little, Roberto had been whispering to her in his native tongue. Gracie didn't mind although she would have preferred to immerse herself in French. But she thought that speaking Italian might help the young man feel less nervous.

Pairing food and wine was one of the major elements of the course, and Chef Pernod took some time near the end of the morning to briefly outline his basic guidelines (more 'rules') on this subject. He explained that the students would be responsible for choosing one wine each evening, to accompany their presentation of the main course. However, Chef Pernod commented that some attention would also be paid to both dessert wines and wines that were best drunk before the meal or with the first course, and that these could be added at a student's discretion. However, he cautioned that if a diner did not like the choice of wine or wines and the way the wine 'married' with the food, it would go against the student's score for their dish.

"The wine should not only enhance the food it is served with, it should bring out new, hidden flavors and layers in it," Chef Pernod cautioned. "Conversely, the food should do the same to the wine. We will experiment a little bit later today, and you will see how different wines work, or do not work, with various types of food. It is important not to reflect the same taste profile in the wine and the food you serve it with," he continued, and Gracie thought she understood what he meant. "The profiles should complement each other, not mirror each other."

chapter Four

Just before the buffet lunch, Claude arrived in the professional kitchen and with a big smile ushered everyone down to the 'lower basement' to see the Château's magnificent 'cave,' or wine cellar. Gracie was impressed: hundreds of bottles were neatly stored in purpose-made wooden racks. Each bottle had a neck tag on which were written the vineyard, grape(s), name of wine and year. This, Claude explained, allowed someone to search for and choose a wine without disturbing the bottles.

He had separated white wines from reds, and dessert wines from dinner wines. Aperitifs had their own section too, and there was a smallish rack which Claude had labelled, 'Les Orphélins,' or 'the orphans.' When Gracie asked him about this rack, he explained that this was where he housed single bottles of some of the nicer wines he'd acquired. "I call it that because they are alone," he said with a dramatically drawn face, "and in most cases, when someone drinks the bottle, that is the end, it is gone." He didn't sound sad, though: Gracie thought he sounded as though he anticipated the enjoyment of these rare single bottles.

Claude was understandably very proud of what he had built up over more than a decade. He noted that he would 'tag along' when the class visited Château Moncontour, since he liked their wines and was nearly out. "I shall bring a couple of cases back, at least," he commented, and looked quite pleased at the prospect.

Lunch was a cold buffet that Monique had put together, offering salads, meats, smoked fish, condiments and breads. It was certainly sufficient, Gracie thought, and allowed everyone to eat as little, or as much, as they wished. It also gave the students another chance to talk among themselves and further the process of becoming acquainted.

Gracie had just put some salad, smoked trout, and a piece of sliced chicken on her plate and was looking around, deciding where to sit, when Angelique, the blonde woman from Toulouse, approached her.

"Would you like to sit together?" Angelique asked with a quick smile. Anna stood slightly behind Angelique, but was smiling at Gracie hopefully. Behind her was Jean Soules, who looked neither happy nor sad to have Gracie join them.

"I'd love to!" Gracie agreed cheerfully, and Angelique led them to a table in a far corner of the room, and the four of them sat.

"I must tell you, I think you are very brave," Anna began, smiling hesitantly at Gracie. Her hazel eyes were wide. Angelique was staring fixedly out one of the tall windows that was to one side of their table: her eyes were the color of chicory flowers and tip tilted, and her blonde hair with platinum highlights was secured haphazardly in a pony tail and stuffed under the little cap. Still, even plain and scrubbed in her chef's uniform, Angelique was very attractive. Distracted, but attractive.

"Brave?" Gracie echoed, and Anna nodded affirmatively as Angelique's attention returned to her lunch companions, and they all began to eat. Jean Soules did not raise his eyes or join in the conversation, but he appeared to be listening as he munched his chicken.

"Yes," confirmed Anna. "You are not in the business," she explained. Her French was heavily accented by what Gracie suspected was her native German. Her kind face was round cheeked, and hazel eyes were accented by laugh lines at the corners. "You are not a sous-chef, or a restaurateur, but a home chef, yet you venture to take this course, with Chef Pernod! Very brave," she repeated with an admiring shake of her head.

Gracie laughed. "Either brave or crazy!" she replied.

"So is Monsieur Zafran," Anna went on cheerily. "He told me he does all the cooking at home, but he doesn't work in a restaurant, either," she offered.

Gracie was surprised, and wondered if Bob Kress had also objected to Philippe's presence on the course's roster. She was about to ask Anna if she knew what Philippe Zafran did for a living, when Angelique coughed suddenly into her napkin.

"Are you all right?" Gracie and Anna asked in unison, concerned.

Angelique gave a couple more muffled coughs, nodded, and swallowed some water. "Fine. Sorry," she whispered.

There was an awkward silence while they all waited to be sure Angelique wasn't choking: even Jean Soules paused in the methodical consumption of his lunch and gazed at his table companion patiently.

Gracie smiled at Anna then. "Entschuldigen Sie, aber wenn Sie nichts dagegen haben, mich zu fragen, Ihre Muttersprache ist Deutsch, ist es nicht?" Gracie asked Anna in formal German. She wanted to know if the woman's main language was German, since she was from Luxembourg, where they spoke both French and German and their own Luxembourgish, which was an offshoot of High German.

Anna grinned. "Ja, meine Eltern sind aus Saarbrücken, obwohl wir leben in Differdange in Luxemburg. Natürlich, ich spreche auch Französisch, Luxemburgisch und ein klein wenig Englisch. Aber ja, Deutsch ist meine Hauptsprache," she replied.

Ah, Gracie thought: Anna's parents were from Germany, Saarbrücken, and that explained why German was her first language. She also spoke

French and Luxembourgish, of course, and a little English.

"You speak German in addition to French?" Angelique asked: she had looked quite befuddled during Gracie and Anna's German exchange.

Jean Soules looked up from his plate again this time fixing Gracie with a look of mild interest.

Gracie shrugged. "I studied German in school," she replied offhandedly, switching back to their common language of French. "So I can get by. I really like languages," she added with another shrug.

That was true: Italian she had learned from her father and French she'd learned in college. It hadn't been too much of a stretch to school herself in Spanish and Portuguese, and she even had a smattering of Russian and Welsh, although the last made her cross eyed and tongue tied.

They chatted companionably for a while as they ate: Anna had learned to cook when helping her mother with their large family: she had eight siblings. To earn money, she had begun waitressing in school, and then at University she had studied Hospitality with a concentration in Food Services. She had been lucky enough to work as a second sous chef in a small family-owned restaurant in Differdange, but wanted to improve her skills.

"At the restaurant where I work, the owner's son wants to open his own restaurant in Luxembourg

City," Anna explained. "He is a very, very talented chef," she said, sounding awed. "And I want to go with him, as his sous chef," she declared, sounding as though voicing her dream could make it come true.

A blush stained Anna's fair complexion and Gracie wondered if the woman wanted to be more than the son's sous chef. Anna was in her early thirties, Gracie guessed, and quite pretty although with no makeup and her hair scraped back in a bun, she would not have caught anyone's eye. Although in their whites, all the students looked more or less the same (except for Brigitte, of course), Gracie thought that Anna's sense of style might benefit from a re-vamp, as well. Especially if she wanted to be sous chef, or something more, to the man she spoke of so reverently. Although of course people should be judged on how well they could do a job, personal appearance always factored in, and to believe otherwise was ridiculously idealistic in Gracie's estimation.

Angelique, on the other hand, was one of those women who could roll out of bed and look great: naturally good skin and high coloring meant she didn't look, as Gracie always thought of herself, like death warmed over, if she didn't wear a little bit of makeup. Although Gracie thought Angelique was a little older than she was—she'd put her in her late thirties or early forties—she was very good looking, and had a figure to match. Not that anyone's figure was really visible in their chef's whites!

"And you want to open a restaurant in Toulouse?" Gracie asked, turning now to the blonde woman. She remembered having heard her say something about that the evening before.

Angelique had been concentrating on her plate of food with her head down and her body turned away from the rest of the room. Hearing Gracie's query, she shook her head. "No—near here, maybe north of Tours." Her voice was low. "My daughter will be going off to the University of Tours in the autumn, and I think that would be a good time to do it," she replied, sounding very proud of her daughter. She took a last bite of her lavishly buttered baguette.

A couple of tables away, someone dropped their cutlery against a plate with a clatter, and Gracie thought that the other students must be quite nervous about that afternoon's session. Although the course had begun that morning, the real cooking would begin in just a few minutes.

"I didn't know you had a family," Anna interjected with a smile. "What does Monsieur Rochambeau do? Is he a chef, like you?" she asked, still smiling.

Angelique lowered her voice even more. "My —daughter's father— my first husband died," she replied shortly. "Long ago."

"Oh, I'm so sorry!" Gracie said feelingly. It must have been very difficult to have been left a single mother at such a young age.

Angelique gave her a quick smile. "I married again, to Monsieur Rochambeau, who is a businessman," she continued. "But we are not together now," she finished.

Gracie wondered if they had been divorced, or merely separated, and when they'd married. She told herself she would google them later, and see what she could find.

"Ah…" Anna sighed. "But tell us about your restaurant!" she urged Angelique, changing the subject to a cheerier one.

"Toulouse has a distinct regional cuisine," Angelique answered. She looked grateful to have another topic to discuss, and shifted her chair closer to the table as she named the famous Toulouse sausages, cassoulet, and confits the region was known for. "I would like to make the Toulousain style better known in other areas of France."

"So, you'd open your restaurant—north of Tours? Where?" Gracie asked, interested. She briefly wondered about Angelique's choice of location, but the fact that her daughter would be here going to University seemed an adequate explanation.

They 'bussed' their table, bringing their plates and utensils up to a large, wheeled cart near the entrance to the prep kitchen. A big dumb-waiter there would ferry the cart down to the kitchen, where the dirty crockery and cutlery would be loaded into the commercial dishwashers.

Jean—who had not said a single word during the meal—nodded silently at them and disappeared, presumably to his room to wash up, as there were about twenty minutes left before they all had to report to the kitchen. Anna also excused herself; Angelique and Gracie walked out to the hallway where Michel's pride and joy, an espresso machine, was standing at the ready. The two women helped themselves to espressos, and stood near the dining room entrance, drinking the small cups quickly, and continuing their chat.

"Well, with my daughter attending University," Angelique replied, facing the windows as she spoke to Gracie, her back to the dining room, "I don't want to cramp my daughter's style, but I do want to be nearby, if you know what I mean?"

Gracie nodded encouragingly.

"So I thought the area south of Paris but north of Tours might be a good spot to introduce people to real Toulousain cuisine. I've been thinking about Blois. They get a number of tourists from all over, because of the mediaeval town and of course, the Château there," she continued, speaking authoritatively. "The trick will be to have the money to finance it," she finished almost in a murmur. "I'm hoping my flat in Toulouse sells quickly."

Gracie nodded: Château de Blois was on her 'to do' list for the few extra days she would spend in the area once the course was finished. "That sounds like a good plan," she told Angelique, who looked less positive than Gracie about it.

They finished their espressos and moved off, towards the grand staircase.

chapter Five

After lunch, everyone re-assembled in the kitchen to learn what they would be making for that evening's dinner.

"This afternoon we will be preparing a version of a classic French dish, Sole Meunière, for the main course tonight," Chef Pernod announced in a haughty tone when the class reconvened. "It will have, however, a distinct Norman twist," he continued, and gave a small yet supercilious nod to Brigitte and Gilles Bernard from Rouen. They both looked surprised, and quite thrilled, and Gracie overheard Gary muttering to himself, 'dead chuffed, those two.'

Chef Pernod explained that not only would the fish be 'enrobed' in a 'Sauce Normande,' it would be accompanied by winkles and samphire.

Oooh, cool, Gracie thought: she'd had samphire a couple of times at some upscale restaurants in the UK, and liked it; she had also tried winkles, which she'd not been very impressed with, to be honest. Perhaps Chef Pernod's treatment of the winkles would improve her opinion of the tiny mollusk.

Chef Pernod then explained that for the starter, the class would be making root vegetable gnocchi which would be served in small dishes, just three or four gnocchi per person, with a dollop of melted butter and salt.

Dessert would be individual apples poached in raspberries, served with raspberry sauce and fennel cream. Gracie remembered seeing fennel pollen in a tin in the massive spice cabinet, and wondered if that would be one of the ingredients. If not, maybe she could use it anyway: she wondered how strong fennel pollen was and what, exactly, it tasted like. It was another obscure spice she had realized was missing from her spice cabinet at home, although she had fennel seed.

Gracie could not help grinning: this sounded like a fabulous menu, and she couldn't wait to start.

Chef, clocking her grin, gave her an imperious frown as if to say, 'let's see if you're smiling when you've finished cooking!' and scowled at her.

Gracie met his gaze but didn't stop grinning: she was too excited!

"Ok, *c'est parti*," Chef Pernod said then, and clapped his hands together.

He really seemed to be a very good instructor in spite of his sharp attitude and sarcasm, Gracie thought as she unlocked the little drawer built in to the work station she had chosen. She withdrew her knives and began setting about her *mis en place* for the gnocchi, which would be made first.

Chef Pernod's commentary that morning had been delivered in an entertainingly mocking tone, and peppered with little jokes that made fun of student chefs past, present and future. He was quite strict, Gracie realized: it was his way, or the highway. Still, that was what she had paid for, and the more she listened to him, she realized that she could learn a great deal if she could just ignore his manner. And his scowls. He was there to teach her how to cook, not how to behave.

Roberto, on the other hand, seemed to shrink into his chef's tunic with each pronouncement by Chef Pernod; Gracie thought she could see the Italian's hands shaking as he set out the small plates and bowls for his *mis en place*. He had better calm down, she thought, or he'd never make it through a week of instruction from Chef!

Since the fish would have to be served as soon as it had been prepared, it would be made last, Chef Pernod explained. Therefore, the gnocchi, which would be served at room temperature and could easily be kept for the few hours until dinner time, would be made first.

Chef Pernod then took five minutes to dispense information about food safety. "It does not matter how beautiful a dish looks or how delicious it may taste, if someone gets food poisoning from your cooking, you don't deserve to wear the chef's whites!" he blasted, frowning at each of them in turn with what Gracie had decided must be his signature glare.

She stared back at him. She had faced down a madman with an assault rifle just a few months before: a scowling chef didn't phase her one bit!

Then, each student received a chunk of butternut squash, a medium purple beetroot, a half a sweet potato, a half a knob of celeriac, a smallish parsnip, a turnip, and some brown rice flour. Chef Pernod explained that not only was the brown rice flour gluten free for those with a sensitivity, it made, in his opinion, the lightest, most delicate vehicle for the root vegetables.

They were instructed to peel their vegetables as needed then wrap them in foil and roast for forty minutes. Everyone hastily did this, happy to begin with something easy, and for several minutes the only sound in the large stainless steel and tile kitchen was that of crinkling foil. Then everyone's veggies went into the roaring hot ovens.

While the vegetables roasted, the students started some prep work on dessert. They puréed bags of frozen raspberries while they listened to Chef's lecture about using frozen fruit for out of season items (quite acceptable, surprisingly). They then sieved the resulting pulp to remove the seeds, blended it with water and some added sugar, and brought it to a boil in individual saucepans on the range tops. This would provide the poaching liquid for their apples.

When the vegetables were ready, everyone turned off their raspberry mixture and returned to gnocchi making. Gracie mashed her roasted vegetables separately according to color once they had cooled, and put the purées in individual bowls. Then she added her rice flour slowly, and blended with her hands until each bowl contained a slightly sticky, different colored lump: one was the squash and sweet potato; one was the beetroot to which she'd added her celeriac just for fun; and the last was the turnip and parsnip.

"La mia zucca è così rigida," muttered Roberto, whose station was next to Gracie's.

She glanced over: his gnocchi dough containing the butternut squash and the sweet potato, both orange, was streaked with un-incorporated flour, and looked very tough, so tough he couldn't knead it properly.

"I think the starchier ones need a lot less flour," Gracie whispered back in Italian. She kept an eye out for Chef Pernod, who would surely berate them both for talking in class and for discussing each other's cooking. He was, however, at the far end of the kitchen, talking to Gilles. "I added the flour a little at a time," Gracie explained quietly. She hadn't known to do that, necessarily: it had just been caution that had prompted her to add the flour bit by bit.

"What can I do?" whispered Roberto in a panic. He knew there were no do-overs.

"Perhaps you can get another half a sweet potato," Gracie suggested, glancing over towards the work surface where the root vegetables had been placed. "You could microwave it, and mix it in, and it might be all right," she finished doubtfully.

"Microwave?" Roberto echoed in scandalized tones.

"Better go tell Chef Pernod, see what he says," advised Gracie.

To her surprise, Roberto returned a few moments later from the front of the room, where he had timidly advanced to tell their instructor of his dilemma. In his hand, he bore a half a roasted sweet potato, and he looked much cheerier than he had.

"Chef said to try adding this and see if I can get the dough to become pliable, become gnocchi," Roberto told Gracie with a smile. "He said he always has a few extra vegetables available in case something happens."

Gracie nodded.

"I suggested your microwave idea, and he said it would have worked, but that the flavor of the roasted is much better," Roberto added happily as he began to mash up the sweet potato and then work it slowly into his stiff lump of gnocchi dough.

Roberto seemed to be succeeding, so Gracie returned to her own work station where she dusted the worktop with flour, then rolled each differently colored portion of dough into a long strip about a half-inch wide. These she cut into pieces about an inch long—she got fancy and did this on the diagonal —and put them on a baking sheet.

Then it was back to the range top to boil a large pot of water. When it was ready, Gracie dropped her gnocchi in a few at a time and cooked them until they floated up to the surface. She cooked her white gnocchi first, then the orangey gnocchi, and the heliotrope-colored beet gnocchi last, so the color would not transfer.

Once cooked, however, the gnocchi were colorfast, so they all went into the same colander to drain.

Gracie was surprised when she looked at the clock to see it was already mid afternoon: there was still quite a lot to be done, and dinner was to be served at seven tonight!

Poaching her apple and making the fennel cream occupied the next hour or so, but Gracie was pleased with her bright red apple that would be set aside until dessert was assembled later that evening. The fennel cream was a bit more challenging. While

Gracie simmered the raspberry poaching liquid on low heat so it could reduce into a syrup, she heated cream with some fennel seeds that she had crushed in a mortar. Next to her, Anna did the same. Both then bloomed a sheet of gelatin in cold water, squeezed it dry and added it to the cream mixture in the sauce pan. They added sugar, stirred, then took the concoction off the heat and cooled it. Gracie transferred her cream into a small bowl, then plunged it into a large stainless steel bowl of ice water to quickly begin the cooling process.

"I'm impatient," she told a curious Anna, who was laboriously stirring her cream to cool it down.

From the other side of the room, Gracie heard a muffled cry as someone grabbed a sauce pan handle without a potholder. The pots were all copper: dreams to cook with, but dangerous if you handled them improperly.

Chef Pernod was instantly solicitous; then, once he had ascertained that the student's hand was not badly burned, he took the opportunity to deliver a strident lecture about personal safety in the kitchen, and admonish them all, noting that at their level, they should be more versed in these things.

Gracie noticed that it had been Gary who had burned his hand on the pot, and was glad that the burn wasn't serious. Gary was dutifully given a large, bright blue plaster, or band-aid, and was warned not to let it come off in any of the foods he would be making. The burn seemed to be more on the base of his palm, though, so it likely wouldn't interfere too much. And the blue color was generally used in professional kitchens so that any such items could be easily spotted if they did accidentally come off. To paraphrase George Carlin, Gracie thought to herself, there was very little blue food.

Gracie's cream-gelatin mixture set up nicely and she covered the little bowl and put it in the refrigerator, labelling it with her initials as they had been advised. Her raspberry concoction was now quite syrupy, too, so she poured this into a small squeeze bottle of heavy plastic and set it aside.

She went to the spice cupboard, then, since most of her prep work was finished: she wanted to taste the fennel pollen and see if she wished to use it in the dessert.

"And what are you doing?" Chef Pernod challenged her as she located the tin of pollen.

Gracie whirled around. Chef fixed her with that ice blue stare and with her peripheral vision Gracie could see Brigitte, smirking, as she watched them.

"I was wondering what this tasted like," Gracie replied mildly, holding up the little tin of pollen. "I've never used the pollen, and since there is crushed fennel in the cream for the dessert, I wondered if this might be good to use as well."

"You are altering my recipe?" Chef asked disparagingly, as though a mere student chef should never dare such a thing.

Gracie maintained eye contact with Chef Pernod. "You told us to be creative," she reminded him evenly. "It's not like I'm substituting blueberries for raspberries or peaches for apples," she added reasonably.

He wasn't going to bully her!

Chef Pernod's blue eyes seemed to get even bluer, if that were possible. "I won't know if it will be a good unless I taste it," Gracie finished.

Chef Pernod took a breath as though he were about to speak, then shut his mouth, gave her a tight smile, and with a exaggerated bow, gestured to the spice cabinet. "By all means, Mademoiselle, have at it," he told her. But his tone was still sarcastic.

By now, their encounter had attracted the attention of several other students, who watched covertly as they finished up their tasks for the afternoon. Brigitte, however, was openly gawking.

Gracie nodded, and reached for one of the small, thin balsa wood sticks that stood in a tall glass jar next to the cabinet. These were tasting sticks, meant to allow for spices to be tasted as needed without contaminating or moistening them. Then she opened the jar of fennel pollen, and touched the tip of her stick into the pale greenish-gold powder, and put the pollen covered stick to her tongue.

It was like fennel magnified and super sweetened, almost too much, but so delicious! Gracie thought she could detect notes of citrus and licorice, which made sense because fennel was in the licorice family. A visual popped up in her head of using a dusting of the pollen as well as a few un-crushed fennel seeds as a garnish for the cream, and she smiled over at Chef Pernod, who stood watching her.

"I think I'll give it a whirl," she told him nonchalantly, and walked slowly back to her work station.

At about five o'clock, everyone took a small break: most dashed up to their rooms and then streaked back down for a fast cup of coffee: Michel was handling the Château's espresso machine this time, and churning out small cups of brown jet fuel as fast as he could. Gracie indulged, and then it was back to the kitchen to begin work on that evening's main course.

Gracie felt that if every day were like today, she would be exhausted at the end of the course, and need a vacation to recover!

chapter Six

They would begin, Chef Pernod explained, with previously made fish stock, to save time. "I presume you all know how to make your own fish stock, of course," he commented, giving Gracie a stare. It was his usual stare, the one she had come to call 'the hairy eyeball.'

She stared back. She knew how to make fish stock: it wasn't brain surgery, after all.

"And I also presume you all know how to fillet a fish," he continued sourly as one of his assistants went around to the stations and plopped down a glistening fish in front of each student. Only Roberto looked slightly non-plussed at the offering before him.

The fishes were gorgeous and fresh, with bright eyes and glistening scales, and no smell at all except one of clean water. Gracie wouldn't have been surprised if one had even given a little wiggle they had so recently been alive.

At Chef Pernod's direction, they began. Gracie pulled out her trusty kitchen scissors as well as a collapsible fish scaler she had brought along, and began to scale the sole. She cleaned the scaler and her station as she went along, and examined the flanks of her fish carefully before continuing, picking off a couple of stray scales that had escaped the scaler's blade. Then she pulled off the skin, removed the fin and the gills, made an incision, and pulled out the sole's guts with her fingers.

Roberto, watching her, shuddered. This kind of thing had never been on the menu at his family's *trattoria*. Still, the reason he was here was to learn, and help his family expand, he thought, and set about the task before him.

Chef Pernod walked among the students, observing, and making little grunts that sounded like either approbation or censure, depending on the skill of the student.

He got to Gracie just as she was running her thin, sharp, flexible filleting knife down the backbone of the sole. Unnervingly for Gracie, Chef Pernod stopped, and watched critically as she slid her knife in, teasing it along the radial bones until a flat, sweet fillet plopped into her hand.

'Beginner's luck,' she thought to herself: normally, she had the fishmonger prep her fish for her, but she'd watched enough times that she had known what to do.

Chef Pernod moved on with a little grunt that sounded to Gracie like a positive, if grudgingly given, comment.

Dredging and breading the fish was simple; then, they set it aside and turned to the winkles. These had been cleaned in cold salted water and were ready to be cooked. After just three minutes in barely boiling fish stock, the winkles were removed, rinsed in cold water to stop the cooking, and drained. These were set next to the sole, and the students were instructed to begin the sauce.

Gracie chose to first chop the mushrooms she would add to the velouté to make the Sauce Normande. She noticed that Gary jumped right in and began making the sauce. However, Gracie liked to have all her ingredients measured out and ready to go first. There was nothing more annoying than having to stop to measure a teaspoon of this or a half cup of that, she thought. It also increased the chances that whatever you were making would suffer while you took the extra time to do what you should have prepared in the first place.

After the mushrooms were chopped, briefly sautéed in a dry, flat pan to remove most of their water, and set aside in a small bowl, Gracie separated two eggs, reserving the whites in case they would need them for something later, and blended the plump orange yolks with a small amount of heavy cream. She used a tiny immersion blender she had also brought with her: useful for frothing cappuccino milk, the blender also was excellent for thoroughly mixing small quantities of liquids and semi-liquids. It created a lovely creamy yellow substance that clung to the sides of the *mis en place* bowl.

Using the same stock the winkles had cooked in, Gracie then began to make her velouté; however, she ran her stock through a makeshift cheesecloth sieve first. She noticed that only a couple of other students—Elspeth and the Bernards—did this as well: the rest merely used the stock as it was. The straining process omitted any bits of winkle or other solids from the finished product, and since it had taken all of two minutes to do, Gracie was glad she had taken the extra step. She could just imagine the brouhaha if Chef got her main course, and found a grain of sand in her sauce!

As she took a measure of clarified butter and put it in a saucepan, she detected a slight scorched smell: someone's roux was burning, she thought—better turn down the heat or it would be completely ruined. Unlike Roberto's gnocchi dough, which had been saved with the addition of more sweet potato, a scorched roux could not be fixed.

Gracie continued starting her own roux: when the butter began to froth a bit, she added the flour that had been provided, a little at a time, and whisked as she did so, until all the grains of flour were incorporated into the butter. Lowering the heat, she continued to whisk as the slurry in the saucepan turned from pale yellow to the deep color of saffron. Then she turned off the heat and quickly added the mushrooms and stirred. A dab of the *velouté* went into the small bowl of the *liaison*, or egg yolk and cream blend. This Gracie mixed carefully, tempering the *liaison* so the eggs would not cook when she added them to the velouté.

She felt Chef Pernod behind her, watching her again, and then felt him move on. She deliberately relaxed her shoulders, then added the tempered *liaison* to the sauce and stirred quickly: it was perfect. She took a deep breath.

Now it was time to sauté the breaded sole, which would only take a few minutes, and the winkles, which would take even less time. While more butter melted in the saucepan, Gracie sliced a juicy lemon and set it aside: just the smell of it brightened her up and energized her. She also took the samphire that had been cleaned and rinsed, and started another shallow pan of water which she would bring to the boil. The samphire needed only a quick blanching before she would drain it, arrange it on the plate, and top it with the sautéed sole and winkles. The sauce would be poured lavishly over the fillet, then drizzled around the rest of the plate for an attractive presentation.

Chef Pernod had advised the students that although the ingredients and recipe was identical for each of them, the final presentation, or 'look' of the dish, would be left up to them.

Chef Pernod added a bit of melted butter to each student's gnocchi, and grated a dust of sea salt on top: these were now ready to serve.

Once Gracie had flipped her fillet of sole, satisfactorily noting that the fish had turned a lovely shade of coppery beige, she added the winkles, then blanched the samphire. Two minutes, and the samphire was out and on some kitchen paper for a quick drain and blot, then Gracie poured the slender green stems onto the serving plate that she had remembered to warm, and arranged them quickly. She squirted the juice from one half of the lemon into the pan with the fish, shook the pan quickly to coat the fillet with the butter and lemon, then lifted the fillet out and placed it on top of the samphire.

Scooping the winkles up with a slotted spoon, Gracie dotted these in amongst the samphire stems. Then she spooned most of the sauce over the fish, and drizzled the rest of it on the samphire and around the edge of the plate. She placed two winkles atop the sauced fillet, along with a tiny tip of samphire she had snipped earlier, and a couple of curls of lemon zest she zipped off on the spur of the moment.

"Et, voilà," she said, loud enough for Chef Pernod to hear.

Glancing around, she saw that most of the other students were also finished with their dishes, some putting last touches on their presentation and only Gary lagging behind, still struggling with his sauce and swearing.   Dinner began with the students still in their chef's whites. Everyone received a serving of gnocchi but since Chef Pernod had also made a few servings of the starter, and these were mixed in with what the students had made, no one knew whose gnocchi were served to whom. Codes on the bottoms of the serving dishes would reveal everything at the conclusion of the meal. Meanwhile, everyone rated each dish according to presentation, flavor, and originality.

The gnocchi Gracie was served were pretty good, but a bit chewy. She had always had trouble with gnocchi, even freshly-made gnocchi from the Italian grocery store: they always seemed slightly rubbery to her. These had good flavor and looked very pretty, so she gave a 4 (the highest score) for presentation and a 3 for flavor/texture, and a 3 for originality, since the gnocchi were all separate colors but arranged conventionally.

Roberto received a serving of pink gnocchi and everyone bit their lips to keep from laughing. Someone had forgotten to cook the gnocchi in color batches or in the proper order, and the purple beets had dyed the other pasta pockets! Still, Roberto said it all tasted good.

The fish came out next, served by the wait staff. Again, a couple of servings had been cooked and plated by Chef Pernod, and no one knew which was which. Gracie tried to look around to find her dish, but she couldn't spot it, since several others had arranged their fish in a similar fashion to hers.

The wine for the evening had been the subject of some debate earlier in the afternoon. Most of the students suggested a white burgundy to pair with the sole, feeling that the wine's acidity and strength would stand up to and compliment the fish and creamy sauce. Other similar chardonnay wines were also suggested, but the Bernards were quite vocal about the Norman winery, Arpents du Soleil.

"They make a range of wine, and a very good chardonnay," insisted Brigitte. "It would make sense to serve a Norman wine with Norman-inspired food," she concluded.

Unfortunately, they could not obtain a shipment of the wine the Bernards had mentioned in time, but Chef Pernod had seemed intrigued by the idea, and promised to investigate the Arpents du Soleil winery and see if they could get some bottles to serve later in the course.

The Bernards had looked mollified.

Gracie, Elspeth and a couple of others had decided on a 2010 white burgundy/chardonnay from Joseph Drouhin that they found in the Château's 'cave,' called La Forêt Chardonnay. Other students had made similar choices, she thought: all white burgundies or chardonnay with only Gary selecting a viognier from Australia's Yalumba Valley. Gracie wondered how the more complex and delicate viognier would pair with the creamy fish dish.

Now, Gracie took a sip of the wine she'd been served with the dish assigned to her and contemplated the plate before her. This wine was lightly mineral, but fresh and with that 'green fruit' flavor she enjoyed. As the wine sat on her tongue, she tasted a bit of softer stone fruit as well, and smiled: the wine was very good indeed.

The big reveal would come at the start of class the next day when they would be told whose dish they'd received and which wine it had been paired with.

At the next table, she heard Elspeth exclaiming over the wine she'd received, and noticed that the woman had drunk nearly half her glass in one gulp. So much for 'tasting.'

Gracie turned to her sole. The serving she had received had the samphire arranged nicely to one side, and the sole and winkles on the other side, topped by the Sauce Normande. She dipped the tines of her fork into the sauce: a tiny bit floury, but the fish was wonderful, and Gracie made little happy noises as she ate. The samphire, naturally salty, played well against the creamy sauce and crispy fish. The winkles were a real trial to dig out of their little shells, and the result was not so wonderful, Gracie thought, that she would go to the trouble again. She had felt the same way the first time she'd ever tried the tiny mollusk. Oh, well: you didn't have to love everything!

Following this course, all the students rushed back into the kitchen to plate their desserts. It only took about three minutes for Gracie to place her apple squarely on the small plate she'd been assigned, squeeze her raspberry reduction around in little blobs and ribbons, and then grab her container of fennel cream from the refrigerator.

Carefully, she tried to make a couple of *quenelles* from the substance, but it did not cooperate, and she was left with thick curls of cream which she tried to arrange somewhat artfully atop the apple. Then, as she had envisioned, she sprinkled a light dusting of fennel pollen on top along with a couple of whole fennel seeds and a single, whole raspberry she had saved. Despite the uncooperative cream, she thought the dessert still looked good. She put her offering on the serving tray and returned to the dining room.

"Well, I think we all did very well, especially for a first try," Elspeth pronounced later that evening. Several of the students had decided to have after dinner drinks in the grand salon, and as they enjoyed the tipples that Claude had to offer, they re-hashed that day's lesson and discussed Chef Pernod—and any student who wasn't present. Jean Soules, Angelique, Philippe and the Bernards had all elected to retire to their rooms.

Gary stared morosely into his glass of brandy, and then nodded. "I have to make myself do the *mis en place* thing," he said, and took a drink. "But I'm just so impatient to start, y'know? I usually don't bother. But I've got to: that's why my roux burned, because I was busy cleaning mushrooms." He sighed. "I don't know who ended up with my dish, but I bet my sauce was awful," he lamented.

Bob Kress, who was one of the group, held his snifter up to the chandelier and looked at the liquid inside it critically. Gracie thought this terribly affected, especially when he closed one eye and squinted at it. "The sauce I got was floury and a little scorched tasting," he revealed in a mild tone. "It wasn't that bad."

"A roux isn't an easy thing to do, even if you make it all the time," put in Henri supportively.

"That's true," Kress agreed. He sipped at his brandy, which apparently met his expectations.

"At least I'm glad that Brigitte didn't get my fish," Gary said feelingly. "Prob'ly would have thrown the plate against the wall!" he quipped, and everyone chuckled: it seemed they all had a similar opinion of the woman from Rouen.

"Well, everything I had was delicious," put in Elspeth with a smile.

"I think you got Brigitte's fish," Peter said to Elspeth, who looked a question. "I watched her as she finished plating and it looked an awful lot like what was on the plate in front of you."

"Oh," Elspeth said, sounding less enthused than she had before.

There was an uncomfortable silence, and then Roberto muttered in accented French, "I do not think Brigitte is very nice."

Everyone snickered agreement, but Gracie, who was sitting near Roberto in one of the padded gilt armchairs, leaned over. "How so, Roberto? Why do you say that?" she asked, concerned. Something in his tone had been quite serious.

Roberto made a face and finished off his small glass of *grappa*. He'd been delighted to discover it among Claude's stock of liqueurs, something from his home country. "She told me today, after lunch, as we were all returning to the kitchen, that she was surprised my tunic didn't have little pizzas embroidered on it," he told everyone. His voice was unemotional, but Gracie could see the hurt on his face.

"Did she mean it as a joke?" Bob Kress suggested. He had found himself secretly quite smitten with the chef from Rouen, even if he did have to admit that she wasn't particularly kind, and led her husband, Gilles, around by the proverbial nose.

"Well, maybe, yes, but even if she did, it isn't very funny, and it isn't nice," Gracie objected, and Kress shrugged in acquiescence. Gracie turned again to Roberto. "Your family runs a restaurant, not a pizza shop," she confirmed, and Roberto nodded.

"Then that was just nasty," Sam pronounced. "I'm glad I'm not next to her in the kitchen, I'd be tempted to..."

"Now, now, let's not get violent," Peter put in with a staying hand on his partner's. Peter, of course, was next to Brigitte in the kitchen. "If I can stand her, you can," Peter added with a wry grin.

The commentary opened up a quick exchange of observations by various people about Brigitte, and it seemed as though no one actually liked her even though Bob Kress made a couple of comments about her style.

"I wish I looked like her," commented Anna, softly.

Gracie wanted to remind her that fashion sense had nothing to do with cooking or character, but she stayed out of it. Inwardly she couldn't help being cheered by the fact that such an elegant woman wasn't also universally loved.

"So, how was your first day?" Jack asked that night as Gracie's call went through.

She was in her half canopy bed in her lovely, quiet room, leaning up against three fluffy pillows, and had decided to call Jack to say goodnight before she fell into what she expected would be a coma like sleep.

"It was amazing," she said, sounding tired but enthusiastic, and shared highlights from the day, including the fennel pollen incident.

"Fennel pollen? Isn't fennel, like, a weed?" Jack asked on a chuckle.

Gracie corrected him.

"So I guess I can look forward to having some on my desserts when you get back, huh?" Jack quipped, and Gracie agreed, noting that she'd already ordered a small tin of it for her own spice cupboard.

"You should see the size of that thing," she told Jack, referring to the cupboard at the Château. "I really don't <u>need</u> something that large, but it's a great idea, so I've been thinking of maybe asking Larry to build one like it, but on a smaller scale," she mused. "I could have him install it on that wall next to the gas fireplace," she continued, knowing Jack would understand the spot she referred to.

"I've seen cupboards that are built into the wall, but only about a foot deep, and they have doors that fold out with racks for stuff," Jack offered, recalling a design he'd seen on an online home woodcrafting site. "Kind of like an accordion," he explained.

"Ooooh, that sounds perfect!" Gracie returned, excited by the idea despite her weariness. "The opposite side of that wall is the pantry, so I think there's room for something like that to fit," she murmured sleepily. She yawned. "I'll email Larry tomorrow."

chapter Seven

The next morning was Market Day, after which, Chef Pernod told them, the results of their scores from dinner the evening before would be posted on a large easel outside the dining room entry.

All the students had a very early breakfast, and Gracie noticed that the level of chatter in the dining room was almost nil. She was tired, too, but still said, 'bon matin' to everyone she encountered. At most, she got a weary grin back, but a couple of people nearly scowled at her! Well, maybe they just weren't morning people, and they <u>had</u> risen very early.

Philippe was standing next to the espresso machine when Gracie approached and poured herself a double.

"You look like you wish it could be delivered intravenously," she quipped.

Philippe gave her an uncomprehending gaze.

"You're miles away," Gracie said sympathetically. "Are you all right?"

He shook himself. "Ah, oui, Mademoiselle, the espresso, yes, it is quite—necessary," he replied obliquely, and poured more of the dark brew into his cup and swilled it down.

They needed two vehicles to go to the Market in Bléré, just a few miles away. Gracie had volunteered to drive, since the Château's van only held a dozen including the driver, Michel. That left three without a ride, so Gracie offered to drive her hire car and bring the other two students.

Monique Lubin, the petite blonde Château manager, asked if she could come to the Market as well, so Gracie's car was full. Gracie had intended to ask Angelique and Anna to ride with her, but before she could, Elspeth ran up and invited herself, commandeering the passenger seat. Gracie had almost expected her to shout, 'I call shotgun!' So Monique sat in the back with Roberto, who was the last to arrive downstairs before they left.

Market Day delighted Gracie, who explained to her passengers that where she lived, although there were Farmers' Markets in the late summer and fall, regular Market Days did not exist. For most of the year, she told them, people bought their groceries at large supermarkets, not open air markets.

Part of the allure for Gracie was the mixture of things available in a European outdoor market. There were, of course, all manner of fresh fruits and vegetables, as well as meat, poultry and fish. But stall after stall of cheese from, it seemed, all over France, lent a pungent air to the damp morning: it had rained again the night before. The dairy vendors also had milk, cream, and all manner of dairy products for sale, too.

And there were flowers: stunning purple irises, bright yellow jonquils and every shade of pink tulips, all arranged in large metal baskets and seeming to call 'bring me home!' The smell of the flowers did not quite dissipate the smell of the cheese, but the mix was not unpleasant.

Because it was mid March, there were apples and pears remaining from the winter, as well as cabbages, brussels sprouts, carrots, potatoes, beets, celery and leeks. Although the only fresh salad greens were endive, 'Good King Henry' which was wild spinach, and wild arugula, greenhouses allowed local farmers to coax early lettuces, and these were also on display at the Market. Early rhubarb and asparagus were also featured.

All sorts of meats and poultry were for sale, including pork, beef, chicken, duck, rabbit and lamb, and it seemed to Gracie that every part of the animal was offered, as well as sausages of every type and combination imaginable.

Chef Pernod seemed really delighted when they found some 'noix de joues de porc' or the center cut of the cheek, called the 'nut.' He bought all of these that the pork vendor had. He also purchased some lamb, and Gracie wondered if a French version of shish-kabob would be on the menu soon.

Equally dazzling was the assortment of fish: from flat fish to shellfish and everything in between.

Muttering to himself, Chef Pernod selected some fresh anchovies, which were much larger than those sold in the States, as well as some halibut.

They would have another Market Day on Thursday, Gracie knew, in Cormery, where they were scheduled to buy enough to last until Sunday, when they would visit the Market in Amboise and have lunch there as well, returning to prepare dinner on the final night of the course.

Gracie loved the emphasis on buying fresh, and buying local, and if it had been up to her, she would have visited the market every morning. However, given the constraints and goals of the seminar, she supposed that three market experiences in a week long course was a pretty good ratio. And of course, on Friday, they would visit the vineyard!

As they toured the Market and watched as Chef Pernod explained his selections and gave his opinion on the goods being offered, Elspeth stuck close to Gracie's side. Not that Gracie minded: the woman was pleasant enough. But Elspeth kept up a non-stop chatter to Gracie in English. Not only did Gracie find this distracting, as non-stop chatter in any language would have been, but she found that it impeded her immersion in French: the more she spoke and heard French, the better her French became. Having Elspeth yammering in English, and having to reply in English, interfered with that. Additionally, since the language of the country they were in, never mind the course they were all taking, was French, Gracie thought it was just a bit rude to converse at length in another language.

About half way through the Market, Gracie leaned over and murmured her thoughts to Elspeth. "My French is so bad I really appreciate being immersed in it," Gracie began humbly. "The more I speak it, and hear it, the better I get at it, too," she went on just above a whisper. "I know it's tempting to speak English, since it's so much easier, Elspeth, but could you do me a favor and stick to French? I'm really trying hard, and speaking English is just making my brain into mush," she finished self-deprecatingly.

"Aye, but your French accent is much better than mine," Elspeth replied, still in English. "I'm very self conscious of the way I sound when I speak French. That's why, I suppose, I want to speak English."

"I think your French sounds fine," Gracie hedged with a big smile.

"Well, all right," Elspeth agreed resignedly.

Secretly, Gracie found herself hoping that having to speak French might also make Elspeth a bit less loquacious.

As they were heading back to the parking area with their purchases, the bakery stalls lured several students to them with the smell of their wonderful breads and cakes. Elspeth was among those who defected towards the scents of yeast and caramelized sugar, and Gracie took the opportunity, now that she was on her own, to detour down the flower stall alley. She chose two big bunches of flowers—orange tulips and yellow daffodils—to bring back, and stood for several moments just breathing in the sweet, and somehow green, air. Did the air ever smell like this at home, she wondered? She was not sure. Perhaps as good, but not the same.

As the vendor was wrapping the flowers in newspaper for her so they wouldn't drip too much on the journey home, Gracie thought she saw Angelique's bright blue raincoat whip around the corner of a stall at the end of the row, and then a man in a dark grey windbreaker hurrying in the same direction.

She turned, but only saw the row of flower stalls.

Maybe Angelique had been buying some flowers, too?

But who had been following her, and why had he been running?

Gracie hastened to catch up with the group, and Elspeth exclaimed over the flowers. "Aren't they just the loveliest things, and so cheery!" she said of the blooms, inadvertently speaking English. Gracie bit her lip and gave Elspeth a pleading look. "You know, back home in Edinburgh, my daffodils are barely poking up through the mulch, let alone in bud or bloom!" Elspeth finished in French, looking chastised.

Gracie agreed that at her home in western Massachusetts, spring was not as advanced as it was here in central France.

As the van pulled out of the parking area and Gracie swung in behind it, she saw Angelique's blue raincoat through a window of the van. She wondered if the man in the grey jacket had been one of the students: she hadn't noticed, particularly, who'd been wearing what that morning as they'd all scrambled to arrange rides.

And so what? It had probably been nothing, Gracie thought, although she made a mental note to ask Angelique about it sometime that day—if they had a moment to breathe, that was. And she reminded herself to look at the other students when they returned to the Château, to see if any of them had a grey windbreaker. She knew Jack would say she was being nosy, but she couldn't help herself.

"I did okay," Gracie admitted in a less-than-enthusiastic voice to Elspeth. They had returned from the Market, taken a short break to change into their chef's whites, and had assembled in the dining room to receive their scores from the evening before. Gracie had found herself once more accompanied by Elspeth, who had come downstairs with Sam and Peter.

Elspeth peered at the tally sheet posted before them and saw that Gracie had received all threes for her gnocchi, mostly threes and one four for her sole, and all threes for her dessert.

"My quenelle wasn't a quenelle, it was more of a curlicue," Gracie admitted, speaking of the fennel cream in her dessert. "But I'm happy no one marked me down for the fennel pollen! How did you get your cream to be malleable?" she asked of Elspeth.

"I took it out of the refrigerator when we began the main course, so it could get soft," Elspeth revealed. "I've used gelatin before and it can set up very stiff," she finished.

Gracie nodded. " My fish may have been a little dry," she added.

Elspeth's scores were similar to Gracie's, and Sam and Peter from California had also done fairly well.

"I think part of the problem was that we had to have the first and second courses done at the same time," sniffed Sam. "In a proper restaurant, we would have done the first course, and then finished the second course in time for it to be served, say, ten minutes after the first course."

"Yes, that might have made the fish a little dry," Elspeth agreed.

"Same thing for your quenelle," Peter advised Gracie. "In a proper restaurant we wouldn't be racing up and down stairs to eat and then serve: we would just be in the kitchen, where we could get everything to the right temperature for serving."

He and Sam, he had confided, had also not used a full sheet of gelatin in their fennel cream, which had made the resulting cream much less firm than Gracie's.

Excusing herself, Gracie moved over slightly, to where Angelique and Anna stood with their table mate Robert Kress, looking at the tally board.

"How did you do Angelique, Anna?" Gracie asked. She turned to Kress and smiled. "And Bob, how about you?" she asked, then turned to look with them at the scoreboard. Kress seemed to be frowning at his scores.

Gracie ran her eye down to his name and saw mostly threes, with a few twos. She resisted a smug smile and concentrated on Anna and Angelique's scores, which were not unlike hers.

As they trooped down the stairs to the kitchen to begin that day's endeavors, Gracie took a moment to ask Angelique if she had bought any flowers at the Market.

Angelique gave her a puzzled look.

"It's just that I saw you—or I thought it was you—at the flower stalls. I was buying some tulips and jonquils, and I thought I saw you, too, and a man, but then you both disappeared," Gracie prodded.

Angelique looked momentarily startled, but then shook her head. "No—it must have been someone else. I didn't buy any flowers," she told Gracie.

Gracie smiled and shrugged. "Must have been," she agreed, but she thought the color of Angelique's coat too distinctive to mistake, and remained unconvinced.

When she had parked her car in the forecourt earlier, the van's passengers had alighted as well, before Michel drove it around to the side of the Château where it was kept. Gracie had lingered by her car, watching to see if anyone wore a grey windbreaker: she just couldn't get the glimpse of the man following the woman in the blue raincoat out of her mind. He had seemed to move with some urgency.

But none of the students was wearing a grey windbreaker, and although a couple of the men had jackets over their arms, they also carried packages and bags from the Market, so it had been impossible to tell if their outerwear matched the one Gracie had seen.

chapter Eight

Because it had been a Market Day, the morning session was shorter than usual. After revealing the wine pairings from the night before, Chef Pernod decided to present a fairly complex lecture on wine and food that would take up most of the morning. Gracie scribbled notes in her own unique shorthand as fast as she could.

The Chef's talk went far beyond the 'white with fish and chicken and red with meat' most people knew by heart. He delved not only into the various flavors different wines could have, from pepper to spice to fruits to mineral and even leather, but also into the layers of flavor in really good wines, and the chemistry behind the tastes and the effect of different foods on wine, and vice versa. He mentioned Gary's choice of viognier to go with the fish dish from the night before, and explained that because the flavor profile of the viognier was more subtle than that of the fish dish, it did not pair really well with it. The evidence was Gary's score for the main fish dish and wine: a two.

"A really good vintage is like an interesting person," Chef Pernod told his class. "And, like an interesting person, a good wine makes you want to know more, to taste more, to find out how it interacts with other things. There are layers of flavor to a wine, just like there are layers of history, emotion, and experience in an interesting person. But just as an intelligent, interesting person will not choose for their best friend someone of a bland nature, so too your wines must be of a similar complexity, and the flavor profile complimentary, to the food's."

Gracie thought that a very apt analogy.

After the lecture, Chef Pernod turned to the subject of what wine they might serve with that night's dinner, and introduced the menu: prosciutto wrapped asparagus with a savory lemon streusel for a starter, and the pork cheeks, braised with potatoes and onions for a main course. Dessert would be fresh strawberries with almond cookies which they would make that day, accompanied by a strawberry almond reduction 'fumé.' Chef's smile was mischievous when he spoke of the dessert, and Gracie wondered what part smoke would play in the dish.

Chef said he would allow the students to choose the starch that would accompany their own dishes of pork cheeks, but the tone of his voice was challenging, not gracious. Gracie decided to use a blend of organic red quinoa and short grain brown rice that normally might be used to make a risotto. Her thinking was that the delicate crunch of the quinoa would be a nice complement to the softness of the pork cheeks, while the rice would absorb the sauce nicely.

Chef skewered each student with those sharp blue eyes again, pausing on each face. Gracie saw Brigitte give the Chef a 100-watt smile, while Henri nodded as though at a comrade; Anna smiled a bit tremulously, but Gracie met Chef Pernod's gaze when it alighted on her, and lifted her chin a fraction. Roberto cowered.

They were given a list of available wines from the Château's cave, and asked to make suggestions for that evening's starter. Gracie noted a non-vintage Vigneau Chevreau Brut. The description said it was a slightly effervescent wine, which she thought might be nice for the opening course. Other students mentioned various citrusy Sauvignon Blancs, a Chardonnay, and a 2012 Château de Bonhoste. This last one was described as a blend of what Chef Pernod had already called the 'three classic white wine grapes of Bordeaux: Semillon, Sauvignon Blanc and Muscadelle.'

"That is a very nice wine, but one must be cautious," commented Chef Pernod, "because the Semillon grape can sometimes negate the citrusy element of the wine," he explained. "And with a vegetable like asparagus we must be careful."

"Why?" asked Sam.

"Does anyone know the answer?" asked Chef Pernod, looking around the kitchen.

"Asparagus contains methionine, and it reacts with most wine," piped up Elspeth, sounding confident. "Just like artichokes contain cynarin. A citrusy wine will handle that?" she finished, less sure.

Chef Pernod stared at her for a nano-second as though not believing such an answer had come out of this somewhat dumpy woman's mouth, and then asked, "but what is it about methionine?"

Gracie cleared her throat: she hadn't known asparagus contained methionine only that it was, in her estimation, a challenge to pair with wine and it usually made people's pee smell weird after they ate it. She had no idea what 'cynarin' was, but recalled that the Greek for artichoke was 'kynara,' and thought the two must be connected. But she remembered her chemistry classes, and knew what methionine was. She also remembered one of Joey's favorite mantras: cooking is chemistry.

"Methionine is a sulfurous amino acid," she spoke up. "I have found that if I blanch and then grill the asparagus before using it in a dish or serving it, it pairs better with wine," she offered. "Also, I think there is a reason asparagus is often used with hollandaise or another lemony sauce," she continued. "I think that helps, too, much as the citrusy wine does."

"Asparagus also contains mercaptan," offered Henri Schilde. "The grilling boosts the sugars in the asparagus, and counteracts the other elements that can clash with the wine," he finished, with a nod of camaraderie over at Gracie.

"Very good!" Chef Pernod declared, looking pleased. Then he focused on Gracie. "And you are correct about the hollandaise sauce," he noted, but sounded surprised. "The cream will smooth out, as it were, the relationship between the asparagus and the wine," he explained, "and the lemon works its magic."

Emboldened, Gracie said, "so, in our dish, we are grilling the asparagus before we wrap it in prosciutto, yes? and the butter and lemon in the streusel, as well as the fat and flavor from the prosciutto, will create that—bridge—between the asparagus and the wine?" she ventured.

Chef Pernod nodded. "Exactly." He looked as fierce as ever, but his tone was quite genial.

With this little lesson having been learned, they all returned to their debate about which wine to serve with the first course. The Château de Bonhoste fell out of favor because of the possibility that the Semillon would make it too smooth. A couple of the Chardonnays became strong contenders and some of the students agreed with Gracie when she suggested the Vigneau Chevreau Brut. "I think the effervescence would be a nice touch, and also good to pair with the asparagus," she insisted.

With a nod of acquiescence that bordered on the mischievous, Chef Pernod then produced a bottle of the Vigneau Chevreau, a bottle of the most favored Chardonnay, and one of the popular Sauvignon Blancs. "We taste, eh?" he invited his students and like a magician, produced a plastic sleeve of small disposable cups like the ones used for ketchup at a fast food restaurant.

Everyone received a dribble of each wine, and was invited to taste them, saving the Vigneau Chevreau Brut for last. All around the kitchen, people sniffed, sipped, swished, slurped and finally swallowed. Brigitte Bernard made a distinct face when she sniffed the Sauvignon. *"Du pipi de chat,"* she muttered, and Chef Pernod, who heard her, laughed indulgently.   Oh, goodie, Gracie thought: was Brigitte becoming Chef's favorite student? Surely that would make her fellow students like her even more, she thought sarcastically.

"Yes, indeed: some of the Loire Sauvignons have a whiff of cat pee, but it is mostly on the nose, not on the palate," Chef Pernod agreed, still grinning. Gracie thought that when he smiled, Chef Pernod was not very fearsome at all, although the rest of the time, his face was quite forbidding. And those ice-blue eyes saw everything, everywhere! "You think it is too much?" he asked Brigitte, actually sounding interested in her opinion.

He sure hadn't been this interested in <u>her</u> ideas about fennel pollen, Gracie thought to herself a bit grumpily.

Once Brigitte had tasted the wine again, she decided that the element added complexity because it was only a small taste of the overall wine. "I have an extremely sensitive nose," Brigitte commented with what Gracie thought was rather affected pride.

Well, maybe Brigitte's nose <u>was</u> exceptionally sensitive to nuances. It was a shame her mind and her mouth hadn't been equally sensitive when she'd made that bad joke to Roberto.

Gracie had noticed from the start that in addition to being a sarcastic snob, Brigitte was a world class whiner: very easily perturbed, she found fault with very small things. That first evening when they had all met and been chatting together, Brigitte had whined that there was no television in their room, or electric kettle. Claude, upon hearing this, had assured her that she had only needed to ask, and these things would instantly be provided. Brigitte had sniffed, and looked somewhat mollified, but Gracie still felt the woman had a real attitude, was overly demanding and quite stuck up.

Now, having heard what she'd said to Roberto and after spending a couple of days in class with the woman, Gracie felt Brigitte also had a mean streak, and not only enjoyed whining and manipulating people—especially Gilles—but also liked to belittle others and thus make herself seem superior.

It came down to the Sauvignon and the Vigneau, and, perhaps fearing the dreaded *'pipi de chat'* the Vigneau was selected for the first course by all the students.

Feeling like she'd achieved a small victory, Gracie turned smiling to the list of wines available to pair with the braised pork cheeks. She had never had pork cheeks, although Elspeth had, and had excitedly told Gracie that they were the most flavorful, tender, melt-in-your-mouth cut of meat on earth. 'Better than tenderloin, better than even the finest filet mignon,' Elspeth had declared.

However, the treatment of the pork cheeks was braising, which meant oil and wine, and it was to be cooked with potatoes and onions, so the flavor of the finished dish would not be delicate. Also, there would be some roundness to the dish, because the gelatinous cheeks would render during the braising process. Gracie thought a nice red with some tannin but overall spicy, ripe fruit flavors would be best.

The class narrowed their selections down to a pinot noir, or red burgundy, and a zinfandel. Once more, Chef Pernod passed around the little cups and everyone had a sniff, a slurp and a swallow. If the class carried on like this, Gracie thought, she would have more fun than she'd expected!

The burgundy had a nose of black cherries with a middle that reminded one of wild mushrooms growing up through damp leaves. It stayed on the palate and finished with a little peppery smokiness that was quite appealing. When Gracie whispered her assessment to Anna, next to her, Chef Pernod overheard and happily agreed: "that is what the sommeliers call 'forest floor'!" he excitedly told them, giving Gracie a look of approval.

Gracie smiled to herself: maybe her palate was a match for Brigitte's 'extremely sensitive' nose.

The zinfandel was the only French zin, a Domaine de l'Arjolle Côtes de Thongue. It, too, was fruity and spicy but the majority preferred the burgundy to pair with the braised pork cheeks.

"I'd drink a bottle of the l'Arjolle over a little ice all by itself," declared Sam, whose partner, Peter, grinned. Brigitte looked highly offended at their remark, but most of the rest of the class chuckled.

Gracie had liked both wines equally, but agreed that the burgundy, a Château du Moulin a Vent Croix de Verillats from 2011, was a better match for the braised pork dish. Once more, all the students concurred.

Those decisions behind them, the class adjourned for lunch, and would return at 2:30 p.m. to begin cooking that evening's meal.

chapter Nine

"You must have really enjoyed the Market this morning," Gracie said to Philippe. It was after dinner on Tuesday, and by mutual consent most of the students had once again gathered in the 'grand salon' for after dinner drinks. Angelique had said she was tired, and had gone up to bed. Brigitte had complained of a migraine, and she and Gilles had also gone to their room, presumably so Gilles could minister to her. But the rest of the students were in the salon, drinks in hand.

Since the clouds had drawn in with the evening and a light rain had begun, Michel had lit a warming, cheerful fire in the huge marble-fronted fireplace, and people now perched on chairs or sat on the two long sofas that formed the main conversational grouping in the high ceilinged room.

Philippe looked momentarily startled at Gracie's comment. "Wh-why would you say that?" he asked in a tight voice.

Gracie smiled to put him at ease. "I just meant, that since you are from Bléré, you must go to the Market every week, and you probably know most of the vendors," she explained, still smiling.

Philippe took a deep breath and appeared to relax. "Oh—yes, yes, of course. Yes, I do—go to the

Market, that is," he answered, and nodded emphatically.

"So—what do you do in Bléré?" Gracie continued. She knew Philippe didn't work in a restaurant, and was curious.

Although everyone had introduced themselves and where they were from that first evening, and although she had learned about some of her fellow students in the course of various conversations, she had not spoken to Philippe at length, and not about himself.

"Ah," Philippe gave a little smile, and touched his neatly trimmed mustache reflexively with his index finger. He cleared his throat. "No, I am not a chef, Mademoiselle," he confessed. "Like you, I am a home cook: in fact, I do all the cooking at my home, as my wife has no talent for it," he explained. "And I enjoy it. It is a wonderful break from work," he noted.

"Oh!" Gracie nodded encouragingly. "Yes, I agree." Again, she wondered if Bob Kress had made a stink about Philippe participating as he had about her enrollment. There was no way to know without asking, and she didn't really want to do that.

Perhaps Kress hadn't wanted to speak against another man, but felt justified in objecting to a woman: there was, after all, still quite a 'glass ceiling' when it came to women becoming top chefs! Oh, well.

"What sort of work do you do?" she asked Philippe again.

He gave a small smile once more. "I am a Police Detective," he revealed.

"No kidding!" Gracie exclaimed, delighted, and launched into a fast discourse on Jack Draper, the Berkshire County Detective, and how they had met in connection with their work, and how she sometimes helped him solve crimes in their region.

Philippe appeared interested, but like all French men, he was usually very courteous when speaking with a woman even if inwardly he was rolling his eyes and tapping his fingers with impatience. Therefore, Gracie was not certain whether he was really entertained by her commentary, or just being polite.

Prompted by Gracie's enthusiasm, however, Philippe explained the way the French National Police, or Judicial Police, force was divided into different regions. Gracie learned that he was part of the squad that served Bléré and the area surrounding it, north of the A-85, the major east west road that led to Tours.

"Excuse me," said Roberto: he had approached Gracie where she sat talking with Philippe.

"Oh, please join us, Roberto," Gracie said with a smile.

Roberto did so, perching on the ottoman to one side of the sofa. "I think I had your asparagus tonight," he whispered, addressing Gracie. "I noticed the way you wrapped the prosciutto, weaving it around the stalks," he continued, smiling at her and at Philippe as well, who looked disinterested, but smiled back.

"Yes: it reminded me of a barber's pole, you know, with the red and white stripes?" Gracie replied, making a twisty motion with one hand.

Neither Roberto nor Philippe appeared to know what she was talking about, so she had to explain it. Then they understood.

"Well, it was very good," Roberto continued. "I gave you a four. And you were right about the wine, too: perfect."

"It was a very good choice," agreed Philippe.

"What did you think of the dessert?" Gracie asked conversationally of both her companions. "I'd never used dry ice before."

Dessert had started out simply enough: plain almond cake and hulled, fresh strawberries. Then each student made a small reduction from mashed, sieved strawberries and almond extract, simmering the liquid until it was syrupy. This was to be drizzled around each serving of cake and berries once they were plated.

The trick, however, had been the use of pieces of dry ice in the syrup. Because the ice converted from solid to gas without becoming liquid, when the students added it to their small pots of syrup, the mixture immediately began to smoke. Each quickly drizzled the syrup, with its accompanying smoke, on their serving plates and covered the plates with a small dome. When the dessert had been presented, these domes were lifted, and the smoke wafted a concentrated hit of almond and strawberry essence up to the diner.

Philippe gave a quick smile. "Nor have I, although I have seen it done," he replied.

"Oh, yes, on television!" Roberto chimed in.

"I do not think I would use it at home: my wife would probably not be that impressed," Philippe confided. "But it was interesting to try here. I think it's better suited to a restaurant setting."

Roberto was nodding. "I could see doing it for gelato," he commented, his eyes alight with imagination. "It might be a unique and fun way to liven up a simple and somewhat dull dessert."

They all smiled in agreement, then Philippe looked at his watch and stood quickly.

"If you will excuse me?" he said perfunctorily, and walked swiftly away.

For a second or two, both Gracie and Roberto wondered at the other student's abruptness but soon forgot all about it: their two table mates, Henri and Gary, were getting into a rather heated argument on the other side of the salon about how each had trimmed his asparagus, and which was the correct way. Their voices had become a bit loud. The other people in the room stopped their conversations and turned to look at the two of them.

Apparently, Gary did not hold with Henri's method of bending the asparagus spears until they broke naturally at the place where the tender part of the stalk began. The Australian felt that slicing off the ends uniformly was the best way to handle the vegetable.

"If you do it your way, you get all raggedy pieces of different lengths," Gary protested in a tone which suggested few worse transgressions.

"But my way uses the best part of the asparagus, with no chewy ends," Henri returned. "And as for the varying lengths, I make all the bottoms the same, and arrange the tops artfully so they look like a bunch of flowers," he finished assuredly. His voice, though firm, stayed quite mild and Gracie was impressed with his self control.

Chefs could be among the most vituperous of participants when involved in a debate over cuisine. Gracie thought Henri was a bit of a know-it-all in spite of the fact that he was a very skilled chef. She didn't think Gary would respond well to Henri's attitude.

She was right.

"Well, if it was your asparagus I saw at the next table, it didn't look like any bunch of flowers I've ever seen!" the Australian exclaimed heatedly, and stood up from the chair where he'd been sitting. "It looked like you'd just thrown the stalks around and tossed the prosciutto on top," he continued, waving one hand to mime scattering the asparagus and prosciutto. "Very sloppy." His voice was deeply disapproving.

"Sloppy!?" Henri, too, stood up, and the two men looked like they might come to blows in front of the large fireplace. Over asparagus? Then again, Henri was nothing if not precise, so to call him 'sloppy' was probably deeply offensive.

"Hold on, hold on, now just calm down!" Gracie said in a fairly loud voice. She stood, and moved swiftly over to Henri and Gary. It seemed the other students were frozen in a tableau, just watching the action. She took each man's arm and shook lightly. "This is not the time or place for criticism like this," Gracie chastised them. "That's Chef Pernod's job, not ours, and he's good enough at it that we don't need to help him!" she added in an effort to inject a little levity into the tense situation. "We're students, and while <u>helpful</u> criticism, advice, and comments are welcome, negative talk like this is not."

She paused, and both Henri and Gary became silent; Henri even looked somewhat abashed at being called out for ill manners. Gary's jaw worked, though, and he looked as though he had plenty more to say, none of it helpful.

"Why don't we bring up the question of the best way to trim asparagus first thing tomorrow, and ask Chef Pernod?" Gracie concluded. "Then we can hear what the expert has to say."

Henri and Gary nodded uneasily, and, avoiding each other's eyes, moved to join different people in the room. In a few minutes, conversation had returned to its previous level and mood.

"That was nicely done," Roberto told Gracie when she returned to the sofa and sat down again.

Gracie shrugged. "It's stupid to argue over something like that, when we have one of France's top chefs teaching us, and can just ask him!" she declared. "Plus, tomorrow when the scores are posted, we can see if the way Henri trimmed his asparagus was preferred to the way Gary did it," she added.

She and Roberto then discussed Italian food for a short while: he loved talking about his native cuisine. Not wanting to be rude and speak Italian in front of the other students, who probably didn't understand it, they had not had a chance to do much talking in Italian. But now since it was just the two of them chatting in one section of the room, Roberto waxed enthusiastic in his own language about classic Italian regional cuisines. Since the others were all engaged in their own conversations, Gracie did likewise, thinking that it would be a good time to practice her Italian. She enjoyed getting some tips from Roberto, and in turn sharing a couple of things she had learned from her father, and was grateful when Roberto helped her along when she was stumped for a word or phrase.

By about eleven o'clock, everyone started to head up to their rooms. Although Gracie had intended to give herself an early night, she had greatly enjoyed the after dinner camaraderie, and didn't regret the late hour. She had also intended to call Jack, but since it was so late, she thought she would just send him a quick email and then get ready for bed.

Her room was on the far end of the Château, snugged into one of the tall towers that guarded the corners of the building. Like proper 'castles,' the Château had once had a moat and an iron portcullis as well as a thick stone outer wall and gate. The gate and portcullis had been replaced by a graceful wrought iron entryway that was more for ornament than for security, and the moat had long since been filled in to make the forecourt where people parked their vehicles, but the towers with their narrow vertical windows still remained.

To get to her room, Gracie needed to climb up both flights of the grand staircase and then turn right; she then had to walk all the way down a long corridor that intersected another, short, corridor which ran perpendicularly to the long one. The Château was laid out in an H pattern, with the long central corridor running along the front of the building and two short corridors on either end connecting the towers to the rest of the Château.

Gracie's room was at the back of the Château, facing the gardens, so when she reached the short corridor, she turned right again, but then she stopped. Faintly, she heard doors opening and closing in the rest of the Château as her fellow students entered their rooms, and she heard a smattering of conversation and several 'good night!s' as well. But she also heard—or thought she heard—raised voices?

Not Gary and Henri arguing over asparagus again, she hoped?!

Shaking her head at the possibility, Gracie turned and tiptoed back the way she had come until she stood in the middle of the long corridor. Claude had installed automatic overhead lights that switched on when motion in the corridor was detected, so

Gracie was bathed in light as she paused, and listened intently.

She chuckled to herself that if anyone happened to observe her from outside the Château, she'd look like an idiot playing statues on her own.

The voices had been louder, but now were subdued. In a moment they became audible once more, and Gracie tried to get a bead on where they were coming from: it sounded like the argument was in one of the last guest rooms on the opposite end of the Château. The towers on that side of the building were part of the Château's Chapel: guest rooms in that section were all off the corridor. Gracie remembered this from the tour Claude had given her.

Now, Gracie stayed still a moment longer, feeling a bit foolish for so obviously trying to overhear something not meant for her ears. She couldn't make out any words since the voices were muffled, but it was clearly a man's voice, and possibly a woman's, though the second voice was so faint it was difficult to know for certain.

With a sigh, Gracie turned around, and tiptoed back to her own room. She passed the doorway to the front facing tower room, and heard rather loud snores emanating through the thick walls and door. Although she didn't know exactly where everyone's rooms were, Gracie knew the occupant of the front facing tower room on her end of the Château was

Henri Schilde. Huh. So it hadn't been Henri and Gary arguing again.

Well, Gracie thought as she unlocked her door and slipped inside, it was no business of hers. If she was going to be bright and alert for class the next morning, she had better wash up and get to bed.

chapter Ten

Unfortunately, the moment her head made contact with the pillow, Gracie knew she wasn't going to go to sleep: at least, not right away. The day had been full of sights, sounds and smells that had energized and excited her. It had also been full of challenges with the cooking class, and there had been that sighting at the Market of the woman in the bright blue raincoat, which still bothered her.

Gracie had believed Angelique at first when she had said that she had been nowhere near the flower stalls, and that Gracie must have been mistaken. But the more Gracie thought about what she had seen, the more she had become convinced that Angelique had, indeed, been the woman she had seen. But who had been the man in the grey windbreaker, apparently running after her? And had he really been following her, or had it just looked like that from Gracie's vantage point? She hadn't been able to get much of an impression of the man: average height, average build—she wasn't even sure what sort of trousers he'd been wearing only that they had been dark.

And just now, the mysterious argument—it had sounded like an argument—between two of the other students. Not that arguments were uncommon:

witness the spat between Henri and Gary over how to trim asparagus.

But that had been, well, almost silly. It had been a show of superiority between two rivals over what was essentially a very trivial thing. Somehow, though, the exchange she had tried to overhear a little while earlier hadn't seemed trivial. Gracie couldn't quite put her finger on it, but the timbre of the voices had seemed far more urgent, and the subject of whatever they had been discussing must, therefore, have been important.

She sighed, and turned over to face her open window. It was a cool night, and clear, and she loved sleeping with the huge old casement windows thrown wide to the smells and gentle sounds of the French countryside at night.

Wondering what stars she could see and mentally trying to figure out which direction her window faced—she determined it faced west— Gracie clambered out of bed and made her way to the windowsill. A handy window seat had been furnished with a small cushion and a couple of pillows, and she knelt on this and put her elbows on the sill, leaned out a little bit and took a deep breath.

There were the stars! She could make out Orion, just about to set, and, higher in the sky, she thought the steady, bright orb must be Jupiter. As Gracie's eyes adjusted to the dark, she could see more and more. If only that light at the far end of the Château weren't on, she thought, her night vision would be really good.

Gracie turned slightly and squinted down the back of the building at the offending light: it made a scalene triangle of brightness on the ground behind the Château. Whoever had that room was certainly a night owl.

What time was it, anyway? Just 11:30 p.m. Well, not that late, then. Let's see, she thought: it would only be 5:30 p.m. at home. Jack should be back from work...

Gracie hopped off the window seat and grabbed her iPhone. Moments later the call went through and she was rewarded with Jack's voice.

"Hey, Gracie, it's good to hear from you!" he answered, and sounded really pleased she had called.

"I'm not interrupting, am I?" Gracie asked considerately.

"Nope. Just got back from taking Woof for a short walk: it's kind of icy and cold so we didn't go far, just in the meadow for a bit. How's it going? You having fun?" he asked anxiously.

Gracie regaled him for several minutes with her recollection of the Market, and of the challenges she'd encountered in the cooking class so far. He was especially impressed with the dry ice dessert. Gracie raved about a couple of the recipes they had cooked, and told him she'd have to find a butcher who could get her pork cheeks. "I want to cook those for you, Jack: you'll love them," she assured him. "Amazingly tender, they melt in your mouth, and the meat is soooooo tasty!" she said with a big smile. She thought that the pork cheeks, surprisingly, were her favorite dish so far.

As she spoke, she realized how much she enjoyed sharing her experiences with Jack. She also realized there had been another reason she had called: she missed him.

"So, how's work?" she asked him.

He sighed. "We had a little problem down on the south side," he replied, meaning the south side of Pittsfield. "People are up in arms about a young man, Lavoriss Johnson," he continued, and told Gracie about a possible case of police brutality that had occurred the day before. A young man had been taken into custody by police for suspected drug trafficking, but some time between his being handcuffed and his arrival at the police station, the man had apparently been beaten: a broken leg, shattered patella and several fractured ribs were among his complaints when he entered the booking room.

"Uh-oh," Gracie noted. "That sounds bad: what police department is it?"

"Lee," Jack answered, naming the town. "There's a lot of tension," he continued. "We've had a sit-in and one march, with more scheduled, and so far it's all been peaceful, but it's like a covered pot that's simmering, right below the boiling point," he explained. "And something is going to turn up that heat and the lid will blow off," he added with foreboding.

Near the turnpike, the southern reaches of Pittsfield were an unattractive mix of light industry and old residences, and those who were part of a lower socio-economic level tended to settle there. Residents rented flats in hundred-plus year old buildings with dodgy wiring and leaky pipes, or places in 1970's era blond-brick low-rise apartment buildings. Most worked in nearby factories or in low-level service jobs.

Although Jack was strict with himself about being racist, he had to admit that most of the people living in the section he spoke about were not Caucasian. Originally labeled 'the Quadrangle' because of its roughly square shape, the area had been called 'the Quad' in the latter decades of the past century, and now was referred to as 'Quadville,' with a distinctly derisive twist. Even the residents of 'Quadville' shook their heads when they pronounced the moniker.

"You've got extra patrols and stuff, right?" Gracie asked, concerned.

"Oh, yeah, sure, the mutual agreement officers are all working overtime. But like I said, it's just keeping the lid on things, it's not a solution." He sighed.

"Do you think the Lee police are, well, guilty?" Gracie asked in a whisper. Part of her wished she were there to cover the story and investigate on her own, and another part of her was happy she wasn't.

Jack made a noise between a grunt and a groan. "I wasn't there," he replied carefully. "So I do not really know." He paused. "But—knowing the officers involved?" He sighed again. "Possibly, yeah, they roughed Johnson up a little too, erm, enthusiastically."

"Ah, well, then they should be disciplined," Gracie judged.

Jack agreed, but then explained that while punishing the cops accused of abusing their suspect while in custody would be the right thing to do, the incident was having a much longer reach.

"Everywhere you go down there, even in my unmarked car, people know you're a cop. They stare at you: they aren't intimidated, they're angry, and they see cops, or all law enforcement really, as the enemy." He paused. "I've arrested plenty of criminals and none of them have ever hugged me or been happy because I arrested them, but I've rarely encountered the kind of hatred I have encountered in the last couple of days," he confided to Gracie. His voice was grim. "This incident just brought all of those emotions out."

"Oh, Jack, I'm so sorry. Please be careful," Gracie put in, her voice very soft.

"I will be, don't worry. But it's not just me: I only go down there to see how things are, and to help out if need be. It's the guys in the local departments, especially the other officers with Lee P.D., and our Sheriff's Deputies: they're on the front lines, 24/7, and it's starting to get to them."

"Well, what do you think is the solution?" Gracie asked.

"I don't know the answer to that question, Gracie," he answered, bleak. Then he changed the subject. "Hey, it must be awfully late over there," he said, and Gracie agreed it was now nearly midnight. "Why are you still awake? Everything ok? Or is it reverse jet-lag?" Jack asked.

Gracie repeated that everything was really fine, she was having a great time and learning a lot, and meeting some interesting people. Then she characterized a few of her fellow students in more detail, and told Jack about the argument over the asparagus.

Jack laughed. "Geez, if that's their biggest problem, they're lucky!" he declared with another chuckle. "They sound like prima donnas."

Gracie agreed. "Well, everyone has a distinct personality," she said kindly. "But most of them are really nice," she added. She mentioned Robert Kress, who had objected to her taking the course, and Jack was insulted on her behalf until Gracie explained that she'd spoken with him, and he appeared to have adjusted his previously negative opinion of her. Plus, she added just the smallest bit gleefully, she thought she was a better cook than he was. "He wants to open a Titanic themed restaurant in Southampton," she continued, her tone even.

"I'd think Southampton would already have one," Jack replied.

"They do, the Titanic Pub," Gracie replied, having gone there before. "I think Bob Kress' concept is more, well, upscale."

Jack snorted in mild derision. "What's he going to call it, the Lifeboat?" he joked.

Gracie gave a short laugh. "I don't know. But with all the people who love the Titanic and anything having to do with it, it might do all right...if the food is good," she added. "His menu is ambitious."

Jack made a humming noise that suggested he didn't have high hopes for Kress' restaurant. "Have you hit it off with anyone in particular?" he asked then.

Gracie told him about Roberto from Genoa, and Anna from Luxembourg, and about Angelique who wanted to open a Toulousain restaurant near Blois, and finally about Elspeth, who it seemed had chosen Gracie as her new 'BFF'. "There's a police detective here, too!" she remembered then. "Philippe Zafran. He's quite nice, although he keeps himself to himself, if you know what I mean," Gracie said.

"Comes with the job," Jack explained. "It's a habit."

Gracie thought for a moment, and then realized he was right. "I wonder if he's ever encountered the negativism you're running into, over here," Gracie continued. "I don't know what the French people think of their 'gendarmes,' " she said, using the common term for police officer.

"It might be interesting to ask him," Jack agreed, sounding intrigued about hearing a foreign policeman's perspective on what could very well be a common challenge.

Then Gracie told him about thinking she'd seen Angelique at the Market, running away from a man. "She seems really nice, and I don't think her life has been especially easy," Gracie mused. "She's got quite good technique, and some really imaginative ideas about food," Gracie enthused. "But, it's funny: I don't know why she'd lie to me and say she wasn't in the flower market. I'm sure she was the woman I saw."

She could hear Jack's shrug over the phone. "C'mon, Gracie, there have to be a lot of women with blue raincoats," he reassured her.

Gracie made a noise that meant she didn't agree with Jack's statement. "But it's a very distinctive shade of blue, not quite royal blue, and with a lot of reddish purple tone in it," she protested. "Like a deep periwinkle, if you know what I mean."

Jack chuckled again. He wasn't color blind, but the nuances among varying shades of blue were lost on him. "Still: a lot of women probably bought a coat like that. And even if it was Angelique, maybe she wants to keep whatever she was doing private," Jack reasoned. "It's no business of yours, especially if you asked her about it, and she denied it," he admonished.

Gracie sighed: he was right. Nosiness—she preferred to call it 'curiosity'—was a failing of hers, although she thought it gave her an edge as a reporter.

But in this case, she probably was making too much of nothing. She needed to learn to leave her job as an investigative news reporter behind her: she was on holiday! She should be enjoying the sights and sounds and smells and tastes of France, and of her course. She should be focusing on this wonderful experience, not seeing mysteries and mayhem in every odd encounter or overheard conversation.

Suddenly, she was very tired, and yawned.

"Well, I see I've had my usual stimulating effect on you," Jack joked.

Gracie apologized, but admitted that she was finally ready for bed. After a few more words, they disconnected.

Gracie almost fell into her bed, and was instantly asleep.

chapter Eleven

When the students arrived at their kitchen stations the following morning—was it already Wednesday, Gracie thought?—they each found four glasses of different sizes confronting them.

"Oh, this looks like fun," Gracie commented to Angelique, who rewarded her with a tired smile.

Elspeth, who had overheard Gracie's jest, turned from her station in the row ahead, and grinned.

"Och, but they've not included a shot glass, for a wee dram!" she commented jovially, in English again. But Gracie just smiled at her and said nothing.

Chef Pernod clapped his hands for silence, and then explained that they would be making a four course meal for that evening, consisting of a wild mushroom soup, a stuffed sardine recipe from Italy, a main course of lamb chops with a spinach and turnip purée, and dessert. "We will make it simple, eh? Fresh fruit and nuts, a bit of cheese, and a dessert wine," Chef Pernod said of dessert.

Gracie suspected that if he wanted to keep dessert 'simple'—and no matter what Chef Pernod said, she knew it wouldn't be 'simple'—the rest of the meal must be quite complicated.

Chef Pernod also explained that they would be working in two groups to make the soup and the appetizer, although the lamb chops would be cooked, as usual, by each student individually, and the desserts composed by each student from the choices offered of produce, cheese, nuts, etc. They were cautioned to keep the earlier courses of the meal in mind when assembling their desserts. "It is important to clean the palate but also leave the tastebuds with something sweet," Chef Pernod advised.

The reason the glasses were at their stations, he continued, was so that they could be thinking about what beverage to serve with each course.

The asparagus debate had been solved earlier, as well, when the scores had been posted and had shown that both Gary and Henri had received a '3' for their first course. Chef had said that both students' approaches to trimming asparagus had merit. Henri and Gary had not looked completely happy with this conclusion, but they had apparently agreed to disagree, since Gracie had seen them shake hands when they'd arrived at their contiguous work stations earlier.

While everyone now was nodding and looked at the range of glasses in front of them, Chef Pernod walked to the middle of the rows of cooking stations and pointed. "These students to my right will be group A, and those on my left, group B. Gather together, please."

Gracie was disappointed to see that her group did not include Philippe: she had hoped to have a chance to talk with him about the police's relations with their constituents here in France. Her group did however, include Gary, whom Chef Pernod had transferred from the other team's side to make the numbers even.

Gracie, Angelique, Anna and the rest of their 'team' as Gracie called them—Bob Kress, Roberto, Gary and Jean Soules—read the directions for the wild mushroom soup. They would make it this morning, then refrigerate it, so they would only need to warm it through that evening to serve.

The first step was to clean and chop freshly harvested wild mushrooms, along with some crimini that would be puréed and form the base of the soup. Bob and Jean worked on this while Gracie put a large knob of butter and a slug of olive oil in a huge flat pan, and warmed it just until the butter melted.

Bob, although he was quite opinionated, seemed willing to work alongside his fellow students, something that surprised Gracie.

Angelique volunteered for the tedious job of clarifying the melted butter, for the soup would be best without the milk solids.

"I'm shocked we don't have some *ghee* handy," Gracie quipped to Bob, who rewarded her with conspiratorial smile.

Gary offered his assistance to Angelique, and Gracie noticed that, while he made a few remarks to her that looked like conversational gambits, Angelique's only responses were tired smiles and a focus on the task at hand. Gracie was too far away to hear what was being said, but the body language suggested that Gary was chatting up Angelique, but that she was not especially interested.

Gracie didn't blame Gary for trying: Angelique was beautiful, and he'd already made several comments to that effect when he had been at their dinner table, and out of Angelique's hearing. Maybe he was just being nice, but Gracie thought he was a bit too much of an opportunist for that to be completely true. And after all, clarifying butter wasn't a team effort!

Once the crimini had been sautéed in the clarified butter and oil, chopped fresh thyme, chives and parsley were added, and a hefty splash of good sherry. The sherry bubbled briefly and the alcohol cleaned the bottom of the pan of any bits of mushroom or herbs that might have stuck slightly. This was then removed to a sauce pan and Anna added vegetable stock and stirred. Then, wielding one of Gracie's favorite kitchen appliances, she puréed the mushrooms and stock with an immersion blender until the substance was as smooth as satin.

Meanwhile, the wild mushrooms (cepes and chanterelles) had been diced—Jean did that—and were sautéed in more clarified butter and oil. When they were nicely caramelized, they were added to the crimini purée.

The soup was now finished, and the discussion turned to presentation. A couple of times Gary glanced over to try and see what the other team was doing, but it was all more or less the same as what they had done. The difference, he advised them in that remarkable accent of his, would be in the final seasoning and presentation. Anna suggested a couple of chives arranged on top of each small bowl of soup. People liked that idea but wondered if there could be more done to make their creation superb—and superior to the other team's.

They had decided to put a couple of large, flat parsley leaves atop the soup as well as the chives, when Gracie suggested a whispered sprinkle of truffle powder as well.

"You've been in the spice cabinet again, haven't you?" Anna asked, her tone indulgent.

Gracie smiled and nodded. "Yes—I don't want to put too much on, but just a little, when it hits the hot soup, well, it should smell amazing…" she explained.

The others seemed only mildly concerned that Chef would object because the ingredient of truffle powder was not part of the recipe.

"He told us to be creative," Gracie repeated convincingly.

Her fellow students agreed, and then they turned to the topic of what wine to serve with the soup.

"We don't want anything overpowering," mused Anna.

"Could we serve sherry?" Angelique asked quietly. "It's in the soup."

"A dry sherry, perhaps," Gary agreed with a smile, which went unanswered by the blonde chef.

"Well, sherry would be one possibility," Gracie chimed in, "but do you think it would be too much the same flavor as the soup?"

"Not if we chose a very dry sherry, no," Roberto offered. "The sherry in the soup is an amontillado. How about a fino? Or a manzanilla?" he proposed.

"I like that idea," Bob Kress said approvingly, and nodded. "And because finos and such are served chilled, I think it would be a good foil for the hot soup," he concluded.

They all agreed, and then turned their attention to the appetizer recipe for the stuffed sardines. This was a more complex dish, requiring the creation of a tomato paste as a first step.

"I suppose we could just use tomato paste from a tin, couldn't we?" Gracie murmured to Angelique, who had returned to her work station after placing their mushroom soup in a container in the refrigerator.

Angelique looked momentarily startled, as though she hadn't been paying attention to the preparation of the next dish.

"Are you ok?" Gracie asked, concerned. "You seem distracted," she added kindly.

"Oh, no, I am fine," Angelique said with a smile. "I just did not sleep very well last night, so I am—spacing out!" she finished with another smile and a small shrug.

Gary was happily chopping and seeding tomatoes while Anna and Roberto dealt with the basil, parsley, pine nuts, garlic and seasonings. Roberto apparently very much approved of the basil, especially, as he kept sniffing it and smiling happily. The tomatoes were sautéed and then reduced, but the result didn't look like tomato paste, as there were chunks of tomato flesh and bits of skin in the sauté pan.

"I think we need to sieve it, to get the tomato skin out and get rid of the seeds and chunks," Anna suggested.

"We should have blanched and skinned the tomatoes!" Bob Kress put in, sounding distressed.

"The recipe didn't say anything about that," frowned Gracie.

Gary whispered, "Yeah, but I noticed the other team did that, though," and he looked at his team mates in concern.

"Oh, why didn't you say?" Anna nearly wailed.

Gracie bit back an acerbic comment that they were only talking about tomato paste, not a global cataclysm.

"The tomato skins will mean more flavor," Roberto put in decisively, and nodded for emphasis.

"That's quite true," Bob Kress agreed happily.

"But the skins won't be good in the final dish," Anna objected.

Gracie pointed out that the tomatoes were supposed to be mixed with the chopped nuts and garlic and spices. "I don't think it's supposed to be a completely smooth sauce," she commented. "But I do agree, we need to remove the tomato skins."

Grinning, Gary approached with a small pair of what looked like long tweezers—they were culinary tweezers, in fact—and, removing the pan from heat as he worked, he diligently removed all the skin he could find in the tomato sauce. Anna helped by using a fork to separate some pulp that stubbornly clung to the skin here and there. Then they ran the mixture through the sieve and decided it was finished.

Satisfied, the team added the rest of the ingredients, and while the stuffing cooled, they removed the heads and bones of the sardines they had been given to prepare. Everything had to be the same temperature: food safety was very important, Gary noted, echoing Chef Pernod's admonishments, and he regaled them with a short but frightening tale of some spoiled taramasalata he had once encountered.

Then they stuffed the sardines, which had been split down the middle, and closed each small fish with toothpicks. These were then wrapped tightly and put in the fridge: they would be lightly oiled then baked that evening, and served on a bed of wild arugula. Gracie suggested a light dusting with panko breadcrumbs to give crunch and texture, as well as visual interest.

They chose a local 'melon de bourgogne' Muscadet-Coteaux de la Loire *sur lie*, with nice body and enough flavor to stand up to the spicy sardine dish. Then, having finished their duties for the morning, the entire class trooped upstairs for lunch.

"Where's Angelique?" Gracie asked as she and Anna filled their plates from the buffet and looked around to decide where to sit. It was a sunny, warm day and the rear terrace of the Château looked inviting. Michel and Monique had set out a few small cast iron tables and chairs, and a couple of people were already out there with their lunches, enjoying the weather.

"I don't see her," Anna answered with a slight frown.

"She said she wanted to get a start on her turnips for tonight," Elspeth put in helpfully, coming up to them with her own plate, and what looked like a double espresso. "I don't think she's feeling quite herself," she added.

"She said she hadn't slept well," Gracie informed them as the three of them headed for the terrace.

"Maybe she'll try to squeeze in a nap before we start cooking for tonight," Elspeth wondered.

"That's not a bad idea," Anna agreed. "I don't know about the rest of you, but I'm exhausted every night!" she exclaimed.

"We are maintaining quite a pace," Elspeth agreed cheerfully, and tucked into her lunch.

"I for one can't wait to look over the cheese and fruit and nut selection," Gracie said eagerly. "The choice of what we select for the dessert plate will affect, of course, the wine we choose too," she continued, thinking out loud. Already she had decided that, since the lamb dish had a good earthy spice to it thanks to the turnips and the nutmeg and garlic that flavored the spinach, as well as a rich Marsala reduction, her dessert plate should be fairly sweet and creamy. She was also excited about choosing a dessert wine to go with her concoction.

Gracie noticed that Gary, Bob Kress and Roberto sat together for lunch, possibly discussing their approaches to the remaining dishes to be made for that evening's meal. Maybe Angelique <u>was</u> trying to get a short nap, Gracie thought as she returned to her own room to freshen up before the afternoon session: she had never come to lunch, at least not that Gracie had seen.

chapter Twelve

By late afternoon, everything was in readiness for that evening's dinner, and the students took a short break. Feeling the need for some fresh air, Gracie quickly switched her chef's white tunic for a knitted cotton cardigan and stepped out into the Château's gardens for a few minutes. The sunny day had continued, and in the west the sun was dropping, and touching everything with a slanted, golden light.

The class was going well, Gracie thought: at least, she was having fun. And she was learning a lot: her technique and skills might be pretty good, but there was always room for improvement. And coupled with those, a great chef needed to have imagination, or what Chef Pernod called 'it,' as in 'you have it or you don't.' Gracie thought of it as talent, or a gift, or even imagination when it came to food preparation and presentation.

As the lessons and discussions had continued, Gracie had had a chance to talk with most of her fellow students, and had formed opinions of many of them.

Elspeth was a bit overbearing, Gracie thought, but she was a nice enough person, and although she didn't seem to be an outstanding cook, she was competent enough. She seemed to get along with the other students, too, although that could just be the result of her forceful personality.

Gracie had liked Angelique and Anna right away, and also felt 'sympa' towards Roberto, whose skills needed polishing, and who always seemed in fear of a scolding, but who tried very hard. Sam and Peter were a lot of fun to be around, and Gracie felt herself gravitating towards them during the students' rare 'down' time, just because the pair were so energetic and always cheerful. They were there, surely, to learn and improve, but it seemed to Gracie that they were also taking this course to, well, have fun and make friends, much as she was.

Gracie couldn't say she really liked Gary from Australia, though. His accent made everything he said seem like a joke, which made conversation with him a challenge, and he was argumentative and surprisingly sexist, something guaranteed to raise Gracie's hackles. He was talented, yes, but not particularly skilled, and Gracie didn't like the way he instantly judged his fellow students, although she had to admit, some of his zingers about Brigitte had been awfully funny.

Gracie had finally decided that Brigitte from Rouen was really, truly a pain, and a master manipulator, especially when it came to her husband, Gilles. He seemed quiet and rather sweet, Gracie thought, but then reflected that, married to Brigitte, how could he be otherwise? She was constantly complaining about something, and nothing was ever quite up to her standards, which were, of course, the best. At least in her opinion, and to Brigitte, that was all that mattered.

Henri, who completed Gracie's table of four at dinner along with Gary and Roberto, was extremely serious and a bit of a know it all. However, he was a really skilled chef although not very imaginative. Gracie thought he would probably go quite far in the restaurant business, so she supposed that he could be given a little leeway when it came to pride.

Gracie had been surprised by Robert Kress: his skills were not very honed but he was very creative. However, he likely wouldn't do the cooking himself at his restaurant: Gracie envisioned him as the 'master mind' behind the operation—or perhaps out in front, dressed in his Edwardian tuxedo, mingling with his patrons!

Jean Soules, a cook in a small Paris restaurant, was almost completely unknown to Gracie, as well as to everyone else: very much a loner, Soules had hardly spoken to anyone, and all people knew of him was his name and where he worked and the fact that he was taking this course because he wanted to become a chef in a larger, more prestigious establishment. Gracie had observed little of him in the kitchen, but she thought he was reasonably skilled and possibly had flashes of inspiration: his presentation of the sole on their first day had been the prettiest of everyone's.

Philippe, the local police detective whose wife let him do all the cooking at home, had been quite friendly, especially during the first evening's reception, when everyone had been new, unsure, and on their best behavior. His work station was just in front of Gracie, so she'd been able to notice that he was quite expert in preparation and great at taking direction.

They had been so busy, Gracie hadn't had a chance to make conversation with Philippe and bring up Jack's current dilemma to see if the French Detective had encountered such negative opinion, too. She hoped, as she trotted up the pleached alley of plane trees back towards the Château, she would have a chance to speak with him soon: maybe it would make Jack feel better, to know that police all over the globe had to deal with the same unpleasant issues.

Monique had placed oblong containers of cheerful pansies along the stone balustrade of the terrace and as Gracie turned to go inside, the bright colors made her smile. She took a moment to study the Château's rear façade, and to see if she could figure out where everyone's rooms were.

There was her room, on the far right: her window was open, and she noted with a giggle that hers was the only one that was. The next window belonged to Anna Guteknecht's room, and the one after that to Gary's room. Robert Kress' room was the next window, and then there was one very large window that Claude had told her had been an eighteenth century addition. This provided a wonderful view of the back gardens to people climbing the Château's main staircase.

On the other side of the staircase window were three more windows, corresponding to three more guest rooms. Gracie thought that one must be Roberto's, and another Angelique's, but she was unsure about the third. The chapel occupied that far end of the Château on both floors.

Three guest rooms were on the front side of the Château's first floor. Henri Schilde's room was the front facing partner to Gracie's, which faced the gardens. On the other end of the Château just next to the chapel was Elspeth's room, and next to her were Sam and Peter from California. Those two rooms actually could be connected to make one very large suite, and apparently the three students had chatted away into the night since they'd arrived, sharing recipes and—so Elspeth said—gossip.

Most of the Château's ground floor windows belonged to the building's function rooms, dining room and salons. These were directly opposite Gracie as she approached the double glass doors off the terrace. However, Brigitte and Gilles from Rouen had one of the large, front facing ground floor suites with a little balcony overlooking the roadway and the town of Reignac. Across the hall from them, Martin Pernod had another suite, but this one faced the gardens and Gracie thought she could figure out which windows were his. But the Château was surprising: some rooms had two windows, and others, like hers, just one where you might expect there to be two.

Gracie let herself in the double glass doors, skimmed by Michel at the reservations desk with a wave and a smile, and began to dash up the stairs to the first floor, where her room was. As she gained the upstairs hallway with its rank of front facing windows, she was surprised to see Philippe, still in his chef's whites, whom she had just been hoping to run into: he was standing at the top of the stairs, apparently about to descend.

"Well, hello!" Gracie addressed him cheerfully, stopping next to him in the corridor. "I was hoping I'd catch you," she continued, thinking that he must have the third room on the far side of the central staircase.

Philippe frowned, and looked wary. "Catch me?" he asked, sounding strained.

Gracie nodded, and quickly reminded him about her friend Jack, back in the United States, who was a police detective, like Philippe.

Her interlocutor nodded shortly and looked uncomfortable.

Gracie continued, giving him a short précis of Jack's challenges with public perception, especially in the wake of what might be a case of police brutality in a small community near her own hometown.

As she spoke, Philippe visibly calmed, although he still looked as though he was in a hurry about something. Gracie thought they still had at least ten minutes before they needed to be back in the kitchen, though. Well, maybe Philippe had something to do?

Gracie finished her summary quickly, and then asked Philippe how French people viewed their police force. "Are they frightened of you, do they think of you as the enemy?" Gracie concluded. "Or do they appreciate the job you do?"

Philippe sighed briefly. "Bien sûr, Mademoiselle, all police must deal with people who think they are the enemy. Franchement!" he declared impatiently. "But it is generally the criminals who think thus, at least in France," he answered with a touch of national pride. "Now, you must pardon me, Mademoiselle," he went on, brushing past Gracie in a determined fashion and hastening down the stairs.

That had been rather rude. Uncharacteristically so, Gracie thought. Philippe had seemed like he couldn't wait to get away from her.

Why?

She checked her watch: yes, ten minutes until they had to start cooking again.

Gracie walked slowly towards her room, thinking. She would have expected that Philippe would have been interested to hear about the work of a police detective from another country. Well, maybe it hadn't been the right time; maybe Philippe had had something to do before reporting to the kitchen.

Henri Schilde exited his room and almost bumped into Gracie, who was frowning and looking at the floor as she walked.

"Must not be late, Ma'm'selle Gracie," Henri advised in an avuncular tone.

Gracie smiled absently at him, and walked directly towards her own room, calling out that she would be down to the kitchen straightaway.

That evening at dinner, the soup and appetizer selections were well received. Gracie thought her team's presentation with the chives, parsley and truffle powder was prettier than the other team's, which had scattered raw mushrooms in a Brunoise dice on top of the soup. And the whiff of truffle powder, even though it was physically all but invisible, was powerfully appealing.

It appeared that everyone's sardines had come out well and it was a very tasty dish. The other team had made little crouton type toasts to go with the sardines, which they had also plated on arugula. Gracie judged that was as nice a presentation as her panko breadcrumb suggestion.

At her table, Henri—who had been with the opposing cooking team—was very complimentary about the food and wine, as was everyone else. Henri especially praised the chilled sherry served with his small plate of mushroom soup. Even Chef Pernod was smiling as he ate and drank the selections placed before him, and Claude became more jovial with each course. Or possibly, with each glass!

Gracie's team agreed that they preferred their choice of wine for the sardines to the choice made by the other group: the 'melon de bourgogne' had a livelier flavor profile than the chardonnay chosen by the other group. Not that the chardonnay was bad, but it was 'uninspired' to use Roberto's adjective.

Brigitte, however, seemed her usual disparaging self. She was at the table with Chef and Claude, and muttered a running commentary to her husband Gilles about each dish put before her. Gracie swore the woman even wrinkled her nose in distaste a couple of times.

Everyone discussed the slight differences in presentation and technique apparent in the two teams' creations, but people seemed in such a good mood, no one took the critique as criticism.

Gracie glanced over to where Sam, Peter, Elspeth and Philippe were sitting: they all seemed to be having a good time, and Gracie caught Sam pouring the table a second glass of the muscadet. It was a really great wine with those spicy stuffed sardines. Philippe no longer appeared impatient or bad tempered, so Gracie mentally shrugged, and put his earlier rudeness aside.

She next received a plate of lamb chops with the turnip purée, spinach and marsala sauce and found it extremely good; she wondered who had been served the dish she'd made, and what they would think of it. The wine Gracie's team had chosen to pair with this course was a classic red burgundy from Chinon with the funny name of "Chiens Chiens." It was dark and berry-rich, with just a touch of minerality that Gary had said reminded him of pencils; it made a perfect foil for the lamb. Gracie's glass contained the Chiens Chiens, so she knew someone from her half of the room had made the lamb dish before her, because the other team had chosen a different wine. Gary received his lamb dish with a glass of rosé; he judged it a good blend, but still preferred the burgundy.

Angelique had appeared for the afternoon session, although she hadn't been at all cheery or focused. In answer to Gracie's query, though, Angelique had again replied that she was fine. Now, at dinner, she seemed ravenous, which Gracie thought was probably quite likely as she had skipped lunch and performed the afternoon's endeavors fueled by more than one espresso from Michel. Anna, at Angelique's table, seemed quite enthusiastic about the food she was served, and Bob Kress looked as though he approved of his meal thus far, too. Jean Soules, as usual, was quiet and calm faced: he ate silently and methodically, marking his scores down and then waiting for the next course with folded hands and downcast eyes. What an enigma!

When it was time for dessert, Gracie instantly spotted who had been given her creation: Claude Barberin, the Château's owner!

"Oh, putain," Gracie whispered, and put one hand to her forehead. Her fingers touched the edge of her little chef's cap and she sighed, and straightened up. She explained her apprehension to her table mates, who were all regarding her curiously. Her offering had been easy to identify because she had been the only one to employ the small, individual hibachi grills that were available for their use.

Gracie's dessert had been unlike anyone else's: skewers of tender, fresh apricot and strawberry halves interspersed with cubes of raclette cheese. She served the skewers with graham type crackers that held a bit of sweetness, and a few macadamia nuts that carried out the creaminess of the cheese. The trick with raclette was that, slightly melted as it was grilled over the little hibachi flame, its inherent creaminess was intensified, and a nuttiness brought out. The fruit, which she had basted with butter, caramelized, too, when heated, creating a taste blend that Gracie thought would be quite good, and different.

She had paired her dessert with a small glass of a sauternes from Château Guiraud: when she'd tasted this medium sweet wine she had realized its cream and vanilla notes would be in perfect harmony with the cheese, while the lemon pie flavor that freshened the wine and kept it from being sticky or cloying would echo the fruitiness of the apricot and the strawberry. She hoped.

"I wonder how they choose who gets which plate?" Roberto mused, looking down at his plate: grapes and almonds and camembert with a riesling. Not too adventurous.

"I asked Michel," Gary offered. "He said they put the numbers we have been assigned—that's how they mark our plates to know who cooked what—into a tombola and just pick randomly."

Gracie had been served a nice looking plate of runny Brie, strawberries and shelled pistachios, accompanied by a small glass of champagne. In her opinion, the choices—except for the pistachios—were fairly run of the mill, and champagne was a really easy choice since it went with just about everything. But it was still very yummy.

"I wonder whose this is?" Gracie asked, looking at her dessert. Surreptitiously, she lifted an edge of the plate to see the number affixed to the bottom on a piece of sticky tape. '5'. Well, she had no clue who number '5' was, as everyone's number was a closely guarded secret: the numbered tape was affixed as everyone submitted their dishes for service, so none of the students knew.

"C'est envoye du pâte!" she heard Claude exclaim then, and, almost frightened, Gracie glanced over at the Château owner. He had slid one small skewer's contents off onto a crisp cracker and taken a bite, then sipped at the wine. Quickly, he put the remaining bite of dessert in his mouth, took a bigger sip of the Guiraud sauternes, and then busily and insistently began making up little mouthfuls for the other people at his table to try. His smile was broad.

"Guess he likes your dessert," Gary commented laconically to Gracie with a grin. Everyone had seen her build her hibachi plate, so everyone knew which dessert had been hers.

"Congratulations," Henri told her, sounding quite genuine, and Roberto gave her a big smile and a thumbs up.

Elspeth waved from her nearby table as did Peter and Sam, and Gracie was surprised to see Philippe raise his glass to her and smile in congratulation.

She took a deep breath and a sip of her champagne, and smiled.

As Gracie was headed up to her room later that evening—no one was gathering for drinks, as they all had an early morning for the Market on Thursday—Chef Pernod called to her from the Library, where he and Claude had been commiserating, totaling the scores for the night.

Gracie pivoted in the main hallway, and took a few steps back the way she'd just come, passing the dining room and approaching the far end of the Château.

"Yes, Chef?" she asked, trying to sound upbeat and ready for anything, but knowing that her voice showed her exhaustion. They were all tired, although so far everyone was keeping up with the pace set by Chef.

"I wanted to say, Mademoiselle, that your skill in the kitchen has surprised me," Chef Pernod began, his voice steady. His arms were crossed over his chest and his legs were spread a bit, and his stance looked quite challenging. Still, the tone of his voice was genuine.

"Thank you, Chef," Gracie replied humbly.

"Your friends, Mr. Battafaglia and Mr. Koch, were effusive in their praise of you," Chef Pernod continued. "So much so, that I frankly doubted you could possibly be as good as they claimed."

Gracie bit her lip.

"But you are. And you have an extremely discerning palate."

"Thank you, Chef," Gracie said again. "I feel like I have so much to learn, and so much to practice!" she told her instructor humbly. Well, it was true.

"Ah, practice is the key," he agreed genially. "But you are quite—fearless—as tonight's dessert showed. You have a good sense of what will work well and what will not, and although you do need to work on your technique, since you have no plans to be in a professional kitchen, it is less crucial than if you did," he judged.

Gracie allowed herself a small smile: she thought Chef had given her a compliment, but that last comment about not being in a professional kitchen had made her wonder.

"If you ever come to Boston, you must stop in at *Mange Tout*," Gracie told him then. "I know Joey and Tyler would be so delighted," she finished.

The Chef inclined his head and said he would like to do that very thing. "And if you have time, before you return to the States, or perhaps if you make another trip to France, I invite you to dine at my restaurant, Éblouisse, in Paris," Chef Pernod told her.

Gracie took a deep breath in surprise. Really? She squinted up at Chef Pernod, searching his face for any sign of insincerity, but found none. "I would very much enjoy that, Chef, thank you," she replied.

Then, still in a bit of a daze, she said goodnight and headed for her room.

chapter Thirteen

Thursday morning, everyone assembled in the Château's foyer to travel to nearby Cormery. It was market day once more, so they had breakfasted early and by eight o'clock everyone except Angelique was ready to go.

"Maybe she overslept," wondered Anna, looking a bit concerned. "I didn't see her at breakfast. Did you see her?" she asked Gracie.

"No, but we were all down to eat at slightly different times, and all ate so fast, she might have gone to the buffet and returned to her room without anyone seeing her," Gracie suggested thoughtfully.

"It is time to go," announced Chef Pernod. Once again, Gracie had volunteered to drive, and once again, Elspeth, Roberto and the Château manager, Monique, would ride with her.

"Let me go up to Madame Rochambeau's room," Monique said in a quiet voice. "I can see what the delay is, and Chef Pernod can meanwhile go along in the van…" she looked at Elspeth and Roberto, and gave a hesitant smile. "Angelique could ride with us—we can squeeze in the back, it's not that far to Cormery," she added.

Roberto took the hint, if it was one, and said he would happily ride in the van with the other students, so that Angelique, the late-comer, could ride in Gracie's car with Monique and Elspeth.

Gracie and Elspeth waved goodbye as the other students hastened to the van, and it pulled out of the Château's forecourt, Michel at the wheel. It was a warm morning, and although Gracie had remembered to look for someone wearing a dark grey windbreaker, none was in evidence.

"I hope we aren't too far behind," Elspeth said anxiously to Gracie once the van had left. "You get the best if you go as early as possible," she advised.

"I'm sure they'll be down any minute: maybe Angelique did oversleep," Gracie answered, thinking aloud. "She's been troubled over something the past couple of days, I think: have you noticed?" she asked Elspeth.

But Elspeth's answer was forestalled by the sound of Monique's running footsteps, clattering down the main staircase. She had her mobile phone in one manicured hand, and was speaking urgently into it.

"Yes, please, as quickly as possible," she said into the device, then hung up. By this time, she was face to face with Gracie and Elspeth, and she looked at them, completely at a loss for words and slightly out of breath. Her blue eyes were huge behind her stylish eyeglasses and her face was white.

"What's happened?" Gracie asked. She had a dread feeling of foreboding from just one glance at Monique's face: it was drained of all color, and she kept licking her dry lips so that only a remnant of her coral lip tint remained.

Monique swallowed. "Madame Rochambeau…" she began, then shook her head as if trying to deny what she knew she must say. "Madame Rochambeau—is dead."

"What?" Elspeth gasped. "You're not serious!" she protested. "You must be joking."

Why do people say that, Gracie wondered silently. No one she knew would make a joke like that.

"Tell us what happened when you went to Angelique's room, Monique," Gracie suggested calmly, and took the woman's elbow, leading her over to the small love seat in front of the reservation desk.

"Elspeth, would you be a darling and get a cup of coffee for Monique, from the buffet table?" Gracie asked sweetly, nodding towards the hallway.

The buffet table was just a few feet away, near the entrance to the dining room, and Elspeth gave a shaky smile and trotted off.

"You're sure she's dead?" Gracie asked Monique quickly, and the woman nodded her answer. "You've called the police?" Gracie asked next, and perched next to Monique. She drew up a little armchair for when Elspeth returned.

Monique nodded again. "I thought it best," she whispered, her lips trembling.

Elspeth came back with the coffee, which Monique gratefully took in both hands and sipped at for a moment.

Elspeth sat.

"Now, what happened when you went to Angelique's room?" Gracie asked again. She knew Monique would give a statement to the police, but she also knew that the more time that passed between the event and the recollection of it, the less accurate the recollection might be. She wanted Monique to say what she had found while the memory was still fresh.

"I knocked on her door," began Monique quietly. "There was no answer."

Gracie nodded. "Go on," she urged.

"So I opened the door," Monique continued. "It was not locked."

"That's odd," put in Elspeth. Gracie nodded.

" The room was very quiet," Monique continued, "and the draperies were still pulled. I walked in, and called her name—'Madame Rochambeau?'" she re-created the moment. "And then I saw her."

"Where?" gasped Elspeth, and Gracie shot her a look: better to let Monique tell it as she recalled it.

"She was on the bed," Monique related.

In the distance, Gracie heard the familiar double tone of the police siren.

"But she was dressed," Monique continued, frowning at the memory. "She had on the same clothes she'd worn to dinner last night: her chef's white jacket and that pair of red and white checked chef's trousers. And her red clogs," she added.

Most of the students wore some kind of athletic shoe to cope with all the standing the course required, but Angelique had worn a nicely broken in pair of red leather clogs, not unlike the ones Chef Mario Batali favored. She swore they were more comfortable than athletic shoes.

"I called her name again, then I reached over and shook her—shook her arm, felt her hand…" Monique continued, faltering slightly. "But—she was cold. And she did not move." She paused and took a breath.

The sirens came closer.

"Ah, they come," she said, sounding relieved.

"Did you notice anything, well, odd? About the room, or about the way Angelique looked?" Gracie asked gently.

Monique shook her head and wiped her eyes. "Except that the drapes were drawn and that she was wearing clothes, no."

"Did you know she was dead?" Elspeth asked.

Gracie bit her lip and stayed silent.

Monique nodded. "Yes. Somehow, I did," she whispered. "I didn't want to believe it, though. I tried to find a pulse, I tried to rouse her. I touched her, and she was so cold, and so still...I think I knew, but I did not want to know," Monique replied, all in a rush. "I just backed out of the room, and grabbed my mobile phone to call the police."

In spite of the circumstances, Gracie found herself fascinated by watching the police operate in another country. She had been to many crime scenes in the course of her job as a news reporter, and much of the activity that shortly began at Château de Reignac was familiar to her. The police pulled into the Château's forecourt, followed only seconds later by the ambulance, blue lights swiveling. About a minute later, a plain, unmarked Renault sedan in a dark blue arrived, and an older man in a navy suit and tie got out along with a younger, blond man in a sports coat.

The police immediately asked Monique to show them up to Angelique's room, and posted one of their number at the Château's front door, with instructions to send the Detective up when he arrived.

The Detective, Jean Valois, was the man in the navy suit and he, along with his assistant, sped up to the first floor after a few quick words with the officer at the door.

"Maybe we should call the others," Elspeth suggested in a stage whisper. She and Gracie were still sitting in the reception foyer.

Gracie shook her head. "I think we should ask the police first, before we do that," she answered. "The fewer people around right now, the better," she explained. "At least until they have finished their preliminary examination."

"I suppose," Elspeth agreed reluctantly. "But it seems a shame to call the police, I mean, Angelique must have had a stroke or a heart attack or something like that, don't you think?" she asked Gracie, reverting once more to English in her upset. "It couldn't have been food poisoning," she added in a murmur, more to herself than to Gracie. "Or more people would have become ill."

Gracie nodded silently.

A plain white van with large blue letters that spelled 'CORONER' —the same in French as in English—drove into the forecourt, and a woman with a white coat over a dark plum trouser suit, as well as two technicians in scrubs, exited. The techs removed a collapsible gurney from the back of the van, and entered the Château right behind their boss. After a fast, murmured exchange with the officer, the three of them went upstairs.

The ambulance departed: clearly, they were not needed here.

Gracie shrugged, and told Elspeth that calling the police was probably the right thing to do, although surely Angelique had died from natural causes. "As you say, a stroke or a heart attack, perhaps," Gracie murmured. "Although she looked quite healthy—although very tired, lately," she added in a worried tone.

"Mmmm…maybe that was because of some illness," Elspeth offered. Then: "Where is Claude?" she asked. Her question echoed off the high plaster walls and tiled floor.

Gracie answered, "Monique said he had gone into Tours this morning," she informed her companion. "I think he left just before we did—or, before we were going to leave," she amended.

After a few more moments of disquieting silence, sounds of activity floated down from the floor above. Voices, doors opening and closing, and then the distinctive sounds of a gurney's wheels being locked into place and rolled down a corridor.

"They'll take the lift," Gracie murmured to no one in particular.

Elspeth nodded. "She must have felt unwell and laid down, and…" Elspeth continued theorizing, her voice quavery.

Gracie nodded, deep in thought. She got up from where she had been sitting, and moved towards the front of the foyer, so she could see through the archway to the landing where the staircase ended and to the hall that led to the dining room and beyond.

A small lift or elevator was tucked into a nook between the chapel and the front tower on that end of the building: it was handy when hauling luggage, but otherwise, most guests just used the grand staircase.

Gracie knew, because she had indulged her curious nature on the afternoon she'd arrived, that there were two other staircases in the Château: one that led up from the kitchen to the ground floor dining room and then up to the first floor hallway on the Chapel end of the Château, and another on the end of the Château where her room was located, that led from the hallway down to the ground floor. Both of these staircases could be found behind nondescript doors sunken flush with the corridor walls on the first floor. When he'd given her the tour of the Château, Claude had said these had been servants' stairways and passages, connecting areas of service with the kitchens, the laundry, and the basement.

Both staircases also continued up from the first floor to the top floor of the Château, which was now where Claude had his flat, with the remaining space used for storage.

The Coroner's assistants had, indeed, used the lift to move the loaded gurney, but the Coroner, a woman of about forty with sleekly coifed, chin-length dark copper hair, was trotting down the grand staircase next to the Detective, and the two were having a hurried conversation in low tones. They had not noticed her.

Gracie took a step or two back so she was out of their sight lines, but caught the words, 'subdural hematoma' and 'trauma.' The Detective's use of the word 'trauma' piqued Gracie's curious—some might say suspicious—nature. What sort of trauma? And where, exactly, was the subdural hematoma?

Gracie immediately imagined a scenario in which Angelique might have, as Elspeth had suggested, felt ill, possibly faint, and had blacked out and fallen and struck something.

But how would she have got herself to her bed, Gracie pondered as the Detective and the Coroner rounded the corner from the landing and gave her brief nods as they headed for the Château's front doors.

Maybe Angelique had regained consciousness and made her way to her bed, somehow, Gracie theorized. That made sense. How awful!

The Coroner left, then, following her two assistants who had scurried out of the Château with as little fuss as possible. Monique, who had trailed downstairs behind the officials, went quietly to sit at the reception desk.

"I must call Claude," she murmured, and picked up the phone.

The Detective gave some instructions to his assistant and the police officers on the scene, and then turned to Elspeth and Gracie, who were now both standing near the reception desk.

"Madame Lubin is summoning Monsieur Barberin and the rest of the cooking class back to the Château," he told them with a small nod. "I am Senior Detective Jean Valois, of the Gendarmerie National," he introduced himself.

Gracie and Elspeth introduced themselves, and then Detective Valois asked them to tell him what had happened that morning. Gracie noted that he was tall and in good shape, and appeared to be about sixty years old. His light brown eyes were kind, and a little tired, but she suspected they also didn't miss much, as they were also very quick. A still-thick head of greyish hair topped a face that would look friendly when relaxed and smiling: at the moment, Detective Valois was doing neither, and his face was grave.

Gracie and Elspeth began their account at the point where they had assembled in the foyer, just before eight o'clock that morning.

"We were all here, except Angelique," Elspeth explained.

"Anna—Anna Guteknecht, you'll meet her when the rest of the students return," put in Gracie, "she suggested that Angelique might have overslept."

"Yes, and she asked if anyone had seen her at breakfast," commented Elspeth.

"And—had anyone seen Madame Rochambeau at breakfast?" asked the Detective.

"No," Gracie answered. "Or, at least, no one said they had," she amended carefully.

chapter Fourteen

It seemed that everyone returned to the Château at once: Claude had sped back from his business in Tours, and Monique had called Michel, who had explained to the students and to Chef Pernod only that there was an emergency that required their immediate return. Then he had gathered everyone into the van for the trip back from Cormery.

Chef Pernod had demanded to know the nature of the emergency, but Michel had not said, because Monique had not told him: she had only explained that the immediate return of everyone was imperative, and that the police were at the Château.

The students, Claude, Michel and Chef Pernod all poured through the Château's front doors, speculating among themselves about the emergency and looking worried. They milled around in the reception foyer, asking Monique what had happened, and continuing to wonder aloud to each other.

Claude ran up to Monique and held an urgent, whispered conversation; Gracie saw Claude's normally ruddy complexion go ashen, and he reached for the back of a chair as though he needed momentary support.

Anna rushed up to Gracie and Elspeth and asked, "where's Angelique?" but fortunately for them, Detective Valois wasted no time calling everyone in to the grand salon, so in lieu of a reply, Gracie and Elspeth escorted Anna towards that room.

The Detective introduced himself, and gave a brief statement to the entire group at once.

"I thank you all for coming back so quickly," he began, standing in front of the empty fireplace. "I am Senior Detective Jean Valois, and this is my Assistant Detective, Noel Malraux," he continued, indicating the young blond man Gracie had seen before. "I appreciate that you are all curious and concerned, so let me explain right away." Detective Valois paused. "Madame Angelique Rochambeau was found this morning in her bed chamber. She is dead." His voice was unemotional and calm but the response to his statement was not.

"Dead!? Angelique?" cried Anna, despite the fact that she had surmised from her friend's absence that the emergency was somehow connected with her, and not a joyful occasion. "Oh, no! That cannot be! But what happened?"

Her questions were echoed by the others, most of whom were exclaiming among themselves, shaking their heads and looking both shocked and saddened. Jean Soules bowed his head, and looked as though he were praying, and Philippe looked stunned.

Well, it was quite a shock. Both Gracie and Elspeth had their arms around Anna's shoulders in support.

Detective Valois put out a staying hand. "Now —now—I cannot give you any details, because quite frankly we do not know much of anything yet," he continued, raising his voice a little so that everyone quieted down. "Myself, my assistant, and members of the Loches Gendarmerie will be speaking to each of you this morning, so that we may create as complete a picture as possible as to what happened, exactly. We will try to discover who among you might have seen Madame Rochambeau last night…"

"Who was the last to see her alive!" whispered Anna in a stricken tone.

Detective Valois nodded.

"Do you know how—?" Claude asked, still sounding shaken and unable to form the horrible words that would complete his question: this was a dreadful thing to have happen.

Detective Valois shook his head. "No. The Coroner has yet to make her examination."

Well, that wasn't exactly true, Gracie thought to herself. Because of what she'd overheard, Gracie was aware that the Coroner and Detective at least suspected that a subdural hematoma was partly to blame for Angelique's demise. Although such hematomae could be anywhere on the body, Gracie knew that ones involved in fatalities were generally on the head. Since Angelique's death was an active investigation and possible suspects had yet to be questioned however, perhaps Detective Valois did not want to say too much right now.

"How about time of death?" Gracie asked quickly.

The Detective shot her a keen look from those deceptively gentle brown eyes. He sighed. "Preliminary time of death is late last night or early this morning," Detective Valois told her, just a little reluctantly. "Once the post mortem is concluded, my office will release a statement which will contain more detailed information, and I am sure the news reporters will announce it on television," he told her, sounding just slightly sour.

Gracie knew that preliminary time and cause of death were usually determined at the scene, at least in the U.S. It wouldn't be much different here. Because of her own experience as a news reporter, Gracie understood that the time of death in this situation was most likely a space of a few hours: other physical markers like lividity and liver temperature would narrow that down.

In response, everyone began to murmur to each other, their voices concerned and just a little bit defensive: even the completely innocent and uninvolved want to distance themselves from a crime, and be certain no one suspects them.

So, then, Gracie thought, when the police began to question everyone, they would be trying to place people not only where they had been that morning, but where they had been the night before. And, as Anna had said, they would try to figure out who had been the last person to see Angelique alive.

She sighed: as tired as they all had been the evening before from the long, demanding day, and with an early Market trip the following morning, most students had not lingered after dinner service. Everyone had likely been in their rooms, in bed asleep or nearly so, when Angelique had died.

It was clear that Detective Valois wasn't going to reveal the manner of death just yet, either. Gracie thought that this detail, too, would be included in the police statement later in the day: once the coroner had done the autopsy, a cause as well as a more precise time of death, as well as manner of death, would be determined. It would most likely be ruled natural causes, Gracie thought to herself as she walked across the marble and tiled floors once more to the reception foyer. Elspeth's theory about Angelique feeling ill and fainting made sense. Gracie shook her head sadly and blinked several times. She felt a real loss.

The remainder of the morning was fraught with tension and concern, as the police used the salons to speak individually with each of the students, with Chef Pernod, and with Claude and Michel. Since the police had already talked to Monique, Gracie and Elspeth, the three of them sat around in the reception foyer, staring vaguely into space and offering half hearted assurances to each other and to the students and staff as they came and went from their interviews.

The Château's reservation inquiry line rang a few times, but Monique let it go to voice mail, and dabbed at her eyes.

Then, she suddenly declared, "oh my," and looked at the clock as though seeing it for the first time, even though she'd been staring at the wall it hung on for the past two hours. "Lunch!"

"I don't think anyone will want to eat," Elspeth commented dolefully.

"Of course they will," Gracie corrected her. "And so will you." She stood. "Come on—we'll help you, Monique. Let's set out the buffet, and we can invite the police and the detectives to join us, too," she suggested, thinking that given the Château's standards, even a buffet would probably be a welcome change for most of them.

Looking more hopeful, Monique led them through the dining room, past the stairs to the kitchen below, and into the small 'prep kitchen' that she used to assemble the breakfast and lunch buffets, and where service for dinners was organized.

With the three of them working, it wasn't long before the remnants of breakfast had been cleared away, and a fresh cloth had been spread on the two long tables next to the dining room entrance. Gracie started the coffee brewing in the large stainless steel urn and prepared Michel's espresso machine, while Elspeth re-stocked the tea caddy and filled the other urn with water to boil. Then they set out a large bowl of freshly tossed greens, platters of hothouse tomatoes, sliced green onions, brine cured Greek olives, hard boiled eggs, slices of roast chicken, ham, and smoked salmon, and tall slender bottles of light green olive oil and dark balsamic vinegar. A loaf of whole grain bread and a basket of fresh rolls went on the table, and wedges of different types of cheese were presented on a wooden cutting board. Elspeth heaped bunches of green and red grapes in a smaller bowl, and then Gracie brought out a large tin of assorted biscuits and cookies that she'd found wedged in the back of a cupboard in the prep kitchen.

"It may not be haute cuisine," she told Monique and Elspeth, "but I think we all need a little sugar after this morning."

Monique chuckled in spite of her sadness, and said she would make sure to watch for Chef Pernod's reaction to the packaged cookie selection.

The atmosphere at lunch was subdued. The police huddled together at one table hastily set up by Claude in a corner of the dining room, ate quickly, and returned to whatever their duties had been. Anna kept glancing at Angelique's empty chair at their table, and biting her lip. Normally quiet Jean Soules was positively mute, and Bob Kress kept shaking his head in disbelief, visibly shaken by the death of his table mate.

As she ate at her table alongside Gary, Roberto and Henri—strangely enough, everyone had taken their assigned seats even though at lunch they did not need to— Gracie tried to recall every detail about the evening before that she could.

Angelique had been tired the previous day because, as she had told Gracie more than once, she hadn't slept well the night before. Might that have been an indication of some kind of illness beginning, just as Elspeth had proposed? Gracie didn't know. But Angelique had seemed very fit and healthy, at least at the start of the course. Still, Gracie had to admit that she really didn't know the woman, and that looks could be deceiving.

Angelique had gone directly to her room after dinner service was over, as far as Gracie knew. No one had lingered, actually, because of the early morning scheduled for the next day, and everyone had gone up to their rooms shortly after their evening chores had been completed.

Gracie regarded her fellow students as they all sat in the dining room. Maybe one of them had seen Angelique after she had gone up, though. Maybe the woman had gone down to the Library to get a book, or had taken a walk.

This morning, Angelique had not been seen by Gracie or by anyone else, apparently, at breakfast, and had missed the van's departure for the Market. Monique had gone to Angelique's room to check on her and discovered her, dead, and fully clothed as she had been the evening before, lying on her bed. The door had been unlocked.

That last fact seemed especially odd to Gracie, and Elspeth had thought so too. Did people usually lock their doors when they entered their rooms? Gracie considered for a minute. Well, not if someone were planning to go out again soon, she supposed. But once people were in for the night, then, yes, she thought they would all lock their doors. So maybe it was wrong to assume that Angelique had gone straight up to bed just because she had finished her work, said goodnight and disappeared from the kitchen. Maybe she had gone back to her room initially, but planned to go back out somewhere. In which case, she probably wouldn't have locked her door.

The library and the walk ideas emerged again on the agitated surface of Gracie's mind.

She savored an olive. Maybe Angelique had returned to her room to freshen up and use the bathroom before going to do whatever she'd planned, when whatever happened had happened: she'd fainted or got dizzy, or whatever, and blacked out and hit her head on something. That would account for the subdural hematoma as well as the Detective's use of the word 'trauma.' That made sense.

Then, maybe Angelique had regained consciousness and dragged herself to her bed, thinking to rest, perhaps, or more likely not thinking too clearly but wanting to lie down. Yes, Gracie thought as she nibbled a piece of smoked fish, that made sense, too.

So where had Angelique been planning to go, and for what reason? Might she have been meeting someone? Gracie chewed on a chunk of baguette that she had slathered with the wonderfully creamy French butter. The answers to those questions could be important, she thought, though she didn't know just how.

She hoped Detective Valois and the police were investigating all those angles; more importantly, she hoped the Coroner would do the autopsy soon and the details about Angelique's death would be released. They all needed to know what had happened to their fellow student. And it seemed so terrible, somehow, that she had died all alone.

Michel and Monique had joined Claude and Chef Pernod along with the Bernards at their table, pulling up a couple of extra chairs and squeezing in. Michel's rangy form seemed to have sunk in upon itself and his mobile face, generally smiling, was somber. Monique—who had declined the offer of a mild sedative—kept squeezing her eyes shut, as though trying to un-see what she had found when she'd entered Angelique's room and discovered her. And Claude just looked shattered: he ate a little, but seemed to be in a daze, saying just a few words to his table mates and not even trying to be cheerful.

Even Chef Pernod looked subdued, downcast.

Brigitte, typically self-absorbed, was yakking away to her husband in her Norman accented French about her dish for that night's dinner, the death of her fellow student apparently gone from her thoughts. And Gilles? He was just listening to his wife and glumly eating the few bits of food on his plate. Coffee and tea were poured, and the humble biscuit tin was passed around from table to table; Gracie couldn't resist a faint smile when she saw

Chef Pernod snag three sugary *palmiers* to enjoy with his coffee.

After lunch, the police and the detectives left, having finished their preliminary questioning. Since all the course participants would be at the Château through that Sunday, when the course ended, Detective Valois said he would be back to speak to all of them again, as needed.

Everyone stayed in the dining room: no one felt like resuming the cooking class. Elspeth, Gracie noticed, began asking her table mate Philippe for his opinions on 'the case,' because, as the Scottish woman pointed out none too subtly and once again in her accented English, Philippe was a Detective. Peter and Sam chimed in, referencing their favorite forensic detective on television in the States and asking Philippe what techniques he thought would be used to investigate Angelique's death.

Overhearing the conversations and questions aimed at Philippe, several other students moved over to his table with their coffees, anxious to hear what he might have to say.

But Philippe shook his head at Elspeth's query, and as the others joined in to ask him to opine, he made a dismissing motion with his hands.

"No, no, I know nothing about this, nothing!" he protested from his seat at the table. He looked extremely uncomfortable and with the students surrounding him and peppering him with questions, he almost appeared trapped.

"Well, of course you do!" Elspeth corrected him insistently.

Philippe's head snapped around as he glared at her. "What? I do not!" he repeated, and stood up.

Those around his table took a step back: Philippe looked quite fierce.

"Well, you must do," Elspeth insisted her voice strident. "You're a Detective, you see things like this all the time, you must have lots of things to say…"

Philippe's frown deepened, and he looked down at his hands, which were still holding his napkin. "Ah," he breathed. "I see." He paused, and placed the napkin on the table, but did not resume his seat. "Well, no, Madame, you are mistaken," Philippe told Elspeth in a calm voice. He looked around including everyone in his remarks. "I do not know anything about this 'case,' as you call it," he directed this remark at Elspeth, "because I am in no way involved in it, in the investigation, I mean," he explained.

Elspeth looked extremely disappointed.

"You mean you don't have a theory? Even take a guess?" Peter asked hopefully.

Philippe still frowned, but took a breath. "Monsieur. Madame. I know no more than you. And I do not believe that guessing is a wise, or indeed, an efficacious approach. The simplest explanation is, generally speaking, the correct one, so perhaps it is exactly what it looks like: an unfortunate but natural death." He paused, and took a breath.

"So do you think that Angelique felt ill, maybe, and perhaps laid down on her bed hoping to feel better and…died?" Elspeth summarized, repeating her theory. Elspeth didn't know about the subdural hematoma, but even so, her idea made sense.

Philippe frowned. "Until all the evidence has been examined, no one knows anything. I will tell you, however, that Detective Valois will find out what happened, as will the Coroner. I have worked with them both for many years," he added, sounding certain.

Elspeth made a disgruntled and dissatisfied face, and drew back slightly. It wasn't what she'd been hoping for, but apparently it was all the answer she was going to get. At least until the Coroner's report and the Detective's statement were ready.

Meanwhile, what would happen with the rest of the course, Gracie wondered. It might be unseemly to bring that up just now, but she couldn't be the only one curious. The week's schedule was so jam packed with topics, study and materials that missing a day, which they were, would be a real deficit. And that presumed the course would continue. Maybe Chef Pernod would just cancel the rest of it and refund everyone's money? No, there were no refunds, Gracie reminded herself, having noted that when she'd applied. But this was a very unusual situation.

Chef Pernod, who had been talking in low tones with Monique and Claude while Philippe had been undergoing his interrogation, seemed to arrive at a decision, for he suddenly clapped his hands together and asked for everyone's attention.

"Eh, bien," he said briskly, and stood. "We will begin afresh tomorrow, and complete the course to honor our fallen comrade," he announced dramatically. "Madame Rochambeau was from Toulouse, and her goal was to open a Toulouse-style restaurant in this region," he continued.

Gracie nodded: she knew he was correct, as Angelique had told her that very thing.

"And so, I shall change a little bit the course structure," Chef Pernod continued. "We will be making Toulousain dishes for the rest of our time together, beginning with dinner tomorrow. We will go to the St. Avertin Market tomorrow morning, then visit our winery on the way back. Then, we shall return, and cook."

chapter Fifteen

Because they were not cooking that evening, the students had spent the early afternoon giving the professional kitchen a thorough cleaning from top to bottom, using white vinegar and plenty of hot soap and water.

Monique had said that the cold buffet from lunch would be available again for dinner that evening, but Gracie had audibly wondered about going into Reignac to get pizzas. Everyone had seemed to grab at the idea and Monique and Claude had both said that 'Brique,' a new pizza restaurant just over the bridge that spanned the River Indre, had an authentic brick oven—hence the name—and was really very good.

So Claude had called in an order for five large pizzas, enough to feed everyone, and asked that they be delivered. Michel had sought out a few bottles of a local Cabernet Franc from Chinon to drink with the pizza. Monique put out a bowl of crisp, cool green salad, and then had run out to a local patisserie. Upon her return she laid several medium sized lemon tarts she had just bought on one of the long buffet tables: dessert!

Now, Gracie was glad to see Chef Pernod dig in to the pizza with the rest of them: he had even abandoned his chef's whites for the evening, and wore a short-sleeved grey henley and oyster colored trousers. Still an imposing figure, he seemed more approachable in civilian clothes, and the more form fitting outfit evidenced quite a buff physique. Gracie couldn't help concluding that the Chef must work out regularly. She also noted that his piercing, ice-blue eyes still surveyed the room, and everyone in it. Much like Detective Valois, Chef Pernod missed nothing.

Despite the fact that their dinner places were all set in the dining room, everyone seemed to prefer a less formal—and cozier—setting. A large sideboard in the grand salon was used to hold the salad and all the various pizza selections, while the big glass coffee table between the two long sofas was where Michel had placed the wine bottles. Everyone's plates and glasses ended up there, too, while people ate, talked and tried to relax in the aftermath of that morning's tragedy. The afternoon had been warm enough, but the evening was cool, and more for ambience than for heat, Michel lit a fire in the cavernous marble fireplace and put some jazz on softly in the background.

"I think it's inspired," Anna said in a brave voice to Gracie as they sampled the pizza.

"Inspired?" Gracie asked. She took another bite of the slice she had selected: mushroom and herbs, different from the pizza at home. And so good!

Anna nodded enthusiastically from her perch at Gracie's side. "Yes. For Chef Pernod to dedicate the rest of the course to Angelique," she elaborated. "Besides, it will be interesting to learn about Toulousain cuisine, don't you think?" she continued.

Gracie smiled. "Yes, I agree, and I'm sure any tips and techniques that were meant to be covered in the course can be taught while we make something from Angelique's home region," she finished agreeably.

Looking around the salon at her fellow students, Gracie realized how interesting—and revealing, perhaps—it was to see everyone in 'normal' clothes. Since that first evening when everyone had been introduced at the reception and dinner, they had all been attired either in their chef's whites, or in super casual clothes at breakfast. Once, Gracie had even been positive that Roberto had basically rolled out of bed and, running late, grabbed breakfast while still in his pyjama bottoms and t-shirt!

But tonight it seemed people had made an effort, maybe not to dress up as much as they had the first evening, but at least to look quite *soigné*, as the French would say. Sam and Peter were in crisp pastel dress shirts and matching dove grey linen trousers; Henri wore a cotton cable knit sweater the color of oatmeal with olive green casual trousers; Gary wore a colorful plaid cotton shirt with jeans; Roberto, true to his Italian fashion sense, wore tight black jeans with a bright blue, finely knit silk V-neck sweater; Bob Kress and Jean Soules both wore jeans and white dress shirts with unbuttoned necks and rolled up sleeves; Anna had put on a pair of grey knit trousers and a flowered tunic-length top in shades of grey and peach.

Elspeth, who sat on Gracie's other side, wore a pink short sleeved top and a pair of tan trousers, and her hair looked as though she'd given it some extra frizz. Gilles was once again all in grey, but without the jacket, and Brigitte wore a black sleeveless silk sheath that cascaded to below her knees in a somber swirl. The scarf she had knotted around the dress' bateau neckline was another by Hermès in tones of black, white and red, and Gracie recognized it as 'Brides de Gala.' She had one exactly the same at home, except hers was in black, white and gold.

Now, Elspeth drained her glass of wine and licked her lips. "Angelique wasn't originally from Toulouse, though," she offered meditatively. "But Toulousain cuisine is lovely: cassoulet, pork sausage, smoked bacon…and duck. Maybe we'll learn to make duck confit!" she finished brightly, and poured herself another glass of wine from one of the bottles Michel had placed on the table.

Across from them and at the opposite end of the other long sofa, Brigitte gave Gracie, Elspeth and Anna a long look. Then she turned to her ever-present husband, Gilles, and said in a whisper that was quite audible nonetheless, "if I had wanted to learn about Toulousain cuisine, I would have taken a course on peasant food."

Anna's fair skin colored, and Elspeth nearly choked on her new glass of wine. Gracie returned Brigitte's stare, meeting the red-head's cool grey gaze with her own snapping black one, and then leaned towards her and said, "Brigitte, we are all affected by what has happened, so perhaps it would be best if you kept any negative comments to yourself." Her voice had been mild, but very firm.

The woman from Rouen looked insulted, and she lifted her chin and stared at Gracie with narrowed eyes. "That was a private conversation between me and my husband," she protested indignantly.

But Gracie shook her head. "No, it wasn't, Brigitte," she corrected her, raising her voice a little. But that was unnecessary as everyone else in the salon had quieted, and was listening to the exchange. "It was loud enough for us to hear," Gracie continued. "And I know from previous experience that you are able to whisper very well when you wish to, because you are always whispering to Gilles," she added, with a nod to the man.

Gilles shifted his feet uneasily and did not meet Gracie's gaze.

"Clearly, you meant for your nasty comment to be overheard," Gracie went on. "And it was. And I didn't like it. So I suggest, as I said before, you say nothing if you cannot say something kind." Gracie punctuated her advice with a smile that was razor sharp.

Brigitte just looked at Gracie as though she didn't know how to answer someone who had not only corrected her, but stood up to her. Then she got up, thrust her plate of half eaten food at Gilles, and stomped out of the grand salon, her beige patent stilettos click -clacking on the parquet floor.

There was a beat of silence in the salon before, one by one, people started chuckling, clapping, and saying things like, 'well done!' and 'thank god,' and 'what a bitch!' meaning, of course, Brigitte.

Gracie took a deep breath, and then a long sip of her wine. Elspeth snagged a bottle and filled it back up to the top.

Oddly enough, Gilles didn't seem at all offended, either by what Gracie had just said to his wife, or by the reactions of the others who had witnessed the exchange. To everyone's surprise, he lifted his glass slightly in a small salute to Gracie, then drained it, and helped himself to another slice of pizza.

Elspeth, who apparently had decided she was the *sommelier pro tem*, filled his glass, too.

Gracie heard the distinct ring-tone of Gilles' mobile phone a moment later. He retrieved it from his pocket, glanced at the screen, and put the phone away again.

Probably Brigitte, she thought, summoning Gilles to her side.

"Was I too harsh?" Gracie murmured to Elspeth.

"Och, no, lass: you were perhaps not harsh enough: that woman needs a good drubbing, always whinging about something and saying cruel things, and have you seen the marks she's been giving?" Elspeth returned with spirit. In English, but Gracie forgave her.

Gracie shook her head and asked—in French—what Elspeth meant: everyone scored the dishes they had been given for dinner. But how could Elspeth know how Brigitte had scored the selections she had been given?

"Sam and Peter have cracked the code," Elspeth whispered to Gracie and Anna, who was listening intently. Elspeth, in French this time, explained that she and her 'neighbors,' as she referred to the two chefs from California, had compared notes on what each had been given for the first two dinners, along with the numbers on the bottoms of the dishes. "Somehow, Sam and Peter figured it out and we know everyone's number now," she continued. "I'm 4. You're 6," she said to Anna, "and you're 9," she told Gracie.

"That's cool!" Gracie said, sounding intrigued. "How'd they do that?!" she continued. "But—how do you know what scores Brigitte gave?" she questioned, frowning.

Elspeth looked coy for a moment, then shrugged as though deciding that telling Gracie and Anna wouldn't matter. "There's a vent in Sam and Peter's room that comes up from the library," she began.

"That's right below their room," Gracie chimed in, thinking aloud.

Elspeth nodded. "Yes." She paused. "And the library is where Claude and Chef Pernod go every evening, to tally up the scores."

"And Sam and Peter overheard them..." Gracie interjected.

Elspeth nodded again. "They did. I'm surprised Claude didn't realize that, about the vent, since he owns the Château," she continued reflectively.

"Well, maybe he didn't think about it, or think about anyone listening in," Gracie returned with a grin.

She got up then, and walked over to the sideboard to choose another slice of pizza. She had liked the mushroom, but there was also a bacon-topped one, one with caramelized onions and goat cheese with fresh basil, and two with the more traditional pepperoni. She was maneuvering a slice of the onion and basil pizza onto her plate when she noticed Philippe helping himself to a slice of the pepperoni pizza. He was wearing a dark green cambric shirt and jeans: the shirt brought out the color of his eyes.

"Philippe," Gracie addressed him, stepping next to him and smiling. "This isn't a question about Angelique, really," she began hastily, and put a reassuring hand on his arm: the man had almost jumped when she had greeted him, and Gracie couldn't really blame him. "I'm sure you can tell me why the Loches Police Department is handling the investigation, not Bléré," she inquired, curious.

Philippe looked relieved as he replied. "Of course. Reignac lies on the dividing line between the region covered by the Bléré police and by the Loches police. And, since I—the Bléré Detective— am here," he inclined his head modestly when he said this, "and not on duty, the Loches police and Detective were the first to respond, and so the case is theirs," he explained simply.

Gracie nodded. "That makes sense. Any ideas when the coroner's report and the report from the Loches Detective—what was his name?"

"Jean Valois," supplied Philippe.

"Ah, yes, Detective Valois—when his report might be available?" she asked innocently.

Philippe shook his head. "I do not know, Gracie: each bureau works at its own pace. But as I said earlier, at lunch, the Detective and the Coroner are very good, and very thorough. And I am sure they will not delay," he added with a faint smile.

"What do you mean, you think she was murdered?" Jack asked later that night. Gracie had called him when she'd got back up to her room, and had told him about the extraordinary events of that day.

Now she lounged on the window seat, casements open wide to the night breeze. "I didn't say that," Gracie protested. "I just said that 'maybe' she was," she clarified. "Trauma and subdural hematoma aren't inconsistent with murder," Gracie said defensively.

"Yeah, but they're also not inconsistent with a natural or accidental death," Jack responded tartly. "I think murder is a real stretch." Sometimes, Gracie's instincts were spot on, and sometimes Jack thought her imagination was a little too wild.

But Gracie had continued to think about Angelique's death for the rest of the day, and to analyze all the information she knew. In addition to the accepted scenario Elspeth had advanced and which everyone seemed to accept, Gracie had also begun to wonder if someone could have hit Angelique on her head and then arranged her body on her bed to suggest a natural demise.

"You're jumping to conclusions," Jack continued, admonishing Gracie. "Not everything is sinister."

"But if it was a natural or accidental death, then why call in the Detective?" Gracie queried. "Doesn't that seem to suggest that they think the death's suspicious? Like, maybe a murder?" she insisted.

Jack sighed. "Until they know exactly what happened and how Angelique died, they will investigate it, and who does investigating? The Detective. It's just like here," he reassured her.

Gracie sighed heavily. "It's just weird: Angelique has been acting, well, oddly, since the start of the seminar," she declared.

"How do you know that?" Jack cut in, still playing Devil's advocate. "You never met the woman before Sunday night. Maybe the way she's been acting is normal for her. You don't know her," he repeated.

"Always the voice of reason," Gracie noted sarcastically. But he had a point, and he was able to be quite objective when examining evidence. It made him a very good Detective. Still, "but she acted as though something were troubling her, really bothering her, and she didn't seem to really enjoy being here, at the class, I mean," Gracie pursued.

"Maybe she was worried about money: didn't you tell me she'd said things were quite tight, at least until her condo sold?" Jack reminded her.

"Yes, but—"

"Or maybe she was really intimidated by Chef Pernod," Jack suggested. "Possible?"

Gracie nodded and told him it was perfectly possible, even though Angelique had seemed quite skilled.

"So, then, that could explain her behavior, couldn't it?" Jack asked in an even tone.

"I suppose…"

"It was probably just like your friend said, an accident, a heart attack or a stroke or something like that," Jack opined. "You'll know when the Coroner's report comes out," he reassured her.

"Well, I <u>have</u> been having trouble coming up with any reason someone might have to want to kill Angelique: she didn't seem the type to make enemies," Gracie conceded. "Now, Brigitte Bernard, on the other hand, I think people would line up to take a whack at her," Gracie told Jack feelingly.

Jack chuckled.

"Mmmmm...I still wonder why Philippe isn't on the case. He's a Detective, too, and he's right here! I would think Detective Valois would be working hand in hand with Philippe to figure out what happened," Gracie insisted.

"Well, didn't you say he'd explained that it's a jurisdictional issue?" Jack asked. "It's probably just that the other police department caught the case and Philippe doesn't want to step on any toes."

"I think Detective Valois might be senior to Philippe, too, I mean, he looks older," Gracie mused then. Philippe was in his early to mid forties she thought, but Detective Valois had to be near sixty.

"That could also be part of it," Jack agreed. "Everything's political," he added wryly.

Gracie sighed again, and scanned the sky outside her window for stars. Nope: it was cloudy. Ah well. And wouldn't you know it: tonight when the weather didn't favor star-gazing, there were no annoying lights from other rooms shining on the lawn behind the Château and ruining her night vision.   Something was tugging at her memory. The other night, when she'd been looking up at the stars and someone's light had been on...when had that been? She hadn't been able to sleep, so she'd done much as she was doing now: gone to look at the stars, and called Jack. That night, she'd told him all about Market day in Bléré…it had been the second night. The night Henri and Gary had argued about asparagus. The night Gracie had heard what she had at first thought was Henri and Gary continuing to argue upstairs, but which she had realized —when she'd heard Henri snoring in his room—must have been another conversation.

That argument—the second one—had been coming from down the long corridor, from a room somewhere on the Chapel end. The light had also been coming from the window of a room in that vicinity, although about an hour afterwards. Whose room had that been? Could it have been Angelique's? Her room was in that part of the Château. Had the argument she'd overheard and the light on in the room been connected? Had Angelique argued with someone and then been so upset she'd been unable to sleep? Had the argument been upsetting enough to bring on a stroke? Or a heart attack?

"Gracie?" came Jack's voice from her iPhone. "You there?"

"Oh, yes, sorry: I got sidetracked, thinking," Gracie replied guiltily.

"I said, well, maybe since this Philippe guy is on vacation, taking this course, he also doesn't want to think about work," Jack repeated. He didn't sound annoyed that Gracie's attention had wandered.

"Mmm…maybe. Well, we won't know anything until we're told cause and manner of death," she noted flatly. "And you're probably right: it was most likely an accident." She filled him in quickly on what she'd been thinking about seconds before: that an argument might have brought on a fatal coronary or similar incident.

"Well, that's a possibility, Gracie—maybe you should mention that to Philippe," he suggested.

"But it's not concrete, just conjecture," Gracie objected.

"I know, but it's observant. Better to mention it than not, and Philippe can do what he wants with the information," Jack reassured her.

Gracie sighed. "Oh, I'll feel so much better once we know what happened for sure."

"Well, of course," Jack put in supportively.

"I think I'm the only one who's even considered that it might be murder," Gracie confessed in a whisper.

"Why am I not surprised?" Jack chuckled.

chapter Sixteen

Friday morning, the Coroner and police finally issued their statement on the death of Angelique Rochambeau. Gracie heard about it when she got up and tuned her in-room television to the 24-hour news channel. It was so early, it was still quite dark out, although some of the liveliest birds were beginning to chirp their greetings to the new day. The sky looked clear with a few fading stars in the violet sky, and Gracie gulped a fast cup of instant coffee and dressed quickly as she listened to the news reports.

The Loches police announcement was a ten second sound byte on the local news, which occupied five minutes at the top of each hour. According to what the news reader said, Angelique Rochambeau's time of death had been narrowed to between midnight and two a.m., and the cause of death was listed as a 'severe cranial fracture which caused a significant subdural hematoma.'

Hah, thought Gracie: so Angelique <u>had</u> hit her head!

The manner of death was, however, labelled 'undetermined,' much to Gracie's consternation.

"How can it be 'undetermined?'" she asked rhetorically as she, Sam, Peter and Elspeth shared a quick breakfast a short time later. They were the only ones in the dining room. She had told her companions of the newscast.

Peter shrugged. "Well, because they don't know how she hurt her head," he replied, smearing some marmalade on a piece of whole grain bread.

"If they knew it had been an accident, they'd rule it 'accidental,' Gracie continued, thinking out loud as she scooped up yoghurt and fresh strawberries. "It would only be labelled, 'undetermined' if they had some suspicion, at least, that it wasn't an accident." She paused. "And, the fact that they are calling it 'undetermined' could also mean that she didn't have a stroke or a heart attack, or presumably some other condition that might have made her black out and fall."

"Oh, but, what else could it be, Gracie," spluttered Elspeth, shaking her frizz. Then she paused, spoon loaded with milk-drenched granola half way to her mouth. "You don't think—someone —" she whispered, unable to finish the horrible thought, and dropped her spoon in her bowl with a splashy clatter.

Gracie nodded. "Could be," she hedged in a non-committal voice.

"But—why?" Elspeth almost wailed. "Who? Everyone liked her…" she protested.

Gracie sighed. "Yes, I know: it seems very unlikely."

Peter shrugged and looked thoughtful. "I suppose it could have been," he said to no one in particular.

"Look, I wouldn't be thinking that," Gracie began anew, "except for the ruling. I expected them to say it had been natural or accidental, but they didn't. That tells me they have doubts. Why they have doubts, I don't know exactly," she admitted. "But if they think foul play was remotely possible, I imagine they'll be coming back here to re-check her room for, erm, more clues." Yeah. Like blood. Or a weapon.

"That's probably exactly what they'll do," Sam offered from behind the rim of his coffee cup, "and then, depending on what they find, they'll issue another statement."

"But who would want to murder Angelique?" Elspeth demanded again, this time sounding annoyed.

Gracie shook her head and kept quiet.

That morning, since she had awakened so early, she'd had time to do an internet search on Angelique Rochambeau before dashing down to breakfast. Although most of the software she owned only worked to uncover personal details and financial histories for U.S. citizens, Gracie had nonetheless been able to find out a few things about her deceased friend.

As Elspeth had said, Angelique had not been from Toulouse originally: her birth record listed her place of birth as Onzain. When Gracie had looked that up, she had found it was a town about a half hour north of the Château. So, Angelique had been a 'local' before moving to Toulouse. She wondered why she had gone there.

Angelique Rochambeau had been born Angelique LaMarque: Rochambeau had been her husband's name. Angelique had told them her first husband, her daughter's father, had died. So Monsieur Rochambeau must have been her second husband.

Unfortunately, Gracie could not find any record of Angelique's first marriage. But further searching, because by then she had been extremely curious, had turned up a marriage license issued several years before, and then a divorce decree for Angelique and Thomas Rochambeau, issued three years later. So since Sophie was old enough to go to University, Gracie had reasoned, this confirmed that Thomas Rochambeau could not be her father.

Perhaps the strain of having an adolescent in the house, a child who was not his, had been too much for Thomas Rochambeau? Gracie had mused as she'd begun to dress that morning. By her reckoning, Sophie would have been about twelve when her mother had married Rochambeau, and around fifteen when she had got divorced. From what Gracie could ascertain, Thomas Rochambeau was still alive and well down in Toulouse: maybe he was the reason Angelique had planned to come back to her home area and open her restaurant here? Maybe she'd wanted to get away from Toulouse, or from Thomas Rochambeau?

Everyone seemed convinced Angelique's death had been an accident because they could not imagine anyone having a motive to do Angelique harm. But could Thomas Rochambeau have had a motive? Could he have murdered Angelique? But why? The details of the divorce that were available online didn't make it look especially complicated, or even contested. But, one always looked at the spouse. Or in this case, the ex.

Gracie had also had time to pull up a basic financial report on Angelique, although a really thorough analysis would have to wait. From what she had seen, it had looked as though her late friend had been in some financial distress: her credit cards were overburdened and although she had put her flat in Toulouse up for sale, it had not yet sold. Angelique had been counting on the money from that sale to fund her new restaurant, wasn't that what she'd said?

Gracie had shaken her head in frustration then, and gone down to breakfast, but thoughts of

Angelique occupied her mind for much of the morning.

The St. Avertin Market was as fascinating as the one in Bléré had been, and Chef Pernod was happy to find some organic pork, some duck, and some goose. He explained to the students that March was not the best time for goose, because goslings are born in the spring, so by the following March, they are very mature. "But we will use their meat, which is rather tough, in ways that will be full of flavor, and which will make it tender," he assured the students.

Chef Pernod also filled his canvas shopping bags with various types of cheese, a number of fresh vegetables and other ingredients which he personally selected. He clearly had a menu in mind, at least for that evening if not for the entire weekend.

Gracie knew Michel had left early that morning to find a specific wine, Corbières, for which Toulouse was famous; sadly, the Château's wine cellar did not stock it, but Michel had done an internet search and located a wine merchant near Limoges who had three cases for sale. The earlier idea of sourcing some Norman wine had apparently gone by the board in the wake of the course's new focus on Toulousain cuisine. Gracie wondered what Brigitte thought of that. Probably nothing complimentary.

In honor of Angelique and Toulouse, which was called the 'pink city' because of the pink bricks used for much of the construction of its buildings, Monique had dressed the dining room in some pink tablecloths and matching napkins that she had found: they would use them for the rest of their time at the Château.

Before they left St. Avertin to return to the Château, Chef Pernod led them all, parade-fashion, into the flower stall section of the Market. As always, Gracie was delighted by the wonderful smells and clean, dewy air that somehow seemed fresher near all the greenery. The Chef stopped before a large stall and surveyed the dozens of conical aluminum holders offering flowers for sale: tulips, daffodils and jonquils, pansies, primroses, irises, even roses and daisies that Gracie thought must be imported from further south. Then the Chef stopped in front of a small, somewhat humble display of lavender violets.

"Do you have white violets, as well?" he asked the stall owner, who nodded, and produced a couple of small paper-wrapped bunches from the back. White violets, Chef explained, were too delicate for display, but often could be found if one asked for them.

The Chef bought two bunches of each color and informed his attentive flock that violets were used both creatively and for their taste in much of the cooking of Toulouse. "We shall be sugaring some, and making a vinegar from some as well as using the prettiest flowers as garnishes," he declared.

Gracie knew from talking to her friend Tyler back at home that sugaring flowers was a tricky task, and she looked forward to having a go at doing some herself.

When they returned to their vehicles—the van and Gracie's car—it became obvious that some people would have to hold some of the purchases on their laps for the ride back, because there was not enough room in Gracie's trunk for everything, and the van did not have much storage space. Elspeth and Anna had traveled with Gracie that morning, but Monique had remained at the Château; this should have meant that half the back seat in Gracie's rented Renault could also be used to store purchases. However, Chef Pernod had apparently requisitioned an entire two bench seats on the van for himself and his most precious finds, allowing the remainder to travel in Gracie's trunk. His actions had left one student without a place to sit and so Philippe found himself sitting next to Anna in Gracie's back seat for the return journey to Reignac.

"Elspeth, I meant to ask you, how did you know that Angelique wasn't from Toulouse originally?" Gracie asked as she drove onto the D 943. A bonus to volunteering to provide extra transport meant that she was getting quite familiar with the roads near Reignac, and could navigate her way around well.

"She told me, that first day," Elspeth answered.

"Oh—you know she's from around here, don't you?" Gracie pursued.

Elspeth shook her head. "No: she never said where she was from, just that she'd moved to Toulouse," Elspeth answered. "I think our conversation was interrupted."

Gracie laughed lightly. "It's almost ironic, really, but it makes perfect sense: she was from Onzain, just up the D 58!" she revealed. "No wonder she wanted to come back here to open her restaurant: it's her home turf."

"How did you find that out?" Anna asked from the back seat, sounding almost offended that Elspeth and Gracie knew things about her departed friend that she did not.

Gracie shook her head and slid a look at Elspeth, but her face was merely mildly curious, no more.

"I Googled her," Gracie replied simply: no need to go into great detail.

"Oh! The internet," Anna commented, sounding both dismissive and awed. Gracie recalled that Anna had a smart phone, but rarely used its internet function.

Philippe cleared his throat and gave a small cough, but said nothing.

"Angelique told me she moved to Toulouse because an elderly aunt there needed someone to stay with her," Anna continued, straight faced.

Aha, Gracie thought, that answers that question. Then she bit her lip. Really? Maybe she was too cynical, she thought next. Maybe Angelique really had had an elderly aunt in Toulouse. Still— "Did Angelique tell you how long she had lived in Toulouse?" Gracie asked Anna.

Anna frowned for a moment. "She said she'd gone right after finishing at the Lycée," Anna replied. "It was a really top rated one, too, and she got one of the highest Baccalaureate Degrees they offer," Anna went on, sounding proud.

Gracie frowned as she made the left turn onto the D 17 in Cormery. "And then she left to go stay with her Aunt?" she asked disbelievingly. It seemed peculiar to her.

As she checked her rear view mirror, she caught Philippe's face: his eyes were shut, and he looked very ill at ease. Maybe he had motion sickness? Probably her driving, Gracie thought, and touched the brake pedal more firmly. She would slow down a bit: they would get back to the Château with Chef Pernod's precious provisions in plenty of time.

"She had studied Hospitality," Anna returned. "She told me she'd got a good job down in Toulouse, which is why she'd stayed there even after her aunt eventually died a few years ago." She shrugged. "And her aunt had willed her the flat, so it made sense."

Of course, it also made sense because Angelique had been married to a man from Toulouse for a while, too, Gracie thought to herself, but did not share that information with her companions.

Elspeth nodded then. "That sounds all right to me," she commented glibly. "She got her experience while she was able to stay rent-free with her relative and then things fell into place, and she decided to open her own restaurant, back near her home town. That sounds like a success story."

Gracie sighed and nodded her agreement. The way Elspeth said it, it did sound like a success. The thing was, Gracie couldn't help wondering about the timing of Angelique's move to Toulouse. She'd have to see if she could find a graduation date for her from the Lycée, and then see if she could find a birth certificate for Sophie.

It wouldn't surprise her if Angelique had been pregnant when she'd finished at the Lycée, and had gone to Toulouse—aunt or not—to have the baby. After all, 'staying with an elderly aunt' was practically a clichéd euphemism for just that situation, even though Angelique had spent years, not months, in Toulouse.

They returned to Château de Reignac just as the van was disgorging its occupants and their numerous packages in the forecourt. Gracie's riders also exited her vehicle and helped to carry everything inside from the car boot. Gracie shot a quick look over at Philippe, but his color had returned and he was chatting amiably enough with Henri as the two men collected the items that needed refrigeration and headed for the larder and fridge-freezers.

Philippe must be one of those men who hated not being in control and who always had to drive, Gracie thought with a smile. She didn't think her driving was nausea-inducing, and anyone else who had ever ridden with her had never complained. Oh well.

She put it out of her mind, and pitched in to get their purchases put away.

Château Moncontour Vineyard and Winery was a beautifully appointed winery that boasted a museum in its ancient caves as well as top of the line, modern tasting rooms in the historic Château. Owned by the Feray family, the Château overlooked the Loire River and its Valley. Because the day was, indeed, fine, the views alone were worth the trip, Gracie thought. Moncontour was one of the oldest estates in the region and its wines were now considered among the best.

Chef Pernod, Claude and the students all gathered in one of the clean, bright tasting rooms and were offered a number of the winery's products, beginning with the traditional Vouvray wines, both still and sparkling. Gracie discovered that she was especially fond of the white Cremant de Loire, a sparkling, rich wine with a nutty aroma that reminded her of freshly baked bread, and a very pale, clear yellow color. She also liked the exceptional, and sweet, 'Nectar,' and could imagine sipping it, chilled, on a warm summer evening while sitting out on her screened porch with Pumpkin, and Jack, and Woof.

A sudden pang of longing told her that she missed them all, and her home, very much.

Because the winery did not ship to the United States, Gracie would have to content herself with bringing the legal limit back in her luggage. The kind staff at the Winery packaged the bottles she chose in purpose made cradles of pressed paper, and attached a signed customs declaration form. Gracie would bring the package in the cabin with her for her flight home.

"We have done this before," the staff assured her, "and there is no problem."

She also bought a bottle each of the Cremant and the Nectar to enjoy while she remained at

Château de Reignac, particularly since she would be there for several more days.

As a special treat, Claude had booked everyone in to a small local restaurant for lunch: Les Gueules Noires. Located in a 'troglodyte' off a very narrow gravel roadway, the restaurant specialized in fresh, local and inventive food, and the class, plus Claude and Chef, took over the entire place. Of course, they couldn't just enjoy lunch: they would, Chef explained, be expected to critique it later that afternoon, once they'd returned to the Château.

Terrace seating outside was fortunately available: although the interior was well lit and atmospheric, its cave like ambience did not appeal to everyone. At Anna's urging, Gracie joined her at a small slatted metal table on the terrace and they enjoyed their three course meal, with wine, surrounded by mature shade trees and the birds of the Loire Valley.

'That was delightful, but nothing I could not have made at home,' Gracie heard Brigitte comment to Gilles as they were leaving the restaurant to return to the Château: a full afternoon of cooking awaited them.

Gracie shook her head and looked at Anna, who had been walking beside her, just behind the couple from Rouen, as they made their way to the car park. Anna just rolled her eyes.

chapter Seventeen

Friday afternoon, the students learned how to make traditional Toulousain sausage. Gracie had once made kielbasa with a Polish friend's family when she'd been at University, so she knew the basic process. However, the ingredients were rather different: they were using ground goose meat rather than pork, and the spices were not at all the same. Chef Pernod explained that because of the time of year, and the less tender goose available, the meat needed to be ground and otherwise augmented so that it would tenderize and be worthy of their cuisine.

The students ground the goose meat—which they first skinned and de-boned— with an old fashioned hand-cranked meat grinder that clamped on to the edge of a table. Smoked bacon, many finely minced cloves of garlic and a considerable splash of red wine were some of the other ingredients in the sausage, which itself would be a main feature of the cassoulet they would be preparing.

"This wine, the La Tour," instructed Chef Pernod, "is the same wine we shall serve with the meal tonight," he said. The emphasis on using wines from Toulouse meant that there was less of a choice, and so Chef would choose the wines for main dishes for the rest of the course. "One never uses inferior wine in cooking, as you all know," Chef continued. "One uses, ideally, the wine one will serve, or one which is less exalted, perhaps, but with similar characteristics."

Dinner that evening was slated to be a cassoulet; the starter would be a simple steamed artichoke with a vinaigrette dressing because the cassoulet was such a heavy, filling dish. Dessert, Chef Pernod had said, would be another Toulousain specialty, caraque.

Elspeth was particularly delighted by the selection of caraque, which was a shortbread biscuit topped with chocolate ganache and iced with green fondant. "I make the best shortbread in Edinburgh," she declared, a statement Gracie nodded and smiled at but privately very much doubted. Surely, Elspeth's shortbread was likely excellent, but the 'best in Edinburgh?'

As the students were busy grinding the goose meat, Monique tiptoed into the kitchen and whispered something in the Chef's ear. Then, with a look of apology at Chef Pernod, she made her way over to Gracie, and whispered to her that the police had returned. "I asked them to park at the side, so as not to alarm anyone," she added with a shake of her head. "But since you asked me to tell you when they came back…" she smiled.

"Oh, thank you," she whispered back to the Château Manager. "I want to talk to Detective Valois."

If Monique were surprised at this, she didn't look it, merely nodded and smiled again.

Gracie quickly tidied her work station and followed Monique up the stairs to find the police: she told no one where she was going, and thanks to Monique's quick thinking, it would be unlikely that anyone else at the Château would realize the police had returned.

Chef Pernod just stared as Gracie left class, but she thought she detected a tiny nod from him.

Gracie found Detective Valois in Angelique's room, standing next to the wooden mantle over the small fireplace. He seemed to be staring intently at the dentilled ornamentation on one corner, and she wondered what the Detective was looking for.

Gracie came to a halt at the crime scene tape that criss-crossed the door, and rapped lightly on the door frame.

"Detective Valois?" she called out in her best 'excuse me but I really need to talk to you' tone of voice.

The tall man turned; he had a small ALS flashlight in one hand, and his warm brown eyes sharpened as he saw Gracie. "Ah, Mademoiselle Barufaldi," he said. "The journalist from the United

States." His tone was not one Gracie would call complimentary.

Apparently, she thought as she pasted her best smile on her face, since the day before, he or his staff had researched the bios of the guests at the Château, herself included. Well, since they were all under scrutiny, she supposed that made sense. And Detective Valois now knew her occupation. "Ah, yes," Gracie agreed, and nodded. "I am a journalist—back home. Here, I am just a cookery student," she told him modestly.

Detective Valois gave her an appraising look.

"I—I just wanted to make sure you—the police, I mean—you knew about Angelique's ex-husband," Gracie continued, sounding less sure of herself than usual. "Thomas Rochambeau. I believe he is still in Toulouse?"

The Detective looked slightly impressed. "Ah, yes, Mademoiselle Barufaldi," he concurred.

"Oh, call me Gracie, it's much easier than 'Barufaldi,'" Gracie interjected.

Detective Valois inclined his head. "Well, Gracie, then yes, we know about Thomas Rochambeau," he confirmed. "The question is, how do you know about him? Were you and the deceased close?" he queried, fast.

Gracie gave a little shrug. "We were getting to be friends," she answered obliquely. "If we had had more time, perhaps…but as for how I know about Thomas Rochambeau, I Googled Angelique, and found out about him," she replied.

Detective Valois nodded.

There was a beat of silence. Detective Valois seemed unsure of what to say or do next, and unaware of the reason for Gracie's presence at Angelique's door. Gracie wasn't entirely sure what she wanted to do next, either. Asking about Angelique's ex husband had been a pretext to what she really wanted to know, since she was quite sure the police were as capable of Googling someone to get information as she was.

What Gracie really wanted to ask the Detective was why the Coroner had chosen 'undetermined' for the manner of Angelique's death. Were there extenuating circumstances that made her doubt that the death had been an accident? And what might those circumstances be? And now that she'd seen him with the ALS flashlight, she also wanted to ask him what he was looking for: blood?

Ah well, the worst he could do would be to not answer her, so she might as well try, Gracie encouraged herself.

"I heard the report this morning on the news," Gracie began, then, with a small smile. "I'm curious about the 'undetermined' manner of death," she added.

"How so?" the Detective queried, looking interested. Or maybe he was suspicious.

Gracie took a breath. "Well, that kinda rules out Angelique having a heart attack or a stroke, or some disease that caused her death, doesn't it?" she began. "The report said 'cranial fracture' so Angelique must have hit her head on something hard and died from the resulting subdural hematoma," she went on, omitting the fact that she'd overheard him speaking to the Coroner on the day of the body's discovery, and had known all along about the hematoma. "The report did not include any further details but I can only conclude that there must be other, erm, evidence, maybe on the body? that made the Coroner wonder about the manner of death, once she had ruled out natural causes," she explained.

"You should have been an attorney, not a journalist, Mademoiselle Barufaldi," Detective Valois offered, returning to formality. Somehow, Gracie didn't think his comment was a compliment.

She shrugged. "I've been in a lot of courtrooms," she agreed. "And yes, I'm wondering if anything was found, any tissue under Angelique's fingernails, for example, or fibers on her clothing, or anything like hair or blood here in her room that might be, well, suspicious." She took a breath. "I see you have an ALS flashlight," she added, and smiled again.

Detective Valois was silent. Was he trying to intimidate her, she wondered? It wouldn't work, and he somehow didn't seem the intimidating type. Maybe he was just waiting for her to say more? All right then…

"The report also didn't mention the size or shape of the wound on her head that caused the cranial fracture. But I'm sure you know the size and shape of it, and from that, have an idea of what the, erm, murder weapon might have been?" she asked, using the term 'murder' on purpose, to see if the Detective denied it out of hand. Or confirmed it.

The clever Detective did neither. "You think it was murder, then, Mademoiselle?" Detective Valois asked sharply. Typical police-craft: answer a question with a question.

Gracie sighed. "I don't know. Angelique did not appear to have any enemies. I can't imagine who would want to hurt her, let alone kill her. So it seemed, until the report, to make sense that her death was a naturally caused, unfortunate accident." She paused for a breath.

The Detective said nothing.

"But if tissue was found under Angelique's nails," Gracie went on, "or if there were bruises, perhaps on her wrists for example, those things might point to a struggle, which could be connected to her death, and if so, could indicate that her death was not an accident," she explained.

Detective Valois nodded. "Quite so."

Encouraged, Gracie went on. "As for blood or fibers, well, that could pinpoint the place where Angelique suffered the fatal injury," Gracie explained. "And any fibers found could be traced, perhaps, to someone who had been with her shortly before she died, and they might know something about how she died," she finished in a rush. Then she paused. "Not necessarily a murder, though... as I said before, I don't know who might have wanted to kill Angelique," Gracie admitted.

The Detective raised his eyebrows as though questioning Gracie's opinion.

Gracie fidgeted in the doorway. "The only red flag, really, is her credit: her cards were maxxed out, and although Angelique's flat in Toulouse is on the market, it hasn't sold yet. I suspect she was quite short on cash," Gracie concluded, and looked down.

The crime scene tape, yellow and black just as it was in the U.S., fluttered in a draft of air.

Detective Valois looked impressed, and he drew himself up, and took a deep breath and toyed with the little flashlight in his hand.

"The details you are asking about, such as blood and fibers and the shape of the wound, were not included in the police statement because they are privileged, Mademoiselle," he said, somewhat stiffly.

"Oh, I see: you don't want to include them because aside from the coroner and the police, the killer is probably the only one who knows them, right?" Gracie asked. It was a familiar enough scenario, and the Detective nodded shortly. He didn't look enthusiastic about having this American interloper involving herself in his case, but Gracie was so used to working alongside Jack to solve crimes, she didn't usually think about how oddly intrusive other law enforcement and investigative entities might think her.

Gracie switched gears then, and focused in on the flashlight he held. An ALS flashlight—alternate light source—had a distinctive lens made up of several small LED bulbs. The flashlights were used at crime scenes to inspect surfaces for body fluids: semen, saliva, urine, and even bone fragments would all show up under an ALS light.

Gracie peered at the Detective's other hand: empty. If he'd been searching for blood stains, he would have had to have spritzed the area with a chemical agent such as Luminol to make any blood that might be present fluoresce. She didn't see a spray bottle anywhere, and was momentarily confused.

Then the door to Angelique's en suite bathroom opened, and the Detective's Assistant, Noel Malraux, appeared. "Nothing in there, sir, beyond the usual," he began, addressing Detective Valois and making a slight face of distaste. He stopped short when he saw Gracie.

Malraux was wearing his sports jacket again, and another pair of khakis.

He was also carrying a spray bottle of Luminol in one gloved hand, and a second ALS light in the other.

chapter Eighteen

"Well, you're right," Jack admitted. It was Friday evening before dinner, and Gracie had chosen to use the short break to call Jack. She had found him in his office, since in Massachusetts, it was not quite lunch time.

Briefly, she had filled him in on the police report, her encounter with Detective Valois earlier that day, and his Assistant's bottle of Luminol as well as the ALS flashlights.

Now, Jack confirmed what Gracie had suspected. "If they were examining Angelique's room with ALS lights and Luminol, they're looking for blood and other things that might suggest that the room was where she hit her head," Jack assessed, sticking to the pretext that the death had been accidental.

"They've had it blocked off with crime scene tape," Gracie murmured. "D'you know, it's the same color here as it is in the States?"

"Hmmm…yeah? Well. They probably taped it off because they found the body there," Jack rejoined. "So maybe Angelique hit her head, oh, I don't know, in her bathroom, or on the sofa in her room—didn't you say there was a small sitting area?" Jack queried.

"Yes. As you enter, the bed is to the left, and on the far wall on the left there's a highboy dresser," Gracie replied, closing her eyes and recalling the furniture placement in her dead friend's room. "Then there's a window with a chair and a footstool. Then on the wall straight ahead opposite the bed there's the fireplace. In front of the fireplace is a small sofa and a little piecrust table on one side. The door to the bathroom is on the right hand wall, and between that and the wall with the fireplace there's an armoire and a little luggage rack."

"Well, then: she could have tripped and hit her head anywhere in there, and then lain down on the bed, perhaps thinking that she would feel better if she did," Jack reasoned.

"But what if it wasn't an accident?" inquired Gracie.

Jack sighed. "Well, then, maybe she was killed in her room, and the killer put her on the bed in the hope that people would think she had died of natural causes. Even though that would be unlikely, because her death was sure to be investigated. And from what you've told me, her head wound would have been noticed once the body was examined, even if it weren't immediately apparent," he continued, analyzing the situation like the Detective he was.

"Yes: Monique—she found the body," she reminded Jack, "she said she hadn't noticed anything weird about the way Angelique looked when she found her, except that she was still wearing her clothes from the day before."

"And except that she was dead," Jack put in wryly.

"Oh, you know what I mean: there wasn't blood all over the place, or anything," Gracie returned, a bit annoyed. Jack seemed to be taking this whole thing awfully lightly.

"Mmmm…well, lack of blood could—I say, could—mean she hit her head somewhere else," Jack mused. "And since your friend didn't notice anything odd about Angelique's face, we can assume that the blow to the head was on the back of Angelique's skull: that wouldn't show when she was lying down on the bed," Jack continued.

"That's right!" Gracie agreed happily. "And doesn't the position of the head wound make an attack more likely than an accidental fall?" she pursued. "I mean, if you feel faint and you fall, you could hit your head," Gracie continued. "But wouldn't you hit your forehead, or the side of your head? You wouldn't fall and hit the back of your head."

"Unless you fell backwards and hit it on something hard," Jack interjected. "Remember that case a while back where the two guys were fighting out in the parking lot and one punched the other, and the guy went down? He hit his head on the pavement, and died from the subdural hematoma," Jack reminded her.

Gracie remembered. "Right. It wasn't the right hook that killed him, but his fall to the surface of the car park," Gracie agreed. "But that didn't happen here: Angelique's face showed no signs of having been in any kind of punch up, at least, not one violent enough to send her reeling to the floor. And her room is fully carpeted," she added, "so if the police think that was where the incident took place, it wouldn't have been the type of scenario you just mentioned."

"Agreed." Jack paused. "And you could be right: the location of the head wound could point to an assailant pushing her head into something hard, maybe, rather than Angelique fainting and falling," he admitted, trying to envision likely scenarios.

Gracie was quiet for a moment, thinking. "The Detective seemed, I don't know," Gracie began hesitantly. "He didn't seem surprised that Malraux—his assistant—hadn't found anything in the bathroom."

"Maybe he'd found something on the fireplace," Jack returned. "Didn't you say he was looking at it closely?" he reminded Gracie.

She sighed. "Yes. At the corner, in particular. But don't you think if he'd found something on the fireplace he would have told Malraux?"

Jack chuckled. "Not with you there."

"Mmmm…well, yes, I suppose. But Detective Valois didn't ask me to leave, or anything, so if he'd found something on the mantel, wouldn't he have done that? So he could have told his colleague?" she asked.

Jack chuckled again. "I just think you can't believe that he might not welcome you as a sidekick in his investigation!"

Gracie made a face at the phone for being called a 'sidekick,' and then told him what she'd found out during her further research on Sophie Rochambeau. The child had been born in the same year that Angelique had graduated from the Lycée: graduation had been in May, and Sophie's birthday was in November. Oddly, the space on the birth certificate for the father's name had been left blank. Also, there had been no record of a Thomas Rochambeau at the Lycée which Angelique had attended; a further search of his background revealed that he had attended a Professional and Technological Lycée in Toulouse. He was a couple of years older than Angelique. Thomas Rochambeau had earned a degree in the French counterpart of the U.S.' HVAC.

"I can see why Angelique might have married him," Gracie concluded. "Thomas Rochambeau had a good education and a good profession. She probably thought he would provide a decent living for her and her daughter, and maybe even support her while she pursued her dream of owning her own restaurant. And he's not bad looking," she added.

"Well, with such a ringing endorsement, I wonder that they got divorced," Jack quipped.

Gracie sighed. It was true that the Rochambeau union didn't inspire romance. "I'm sure the police will ask Mr. Rochambeau that question," she said sourly.

"Prob'ly," drawled Jack.

"I miss not being on the inside of the investigation," Gracie admitted.

The chat with Jack had been all too short, Gracie thought moodily to herself a short while later. She sped back down to the little prep kitchen to begin that evening's dinner service. She hadn't really even had time to ask him how he was or how the situation on the South side was developing.

Well, she'd be home in a few days, and she had no doubt they'd have a nice, long, heart-to-heart when she was back. She was looking forward to that, she realized. And to going home. Even though she was having a fabulous time here, at least until

Angelique had come to harm. And even now, it seemed important to her and to everyone else to carry on.

Assembling the artichoke starter was not complicated. The vegetables had been rinsed and trimmed, then cut flat so they could stand easily in the large pot to boil. They had cooked for a little over a half hour, or until a knife inserted in the base of each one could be removed easily. The artichokes had been drained and left to cool to room temperature while a butter and lemon emulsion had been made to accompany them.

Gracie placed her artichoke on a pretty dish, alongside the small bowl of the emulsion, then looked critically at the presentation. A bit boring. Carefully, she pulled a leaf from the bottom of the artichoke near the back, and placed it whimsically on the side of the sauce bowl, just dipping into it slightly. Better.

Dinner progressed well, and everyone seemed to enjoy all the food set before them. Even Brigitte was not overheard complaining or making derisive comments as she had after lunch, and Gracie snickered to herself that miracles could happen.

Gracie told Monique that the dining room looked very pretty indeed with the pink tablecloths and napkins she had found. Monique looked pleased, and Gracie was happy to see that the tender-hearted woman was getting over her shock at finding Angelique's body.

The cassoulet had been an adventure to make and fabulously tasty to eat. Chef Pernod had lectured them about the rivalry among the cities of Toulouse, Castelnaudary and Carcassonne, each of which claimed to have founded the original cassoulet. Of course, each mediaeval walled city also insisted on specific ingredients that a 'real' cassoulet contains. Chef even told his students about the *Académie Universelle du Cassoulet* which had contests and gave medals for the best dish. Gracie hardly believed him, but a quick search on her iPhone had revealed that Chef was not pulling his students' collective leg: there really was such an entity.

The cassoulet the students made was largely Toulousain, although its goose sausage base showed some influence from Carcassonne. Cubed bits of mutton were first seared in rendered salt pork and then included in the traditional tapered cassoulet pot which Gracie described as a 'vat' because it was so huge. The shape, she learned, was important because the tapered ends meant a larger surface to volume ratio which meant more room for evaporation and thus, more crust and more browning. She made a mental note to order one for herself.

Chef explained that historically, duck had been used for cassoulet because duck legs had been plentiful and preserved through salting and cooking, then packing it in its own fat: the classic confit. However, a confit was not, necessarily, the base for cassoulet, and therefore they would not use it. Instead, some inexpensive chicken legs were tossed into the vat, and then finally the sausages.

Everyone worked together: adding the meats, dicing onions, adding the other aromatics and draining the dried beans that Chef had soaked in salty brine overnight. They used home made chicken stock that the Château provided. Then the cassoulet cooked, low and slow in the oven, until the meats and the beans had tenderized to creamy perfection, and the cook pot had developed a deep brown crust atop the stew.

Chef explained that the cook must remove the cassoulet pan seven times and break the crust that had formed thus far on the top: this allowed more juices and liquids from the stew below to flow outward on the surface and harden into a progressively thicker crust each time.

"That is the secret," he declared with a mischievous grin.

They served the cassoulet in large, shallow bowls, being certain that each dish got a good amount of the chewy crust. Chunks of whole grain bread accompanied the cassoulet, and Gracie saw more than one person wipe the bowl with the last piece of bread, the taste was so remarkable.

The caraque for dessert was delicious. They had all worked together to bake the shortbread under Chef Pernod's instructions, and Elspeth had admitted that the resulting product was 'as good as my own.' Then, the students had tried their hands at making the chocolate ganache and the fondant, adding just enough food coloring to the latter to get it right.

Gracie had never considered herself much of a pastry chef: Tyler handled anything really tricky she'd ever served at one of her Open House parties. However, she was quite pleased when she ended up with a beautiful, shiny ganache.

The fondant had been simple: just sugar and water. But it had required a lot of time over a hot saucepan until the mixture evaporated enough to get to the 'soft ball' state. Then the mixture had to be kneaded until it was the consistency and elasticity of dough. Gracie accomplished all those steps pretty well, then she added the coloring, and kneaded the mixture again to distribute the color evenly. That was where she ran into trouble: most of the other students' lumps of fondant were becoming a perfect shade of spring green, while Gracie's fondant was streaky and spotty, with some parts darker than others and some parts hardly colored at all.

"You should have added the color bit by bit," critiqued Chef Pernod with a 'tut tut' and a shake of his head at Gracie's efforts.

Gracie sighed. Yes, she should have. But, whether she was becoming over confident or was just tired or distracted, she hadn't been as cautious as she had the first day, with the root vegetable gnocchi.

When she trimmed her caraque, though, she cheated and used the parts of her fondant that were more or less all the same shade of green. It took extra time to cut and shape specific sections of the mixture, but the result was, if not perfect, at least quite pretty. And who knew? Maybe she'd start a new trend of having marbled fondant on caraques!

Everyone seemed to think all the caraques were delicious, and whoever received Gracie's offering didn't exclaim in disgust and run out of the dining room, so the dessert must have been okay. After dinner, nearly everyone retired quite quickly after they finished, in order to get a good night's sleep before the next day's lessons.

Before heading up to her room, though, Gracie went to the small salon, to look over the display of area attractions. She had resisted the temptation to join Sam, Peter, and Elspeth in their heating vent eavesdropping party while Chef Pernod and Claude tallied tonight's scores, even though she'd been invited. She would be staying on at the Château for a few days after the course ended, and wanted to visit some local Chateaux and wineries before heading back to Paris and flying home. Therefore, she'd wanted to look through some of the brochures the Château had available, and get an idea of where she might want to go.

She was just leaving the small salon on her way to the grand staircase when she heard a knock at the Château's front doors. These had been fashioned, in the 18th century, as graceful wrought iron and glass double doors, and they sat atop a sweeping stone stair that curled on either side down to the front courtyard.

She turned.

Michel, who had been sitting behind the Reception desk, jumped up and hurried towards the front doors.

"Who is that?" Gracie asked, curious. She had thought that the Château was completely filled by the students and staff of the cooking class, and closed this week to outsiders.

"It's Angelique's daughter, Sophie Rochambeau," Michel told her in a whisper. "She came up, of course, once she was notified of her mother's death. And the police will want to talk to her, to see if she can shed any light on her mother's— accident," he finished diffidently.

"Oh!" Gracie cocked her head at Michel. "Is it a secret? That she's here, I mean...only you're whispering. Why didn't anyone tell us she was coming, and staying here?" Gracie queried.

Michel smiled. "Oh, it's not a secret," he told her. "I just don't think she would want a bunch of people all rushing up to her at once with their condolences, if you see what I mean," he explained.

Gracie supposed she did, but still wondered: "why is she staying here? Isn't it—I mean—wouldn't it be—won't it make her sad, to stay in the place where her mother died?" she asked directly. There was a nice B&B, she knew, in Reignac.

Michel shrugged. "She asked Claude if she could stay here," he told her, one hand on the brass doorknob. "She said it will make her feel closer to Angelique."

Gracie looked doubtful. "I thought we were full?"

Michel shrugged again. "Full enough. There is, actually, one more guest room, and it is vacant," he told Gracie, adding that it was quite small, and tucked into a corner of the ground floor, next to the chapel, and facing the gardens.

Gracie knew that Chef Pernod had the back-facing ground floor suite. There must be another guest room to the right of Chef Pernod's suite, then, Gracie realized. Her tour of the Château had, of course, not included an introduction to every guest room.

"Oh, well, I'll let you open the door, and welcome her, then," Gracie told Michel considerately, and walked swiftly off towards the grand staircase.

chapter Nineteen

It was a busy morning on Saturday in Château de Reignac's large professional kitchen. The students were preparing the duck confit which would be the main course on Sunday. They were also making a 'pâté de campagne' which had to sit, refrigerated, for at least eight hours prior to serving. Since the pâté would be that night's starter, it had to be prepared early as well.

The pâté's ingredients were quite simple: boneless pork shoulder, diced quite small, some pork liver—which Chef Pernod explained was preferable to chicken liver because it kept the pâté more moist since it did not need to be cooked to as high a temperature—onion, parsley, spices, and eggs. Then things got interesting: Chef Pernod's pâté de campagne, or 'country pâté' also included brandy, heavy cream and green peppercorns. Optional additions were juniper berries, finely diced mushrooms and nuts. Gracie chose the berries and the mushrooms for her little terrine.

The traditional 'pâté spice' mix of cloves, ginger, coriander, pepper and similar flavors also went into the mix. The utensils and ingredients had to be kept very chilled during the mixing process, to avoid any possibility of bacterial growth. Since it was very cold in the subterranean kitchen, whose eyebrow windows gave onto the north and east and admitted light but no heat at this time of year, Gracie thought that would not be a problem. They usually shivered through the first few minutes of class, anyway, at least until the big ovens and range tops were fired up!

The pork was divided and half was ground fine. Then the larger diced pieces of pork were added along with the liver and spices. Next, they made the 'panade,' which Gracie realized was the binding agent. This consisted of flour, eggs, brandy and cream. The *panade* was mixed with the ground meats and spices—Chef Pernod advised using the hands to do this, and as the students' fingers squished and blended in the chilled aluminum bowls, the Chef gave a short discourse on the importance of touching the food one prepares so that the care the chef feels for the food and the people for whom it is meant goes into the preparation. Gracie, for one, knew her hands and nails were scrupulously clean, and thanks to blitz inspections by Chef, so were everyone else's. The importance of trimmed nails and clean hands— up to the elbows! just like surgeons!—had been part of the first day's 'rules' lecture.

Had Gracie's forearms not been aching from the cold, she might have given more credence to what the Chef was saying, since it fit in with her world view. However, she was just happy to be ready to line her terrine pan with strips of streaky bacon, and then empty her pâté mixture into it.

The students were told to pack their mixture well, to get rid of any air pockets, then top the terrine with more bacon slices, and cover it with foil. Following this, everyone's terrines went into several large, high-sided roasting pans which held hot water, and went into the oven. The terrines would cook in the *bain marie* for about an hour. They would use meat thermometers to determine when the interior had reached 65 degrees Centigrade or 150 degrees Fahrenheit.

Once the terrines were all cooked, they would be taken out of the *bain marie* and weighted down as they cooled.

Chef Pernod also gave each student a list of the different types of creations similar to what was generally called a pâté or a terrine. Looking over it, Gracie noted there were also ballantines, galantines, pâtés grandmères, mousses, aspics and several more. Each was just slightly different in contents and in preparation, although most were served in similar ways.

Once everyone's terrines were safely in the refrigerator, Chef Pernod immediately set the students to making the duck confit.

"No rest for the weary," groused Elspeth as she rubbed a duck leg with a mixture of salt, garlic and thyme.

"Yes, but now it just gets refrigerated," Gracie replied with a smile. "We don't have to cook it until tomorrow!"

That evening's main course was to be a roast duck breast that each student would stuff with a blend of ingredients they would choose independently. Gracie liked the fact that Chef Pernod was giving them more leeway to be creative: how else would they learn? She chose strawberries, chopped hazelnuts, minced shallot and some of that lovely Selles sur Cher goat cheese she'd discovered at lunch, with the greyish rind. This, she had learned by chatting with her fellow students, was a mix of natural processes and charcoal dust. Although she didn't want her duck breast to taste like an old Smokey Joe barbecue pit, Gracie had liked the cheese when she'd tasted it, and thought it would be an interesting flavor to include.

So far, when everyone's scores were posted each morning at breakfast (what a way to begin the day!) no one had scored dramatically low. Even Roberto had done reasonably well, although he continued to be very unsure of himself.

Brigitte and Gilles had generally scored at or near the top of the class, but only Brigitte looked smug about it. Gracie usually placed just above the class average. This, Elspeth, Anna and poor Angelique had all told her was excellent for someone who was not 'in the business.' But of course, Gracie wanted to do better. Maybe she couldn't come in first, but she'd like to be nearer to the top.

Each day's individual scores were posted, but every day the students' aggregate average scores also went up on the 'leader board.' The Bernards, Henri Schilde, Elspeth and Angelique had all flip-flopped among the top spots. Gracie, Sam and Peter, Robert Kress, Philippe, Anna and Jean Soules had usually been in the next group. Roberto and Gary generally were towards the bottom of the scoreboard, but it was worth noting, Gracie thought, that the scores were separated by only one or two points, at most.

"Why do you suppose they do that?" Anna asked Gracie on Saturday morning when they were finally released from the kitchen for ten minutes. The two women had dashed up to the dining room to get coffee, as nearly everyone had, and Anna had gone over to study the scores. She sipped moodily at her cappuccino.

Gracie shrugged. "You mean, why do they do the scoring? I guess so we can judge ourselves against each other," she suggested calmly. "Maybe it's Chef Pernod's way of inspiring us to do better."

Anna gave an unladylike snort. "I didn't come here to be judged," she muttered, sounding almost mutinous.

Gracie gave her a hard look. "Are you okay?" she asked solicitously. Anna had been the closest to Angelique: even though they hadn't met prior to the course, it seemed the camaraderie between them had been instantaneous. It was certain that Angelique's death had impacted and affected them all, but Anna probably felt her death most keenly. Plus, Gracie thought that Anna was a kind-hearted soul, who was easily wounded. "I'm sure you're very upset about Angelique," she continued now, her voice soft. "I mean, we all are, but you must be especially, because you and she were quite friendly."

Anna swallowed hard. "We were. And it just seems so…" she struggled for words.

Gracie put an arm around the woman's shoulders and gave her a fast hug. "I know," she said consolingly.

That afternoon, the students made croquants, a kind of thick sugar cookie that featured almonds and caramelized sugar. These were usually topped with chocolate or fruit, but Chef Pernod had decided that sugared violets would be the topping in this case.

The class went smoothly and most of the students still seemed a bit subdued. The only hitch was when Roberto's sugar nearly burned because he had the flame up too high trying to caramelize it. However, he snatched the small saucepan in which he'd been stirring his sugar off the heat just in time, cleverly immersing the bottom of the pan in a nearby sink full of dish water. This cooled the pan and the contents almost immediately and meant that the cookies Roberto made were as tasty as anyone else's, and not a disaster.

As Gracie prepared her egg wash, and then painted each little flower, stem and leaf with it, using what looked very much like an eyeshadow brush, she pondered further the demise of Angelique.

Because of the police activity the day before, and despite her conversation with Jack who was still sticking to the accident theory despite some details that even he had admitted could point to murder, she was becoming convinced that the death had not been an accident. The more she tried to convince herself that the initial assumption was the right one—that Angelique had fainted, fallen, hit her head, and dragged herself to her bed—the more unlikely she found it. Especially since the report had not indicated that Angelique had suffered any kind of physical or neurological event that could have made her black out and hit her head. She thought that if this had happened, the report would have included it, even by noting that her death had been 'secondary to' a cardiac event, or similar language.

She was eager for the police determination of manner of death to be decided: a tragic accident was better, if any sudden death could be said to be 'better,' than a murder, certainly. But she would be surprised if that were their conclusion.

Gracie wished she could have somehow had a chance to see the autopsy report: the facts that had been released had been a mere summary. She didn't know if autopsy reports were public record here in France, as they were in the U.S. Even if they were, however, she doubted that anyone would be allowed to see Angelique's because the death was still being investigated.

But, if Angelique's death had been a murder, and not an accident as Gracie still hoped, who would have had a motive to kill her? The means—some kind of heavy object—seemed less important, somehow: anyone could find a big rock or a heavy pipe or some similar item to whack someone on the head with. As for opportunity, well, since Angelique had died between midnight and two a.m. on Thursday, she had most likely been injured, either accidentally or on purpose, some time Wednesday evening. That meant that almost anyone at the Château could have killed her.

The Château had an automatic alarm system, and all the ground floor doors were alarmed. The small basement door which led out into the gardens was usually locked, and it was the only door not connected to the alarm system. However, the police had not discovered any signs of forced entry at that door, or anywhere else.

When Claude had given Gracie the 'grand tour' of the Château, he had pointed out this door, which led to a short, narrow stone staircase he explained had been part of the original 15th century edifice. The stair was now connected by a short hallway and two doors to a little washroom and the games room at the far end of the Château's ground floor. The stair then extended up to the first floor, opening onto the first floor hallway near Gracie's room, and continuing up to the top floor and the storage area.

Claude called it the 'secret' door because usually only Château staff used it, or even knew about it: in centuries past, it had been another one of the routes used by the Château's servants to come and go to and from the main part of the Château virtually unseen. Monique in particular liked the door, because in rainy or very chilly weather, it made the walk to her house, which was only about fifty yards away, quite short. Additionally, the door was almost totally obscured from the outside by the thick growth of grape vines that grew adjacent to the

Château's walls and sought purchase against its façade.

It seemed, then, that if Angelique had not died of natural causes, her death had been either intentional or accidental. Either way, someone at the Château had to have been involved. The challenge now was to figure out who that might have been.

chapter Twenty

At dinner that night, Angelique's daughter Sophie was introduced to her late mother's fellow students, and invited to dine with them. For dinner, she sat where her mother had, and Anna immediately took her under her wing. Gracie smiled at that, and noticed that Anna more or less monopolized Sophie throughout the meal.

Gracie had put two slices of her terrine on a bed of torn butter lettuce, and had arranged finely chopped pickles, capers and bright grape tomatoes in individual groups, whereas most of the other students had scattered these accoutrements evenly over the lettuce leaves. As the starter was served, Gracie thought that her dish was presented to Brigitte; although she could not be certain, she watched closely to see the woman's reaction.

Brigitte seemed to like Gracie's pâté quite a bit, even giving a taste of it on the tip of her fork to Gilles, who of course nodded amiably.

It was impossible to distinguish among the duck breast platters, because everyone had plated them in more or less the same fashion: the stuffed duck breast at one side, with the sautéed leeks, kale and sun dried tomato accompaniment on the other side. Equally similar looking were everyone's violet croquants. Gracie was given a cookie with rather stiff and crunchy violets: tasty, but she knew her flowers hadn't come out quite that hard and wondered if they had been supposed to.

As she nibbled at the croquant and tried not to break a tooth, Gracie mentally reviewed what she knew about all her fellow students, to see if she could come up with any motive—no matter how tenuous—for murdering Angelique, or remember anyone who might have mentioned a past association with the dead woman. No one had appeared to be particularly chummy with Angelique in the way of old friends meeting up again, but perhaps someone had known the dead woman at an earlier time, and for some reason had not liked her.

She eliminated Claude, Monique, Michel and Chef Pernod: none of them had ever mentioned knowing Angelique before this week, and Gracie somehow felt that they would have. Brigitte and Gilles could have met Angelique before. Brigitte had been quite vocal about the fact that she and Gilles took at least two food and wine seminars or courses every year similar to the Cordon Bleu class they were attending now. Maybe they had met Angelique at one of them? Still, Gracie felt Angelique might have said something, particularly as she had discussed Brigitte's sour nature with Gracie, Anna and Elspeth a couple of times.

Gilles seemed too nice a person to kill anyone, and no one had mentioned that he had known Angelique. Sam and Peter from California had definitely not known Angelique: they had chummed up to Elspeth at once because their rooms were cheek and jowl, and connected, and they had commented early in the course how nice it was to find a 'sympa' neighbor among strangers. Ditto for Elspeth: with as much chatting as the woman from Edinburgh had done, Gracie was certain that Elspeth would have told her if she had known Angelique before.

Gracie's eyes fell on Philippe. Angelique had been from Onzain, not very far from Bléré, the Detective's home town: had the two known each other, perhaps as students? But if the Detective from Bléré had known Angelique before the course, it seemed to Gracie that he would have made it a point to greet her especially, maybe even express surprise at seeing her, and perhaps share their common history with the rest of the class. Certainly, once she'd been found dead, Philippe would have mentioned having known her before, if he indeed had.

None of that had transpired, so Gracie thought Philippe was probably as much a stranger to Angelique as anyone else. He'd been quite affable throughout the course, although in the last couple of days he'd seemed 'off.' Then again, everyone had.

Henri Schilde talked of very little that was not connected with food, cooking or the specific recipes they were making. He had not said one word about Angelique that Gracie could recall, and so she omitted him from her list of those with a motive.

As for Roberto, as ill at ease as he had been throughout the entire course, Gracie thought that if he'd known someone from a previous class or restaurant, he would have made a beeline for that person, seeing them as a security blanket. He had not mentioned Angelique at all. Another strike.

Gary from Australia had only made admiring and somewhat risqué comments about Angelique's face and figure: Gracie recalled that he'd shaken his head that first night and whispered to Gracie, Roberto and Henri that it was a shame that 'such a bonza chickie babe' would be 'wasted in a kitchen.' Gracie had presumed that 'bonza' meant pretty, and had only wrinkled her nose at the chauvinistically diminutive 'chickie babe.' And since then, she recalled, Gary had taken what opportunities had arisen to be near Angelique if possible, and to speak to her.

Hmmm, Gracie thought to herself as she finished her croquant. Had Gary perhaps come on to Angelique? Would she have said anything to Anna or to Elspeth or to her? Probably not. Would she have rebuffed Gary's advances? Very likely, Gracie thought. Angelique had been focused and determined: she wanted to open a Toulousain restaurant near her home town, be successful, and provide a good life for her daughter. A proposition from Gary would most certainly have been rejected, but almost as certainly dismissed by Angelique as something of no consequence.

Could such a rejection and reaction have spurred Gary to murder?

Covertly, Gracie regarded her table mate as he ate his croquant in two bites, pronounced it 'ace' and began to slurp at his cup of tea. He was brash and opinionated and sexist, but that didn't make him a murderer. He was good looking: maybe he was not used to hearing 'no.' And he was impatient, and had a temper: Gracie had seen that in the kitchen. Could it be enough of a temper to make him kill? Even in the heat of the moment?

As dinner ended, Anna came over to Gracie with Sophie in tow.

"I don't know what you've planned for this evening, Gracie," she began hesitantly. "But I thought I'd give Sophie a little tour of the Château, you know, show her the kitchen and so forth. I know Claude gave you an extensive tour of the place when you came, since you got here early, and I thought you might know more about it than I would. Poor Sophie —she's been with the police all day, so she hasn't seen a thing besides her room, the front hall and the dining room, isn't that right, dear?" she turned to the young woman beside her.

Sophie was seventeen years old, and had the same lovely features as her mother had: thick, sun streaked blonde hair, and naturally rosy cheeks and lips. She had large, round green eyes, whereas her mother's had been slightly tilted and blue. Sophie's were fringed with long, light brown lashes that needed no mascara, and her figure was enviably slight, although she was tall. Gracie would describe her as 'willowy.'

The young woman nodded, and smiled at Gracie. "Anna tells me you were friends with my mother, too, yes?" she asked Gracie, who agreed that yes, she had been.

"I think that is what makes me the saddest," Gracie told Sophie earnestly. "The fact that I think your mother and I might have formed quite a fine friendship, and now we never will have that chance. Particularly in this day and age of Skype and email and texts and SMS, people from all over the world can get to be friends, and stay friends, despite distances between them." She paused. "I would have liked to have had that with your mother."

Sophie's eyes shimmered with tears and Anna patted her on the back and handed her a tissue.

Gracie wondered privately if a tour of the Château would have been the way Sophie would have chosen to spend her evening: she looked quite exhausted. But she seemed willing enough, and Gracie thought it might be a nice distraction for the girl as well.

She wondered how much longer Sophie would need to stay nearby to speak with the police, and what her plans were now, since her mother had died. Surely she would still go on to University. But where would she live? With her mother dead, who would look out for her?

It wasn't her problem, Gracie told herself sternly. Still, she could at least chat with the girl while they explored the Château, she thought, and suggest ways Sophie could handle what was sure to be a demanding time, left so suddenly on her own.

chapter Twenty-one

Gracie and Anna began their informal tour of the Château de Reignac in the basement, in the large professional kitchen where the classes were held. Sophie admired the equipment, but confessed that her culinary skills were limited, unlike her mother's had been.

"I can make toast, and tea, and passable coffee," she related with a small smile. "I eat a lot of instant noodle soup, and salad, and sometimes I treat myself to a rotisserie chicken already cooked that I can eat as is, and use to make sandwiches and so on." She paused. "I'm afraid my mother's cooking gene didn't get passed down to me," she finished, sounding sad.

"You must have loved it when you were home, and your mother would cook for you," Anna suggested as they trudged up the stone steps to the ground floor to continue their tour.

Sophie nodded. "Yes: she often tried out new recipes on me. Called me her 'guinea pig,'" she laughed a bit, then looked solemn at the memory, now never to be repeated.

"Did you enjoy dinner tonight?" Gracie asked, changing the subject.

Sophie nodded enthusiastically. "Oh, yes, it was delicious!" Then she frowned. "I didn't quite understand the scoring part, though: do you do that every night?"

"Every night, on every course," Gracie confirmed, and explained that the students' individual scores as well as a running tally ranking everyone from highest composite score to lowest were kept by Chef Pernod and Claude. "Your mother was quite near the top, doing very well," Gracie finished with a smile.

Sophie nodded. "Well, I'm glad of that, at least."

On the ground floor, Sophie found the two salons quite inviting, but was intrigued by the games room on the far end of this level. Decorated with souvenirs from Claude's many trips to such exotic locales as Africa, India and the Far East, the room had a gaming table, a pool table, a full bar, and several extremely comfortable looking leather club chairs.

"How fascinating!" Sophie commented, stroking the preserved nose of a stuffed impala head.

Gracie did not point out the little wooden door that led to the hall, the staircase, and the 'secret' door to the gardens.

The student was also understandably charmed by the Château's library.

"Wow, check out all the books!" she exclaimed, going over to the rolling ladder that allowed access to the top most shelves. These grazed the ceiling, and as she had on the day of her arrival, Gracie wondered if anyone ever dusted up there.

They then passed several guest rooms, including Sophie's room, tucked away in a corner adjacent to the Chapel.

"Claude showed me a lot of stuff in the chapel," Gracie said as she opened the heavy, old wooden door and found the light switch. "It's dedicated to St. Louis," she added.

The Gothic Revival chapel was illuminated by an antique-looking chandelier fitted with low-watt electric candles, and a couple of more modern floodlights behind the altar. The grey stone of the interior seemed to absorb the light, however, and since it was night time, no light from came in through the delicate stained glass windows. "I wish there were another light switch," Gracie murmured, glancing around. She found none, however.

A few rows of small chairs supplied seating, and were arranged to make a center aisle. Gracie, Anna and Sophie walked down this path, and then Gracie led them past the altar rail and off to the right.

"Here's the tomb of Louis de Barberin," she informed them, sounding like a tour guide. She explained that the man had been an ancestor of the Marquis de Lafayette, and had been given the land by the King of France. The Château's present owner, Claude Barberin, was a direct descendant. "Louis made a lot of renovations to the existing fortification when he inherited the land. He filled in the moat, put in the extensive gardens, and built, among other things, this chapel," Gracie continued, waving her hand to encompass the entire structure.

"Wow, 1717!" Sophie exclaimed, reading the dedication plaque on the wall.

"Mmmm…yes, well, the earlier structure—a bit of wall and the round towers are all that remain of that—was from the 1400's," Gracie put in with a smile.

"Do they still use the Chapel?" Anna asked: she hadn't had time for more than a perfunctory tour upon arriving at the Château.

"Yes," Gracie answered, nodding. She explained that Claude had told her that weddings were held here a few times a year, and that twice a year, Mass was celebrated. "I think they have done some baptisms, also," she said.

"Who are these people?" Anna asked, pointing to the stone statues on either side of the central stained glass window. Together, these three features served as a reredos.

Gracie gazed up at the stone faces and recalled what Claude had told her. "That one is Saint Louis," she told Anna, pointing. "This one is Saint Joseph."

Anna and Sophie nodded, pleased.

"And is that another tomb?" Anna asked, pointing to the large horizontal plaque that dominated the opposite wall of the chapel, and sounding as though she hoped it wasn't.

"It is," Gracie confirmed cheerfully. "It's the tomb of Mayor Lesage, the first Mayor of Reignac, back in the 1820's." She sighed. "He predeceased his wife by two decades, and when her time came, she begged her children to bury her with him, here. But the children did not wish to spend the money, and so she was buried in the public cemetery in Reignac."

"How sad!" Sophie exclaimed. "I wonder if her children regret their decision now: I mean, how expensive could it have been?" she asked rhetorically.

Gracie shrugged and shook her head.

"Maybe the Chapel is haunted!" Anna suggested. She sounded as though she were trying to make light of it, but Gracie somehow thought the woman might be quite superstitious.

Sophie and Anna began to cross the slightly faded oriental carpet towards the far side of the chapel, with Gracie following. Then something caught Gracie's eye.

Although it was not very bright in the Chapel, she could see what looked like a darkish smudge on one corner of the rectangular marble altar. It looked out of place, and Gracie quickly gained the three shallow carpeted stairs that led up to the high altar, and peered closely at the stain.

"What're you looking at?" Anna asked from the far side of the chapel.

"I'm not sure: it's probably dust or dirt or something," Gracie replied offhandedly. Quickly, she scanned the rest of the altar: clean white altar cloth, gold candelabra, silk flowers in a small vase, but no other dark smudges.

She pulled her iPhone out of a pocket and switched it to the 'flashlight' feature, and aimed it at the mark. With a quick intake of breath, she just as quickly shut the flashlight off and jammed her phone back into her pocket.

The stain was not black, but dark red, mahogany in color. Could it be blood? Could it be— Angelique's blood? Had she found the crime scene?

Jack would tell her she was jumping to conclusions again, Gracie thought with a frown. But she had a feeling...

Gracie moved away from the altar and joined Anna and Sophie in front of the Mayor's tomb. Fortunately, neither of the other women had noticed Gracie's actions near the high altar, or had not cared if they had.

Gracie turned to her companions and said, "well, I think that about does it for the interior of the Château." She paused. "The gardens are definitely worth a look tomorrow, when it's light, and if you want to come see my guest room—I'm in one of the 15th century towers—you're welcome, Sophie," she added kindly.

Apparently thinking nothing of Gracie's somewhat abrupt conclusion to their tour, Anna and Sophie followed Gracie back down the center aisle and out of the Chapel. Gracie said hasty goodbyes and then she and Anna headed up to the first floor where their rooms were, and said goodnight. Anna turned at the door to her chamber, and Gracie continued walking swiftly to her little tower room at the end of the hallway: she needed to call Detective Valois. But first, she wanted to get a photo of that stain. She would have done it while they had all been in the Chapel, but in case the mark did turn out to be Angelique's blood, Gracie hadn't wanted to call Sophie's attention to it by taking a photo of it.

Gracie reached her door, waited ten seconds, then once she heard Anna's door close, she tiptoed back along the corridor. Maybe she should enlist the help and advice of Philippe, she thought. He was, after all, a police detective, even if he had been very reluctant to assume that rôle, even unofficially, when it came to Angelique's death.

Wasn't his room on this floor? She recalled having seen him come down from the first floor on one of the first days of the course, so she had assumed that his room was on the same level as hers. Mentally, she tried to recall the occupants behind the closed doors: on her end of the Château there was her room and that of Henri Schilde. Anna's bedroom was here, and next to her was Gary, and then Bob Kress. Roberto's room was along there, and then Jean Soules in the next room along the corridor. Finally, there had been Angelique's room. Across the hall were Sam and Peter from California and Elspeth, with their connecting rooms. The far end of the hall contained a door which led to the balcony of the Chapel.

"Huh," Gracie grunted, then tiptoed down the stairs. It was just eleven o'clock, and the large ornate clock in the main hallway began to chime the hour. A glance out the tall windows showed mostly darkness, with a couple of pinpricks of light from the neighboring town of Reignac, and a few spotlights in the shrubbery at the front of the Château. It was overcast, and what Gracie knew was a waxing gibbous moon was obscured. It would probably rain the next day, she thought to herself with a sigh.

So if Philippe's room wasn't on her floor, he must be on the ground floor, Gracie determined. Had she known that? She shook her head: it had been confusing, trying to learn not only the layout of a new place, but where all her fellow students' rooms were. She knew Monique lived in a small stone cottage just a few yards away from the remains of the

Château's 15th century wall, and Claude had an apartment on the Château's private second floor, the remainder of which was used for storage.

Gaining the ground floor, Gracie turned towards the Chapel end of the Château. The Bernards' suite was to the right, along the front of the building. It was, of course, arguably the nicest at the Château. She knew Chef Pernod had the rear facing suite opposite. Ah, this room to the left of the Chef's must be Philippe's, Gracie thought, since Sophie's was the small room to the right.

Should she knock? Gracie hesitated in front of the door to Philippe's room. It was quite late. And she wasn't even sure what the stain was! Maybe, she thought, withdrawing the hand that had been raised to knock, she should take her photo and then go to bed. She could call Detective Valois in the morning, and maybe ask Philippe to take a look at the stain then as well: it would be daylight. Maybe he could determine whether or not the stain was blood.

Gracie took her picture and returned to her room without incident. Then, she emailed the picture to Jack, got ready for bed, and picked up her iPhone.

"I just got that photo: what happened?" Jack answered his phone with a question. "Are you all right?"

"Yes, I'm fine: why?" Gracie returned, confused.

"Well, you just emailed me a picture of a bloodstain," Jack replied. "I thought maybe you'd cut yourself in the kitchen."

Gracie reassure him that there hadn't been any mishaps of that nature during the course, just a couple of minor burns and a near miss with Roberto's caramelization.

"So—that's a bloodstain?" she asked him, sounding quite happy.

"Well, I can't be positive of course, not from a photo, but it sure looks like one," Jack replied.

chapter Twenty-two

"Philippe, if you have a moment…" Gracie murmured the next morning as she was leaving the dining room after breakfast. Philippe was also on his way out, and as she had planned to, Gracie snagged his sleeve.

He looked sharply at her. "Oh! Gracie. You startled me!"

"Oh, sorry, Philippe," Gracie apologized, and gave him a winning smile. "But I need the benefit of your expert opinion."

Gracie had called the Loches police station and left a message for Detective Valois before she'd gone down to breakfast. The woman who had taken her call had assured her she would tell the Detective the moment he came in or called in. However, she had not heard from him yet. Well, Gracie supposed, there were probably other cases besides this one that Detective Valois had to investigate.

Now, Philippe Zafran, the Detective from the Bléré department, was looking at her and frowning. "My expert opinion? On what?" he asked brusquely.

Gracie led him down the corridor towards his room and towards her goal, the Chapel. "There's something in the Chapel I need to show you," she answered obliquely.

"In the Chapel?" Philippe parroted again, slowing as his feet came level with his chamber door. "How could I have any expertise about the Chapel?" he asked. Then, not waiting for an answer, he continued in a rush: "I am sorry, Gracie, but I need time to get ready for class…" He came to a stop in the hallway.

"Oh, please, Philippe: I—I'm not sure what it is. I thought, being a detective and all, you could help me figure it out," she finished, sounding suppliant.

"But, Mademoiselle, I told you I have no expertise in religious—" Philippe protested once more, but Gracie cut him off.

"Oh, it's got nothing to do with the Chapel itself," she reassured him. "That's just where it is," she explained, and beckoned him again. "Please? It'll only take—two minutes, I promise! And then you can get ready for class…"

Apparently mollified by Gracie's deferential attitude, or possibly realizing that if he didn't go with her, Gracie would keep pestering him, Philippe followed Gracie into the Chapel. She switched on the lights, and led him up the aisle to the altar. With daylight—albeit cloudy daylight— now coming in through the windows, the stain on the corner of the high altar was much more apparent, although its color was still somewhat doubtful. Only the flash from the camera on her iPhone had shown Gracie the smudge's true dark red tint.

"Here—what do you think this is?" Gracie asked Philippe, pointing to the stain.

Philippe stared hard at the mark, then blinked, slowly, once. Then he seemed to pull himself up and he turned his gaze to Gracie.

"It looks like dirt, or grease, perhaps," Philippe told her flatly, and shrugged to suggest the mark's unimportance.

"Oh." Gracie was clearly crestfallen. "I thought —I thought it could be blood," Gracie confessed in a small voice.

"Blood?" Philippe exclaimed, sounding as though the thought were ridiculous. "Blood? Where did you get that idea?" he challenged on a laugh. Gracie shrugged. "I don't know…exactly…I thought maybe it could have something to do with… Angelique?" Gracie replied uncertainly.

"Angelique?" Philippe's voice was incredulous.

"Oh, Philippe, I know you don't want to get involved in her case," Gracie began, speaking rapidly. "I know you're on holiday and you want a break from work, and that makes sense. And the investigation into Angelique's death is Detective Valois' job, not yours: I know all that," Gracie continued. "But the police seem to have ruled out Angelique's room as the place where she got hurt, so when I saw this mark last night, I thought maybe something had happened to her here..." she trailed off, disheartened by her confidant's disbelieving stare.

Philippe raised his eyebrows. "Last night?" he queried sharply.

"Yes." Gracie explained about the tour she and Anna had given Sophie.

"Did Sophie—see this?" he asked, indicating the stain.

Gracie shook her head. "No. I didn't want to call attention to it," she explained, adding that neither of her companions had noticed the mark. "But I thought that maybe you could tell me what you thought? I mean, you're a detective, you must have been at lots of crime scenes and seen lots of blood stains."

Philippe seemed to relax, and he nodded. "Well, of course, Mademoiselle. But it would be very unprofessional of me to become involved in another Detective's case," Philippe said, repeating what had become his mantra of late.

"Well, okay, then: don't get involved, just tell me what you think," Gracie returned hotly. It seemed to her that Philippe was just being stubborn, now: surely he could tell her his opinion. That wouldn't be interfering in Detective Valois' investigation. And after all, everyone else at the

Château was speculating amongst themselves, why couldn't Philippe give her the benefit of his experience? "Tell me what you think! Is that stain blood, and do you think it might be Angelique's?" she repeated, raising her voice.

"Oh, don't be ridiculous!" Philippe snapped. "You've wasted my time with this nonsense! Tell you what I think? All right, this is what I think: that mark there," he pointed at it and shook his finger, "has nothing to do with anything. It's just dirt. It has nothing to do with Angelique." He paused, then turned on his heel and stomped back up the aisle. "And it's certainly not blood!" he tossed over his shoulder as he left the chapel.

Gracie sighed. It was odd, she thought, that Jack had instantly thought the stain was in fact blood, the moment he'd seen Gracie's photo.

Well, now she'd offended Philippe. Like many men, he was very sensitive, it seemed, when he thought his dignity might have been impugned. Apparently, asking him to analyze what he thought was a smudge of grease or dirt qualified since he clearly felt that would be beneath him. And wow, had he been angry!

Gracie had expected him to at least be curious about the stain, but he hadn't been, not at all. Was she just over imagining things, putting a macabre twist on something that was really pedestrian?

Gracie didn't know. But Jack hadn't thought identifying the stain as blood had been out of the question. She and Jack had been the only ones who'd seen the stain in the bright light from her iPhone's flash and therefore been able to note its true deep red color.

Gracie knew all about disturbing evidence. She hadn't touched the smudge for this very reason. However, her curiosity was getting the better of her now, and she needed, somehow, to prove that the substance on the altar was blood, even if it were just for her own satisfaction. Even if it had nothing to do with Angelique.

She leaned over and sniffed deeply at the stain. It was too dried to get any whiff of scent. What if she just dabbed at one end of it, and checked it to see if it had blood's tell-tale metallic tang? She could always tell the police what she'd done: they might not like it, but a tiny fingertip would hardly compromise the evidence, would it?

She licked her left forefinger, and dabbed it lightly on the right side of the stain, just past the corner of the altar. Then, delicately, she sniffed at her finger. Her saliva had moistened the dark red substance enough so that she could smell a faint trace of—yes, she was sure. Blood.

Peculiar though it may be, Gracie felt quite happy that she'd been correct.

When would Detective Valois get here, Gracie wondered yet again as she hurried from the Chapel moments later. Gracie only had a couple of minutes now before class would begin, and she still had to change into her chef's whites.

It was Sunday, she realized as she walked swiftly along the main corridor: the course would end that evening. Perhaps Detective Valois went to church on Sunday? Maybe that was the delay? Still, he was in the middle of a murder investigation, Gracie thought to herself with a frown. You'd think...

'I do not think we will be paid, and although her Estate will settle her debts, it will not be anything close to what she should have paid us for the week,' came Claude's voice from the entrance foyer, echoing off the marble walls and floating down the corridor to Gracie's ears. He sounded sad.

'But I have already bought everything, and ordered the work to be done!' exclaimed Monique's voice.

Clearly, the two were discussing something in the reception foyer, unaware that Gracie was late, and at the foot of the grand staircase just a few feet away. They probably thought that all the students had already gone to the basement, and that they were alone and not overheard.

Gracie stopped, and held her breath.

'I should have known—not that she would die, of course—but that she was not able to afford to take this course. Not really,' came Claude's voice.

'Why do you say that?' Monique asked.

'The very first evening, just before we all went into dinner, poor Angelique came to me in a panic and said she really needed to leave, to not take the course. As you know, there are no refunds, and I reminded her of this,' Claude's voice continued, explaining. 'She sounded so pathetic, I very nearly did agree to refund her something…'

'I'm happy you did not!' Monique rejoined with spirit. 'At least we'll get some of what we are owed: didn't you tell me that the Cordon Bleu had allowed her to pay half the cost of tuition and room and board when she registered, and that she had promised to pay the other half at the end of the course?'

Gracie could not hear Claude's reply, so she assumed it had been a silent nod.

'We had a very quiet winter, Claude, and we need every penny to do the renovations, and do them in time for our busy season!' the Château manager reminded him.

'I know, I know. Well, never mind, we'll find the money somewhere,' Claude's voice reassured Monique. 'I imagine the Cordon Bleu is in the same predicament we are,' he mused.

Monique asked something Gracie didn't quite catch, in a very low voice.

'She told me she had charged a partial payment on her credit card, and begged them to charge the remainder on the card as well but not process the charge until next month,' Claude clarified in response to whatever Monique had asked. 'But no one will see that second payment,' he concluded. 'When poor Angelique begged me Sunday evening to let her leave the course, she told me she was flat broke, owed money everywhere, and that her credit cards were at their limits.'

He paused and Gracie heard Monique mumble something else. She sounded annoyed.

'You may well say that, Monique, but I think she felt this course was her chance to get the resumé, and perhaps the confidence, she needed to finally open her own restaurant. I think she would have been a success,' he continued. 'She was no stranger to hard work, having been a single working mother for much of her life. All she was waiting for was her flat in Toulouse to sell, and then she would have been on her way." Gracie could almost hear him shake his head in regret.

'Well, we will never know, now,' Monique finished brusquely, but her voice quivered. She wasn't an uncaring woman, Gracie knew, and she had been distinctly unnerved by her discovery of

Angelique's body. But Monique was very practical, and concerned with day to day realities, like finances. Worry over money made her short tempered.

At the sound of Claude's steps turning towards where she stood, Gracie quickly ran up the grand staircase two steps at a time on the tips of her toes. She succeeded in gaining the landing just as Claude entered the small adjunct foyer, and thus she avoided being seen.

She sped back to her room and changed almost mindlessly into her chef's whites. What had that conversation meant, exactly? Gracie wondered as, properly attired now, she ran back downstairs, and down to the basement.

Claude and Monique had clearly been speaking of Angelique. She had mentioned that she needed her flat to sell quickly and for a good price. Although Angelique had not been specific about financial troubles, it was not unimaginable that she had had them. Gracie had pulled her basic financials, and knew that Angelique's credit cards had been at or near their limits—but so were many people's, and it didn't necessarily mean financial ruin. But Angelique was dead, and if she had been deeply in debt it was likely that her Estate would settle for pennies on the dollar—or euro.

Could that have been a motive for her murder? No, that didn't make any sense to Gracie, and it never had: why kill someone who owed you money? You'd never get your money from a dead person. And besides, Gracie couldn't envision creditors tracking Angelique down to the Château and then killing her.

Sighing, Gracie forced herself to pay attention: Chef Pernod had already begun the instructions for that evening's meal, and as Gracie skidded into place at her work station, he glared at her.

"So kind of you to join us, Mademoiselle," he said sarcastically.

Gracie bit her lip. "My apologies, Chef," she said, low. "It won't happen again."

"And WHAT is that SMELL???" Chef Pernod demanded next, looking around at his students and sniffing loudly.

Everyone looked confused, and started sniffing, too.

Gracie looked momentarily insulted: was Chef Pernod saying she smelled? She didn't smell much of anything except the usual smells of a clean kitchen, but just to be sure, she sniffed at the sleeve of her tunic: nothing.

"I smell BLEACH!" Chef Pernod exclaimed accusingly. "Who has been cleaning his work station with bleach?" he continued, and began to sniff at each student's place, determined to find the culprit.

Early on, the Chef had explained that while cleaning with bleach was done once a week in professional kitchens, usually the evening prior to the day the kitchen was closed, daily disinfecting was accomplished with copious amounts of white vinegar and elbow grease. The students now knew that firsthand, since they cleaned the kitchen every night. Chef had explained that the fumes from the bleach would linger, and not only affect the chefs' sense of smell, but possibly the way the food tasted.

Apparently, Gracie thought, someone had been over zealous when they'd all cleaned up the night before. She didn't recall anyone using bleach, but then, they all cleaned their stations at somewhat different times, and she hadn't really been paying attention to what the others had been doing.

Chef Pernod, although he walked up and down the rows of work stations, did not succeed in discovering who had wiped his or her station down with bleach; the smell had apparently dissipated almost as quickly as it had been noticed.

Chef Pernod continued with his instructions for that evening's meal, but he was in a foul humor. They were to make curried courgette, serve the duck confit they had begun the day before, and make something called 'fenetra' for dessert. Since the courgettes would be cooked just prior to serving, as would the duck confit, they would spend the morning making the fenetra, which Gracie learned was a type of cake. Almonds made up the base, then came lemon flavored cake layers, with apricot jam as a filling.

Gracie began to measure out her flour and sugar, got the right amount of butter and two lovely, brown local eggs ready to use, and was just about to crack the eggs into a small bowl when Monique appeared at the front of the kitchen. She murmured something to Chef Pernod, who looked completely exasperated, and made an impatient motion with one hand.

"Mademoiselle Barufaldi," Monique called, and Gracie stopped, hand suspended above the bowl. "Please come upstairs."

Carefully, Gracie laid down her eggs, took off her apron, and followed Monique up the steps to the prep kitchen, then through the dining room. She was sure she could feel Chef's eyes on her back as she left the kitchen. Thank goodness the course was almost finished: she wouldn't be surprised if Chef booted her out this very afternoon!

"What's this about?" she asked Monique as they reached the main hallway.

"The police are here. At your request, I understand?" Monique continued, sounding peeved.

Why should she be annoyed that Gracie had called Detective Valois?

It seemed everyone was in a bad temper this morning.

Detective Valois and his Assistant Detective, Noel Malraux, were with Claude in the entrance foyer. They turned when Monique ushered Gracie in.

"Ah, good morning, Mademoiselle," Jean Valois said, cheerily enough. "You wished to see us?" he asked, a pleasant look on his face. Malraux, too, looked interested, and gave Gracie a small smile.

Well, at least they were in decent moods.

"Yes. Thank you for coming so quickly," Gracie said in response. "I know it's Sunday. I have something I think you need to see," she explained, and with a gesture for them to follow her, led them down the main hall to the Chapel. She noticed that Monique and Claude followed along behind them. Gracie didn't especially want the Château owner and his Manager there when she showed the stain to the police, but she supposed that since Château de Reignac did belong to Claude, and since Monique ran the place, they had a right to know what she'd found.

They all trooped down the Chapel's center aisle, and Gracie led them up to the high altar, and came to an abrupt stop.

"It's gone," she said, sounding disbelieving.

"What's gone, Mademoiselle?" Detective Valois inquired curiously.

Gracie sniffed the air, much as Chef Pernod had done a short time before.

"Bleach," she replied cryptically, then turned. "Detective, did you bring that handy little ALS flashlight you and your assistant were using the other day?" she asked.

The Detective nodded, and said that they always brought their crime scene kit with them: it was standard procedure.

"Well, could you go get it? I need you to examine this area, here," she pointed to the corner of the high altar. The white marble gleamed, not a trace of the smudge to be seen.

"But, why, Mademoiselle?" the Detective queried, genuinely confused. Still, he motioned for his Assistant to go get the device.

Gracie took a deep breath. "Because, last night when I was giving Sophie Rochambeau and Anna Guteknecht a tour, we were in here, and I noticed a dark smudge, or stain, just here." She pointed, then paused. "And now it's gone."

"A stain? What sort of stain? The cleaners come once a week, every Sunday morning…" began Monique, indignant.

"Not a dirt type of stain, Monique," Gracie interrupted her in an impatient tone. "I think it was blood."

"Blood?!" exclaimed Claude. He was echoed by the Detective. Monique closed her mouth with an audible clack and looked shocked.

"Why do you believe that?" Detective Valois asked Gracie.

"Because I took a photo of it, and it was dark red in the photo, although it was hard to tell the color in the low light of the Chapel. It wasn't even that obvious, unless you looked directly at the altar. But the flash showed the stain, and showed its color. And — I wet my finger and touched a tiny corner of the smudge," she confessed. "And it smelled like blood. You know: that metallic tang?" Gracie continued.

The Detective gave her a look that clearly indicated he was not at all sure of her sanity, and shrugged. "But, where is this stain now, Mademoiselle?" he asked reasonably.

Gracie sighed. "Someone must have cleaned it. With bleach."

Monique drew her breath in sharply, and everyone looked a question at her.

"As I said, the cleaners come every Sunday morning," she repeated in a small voice.

"Do they clean the Chapel?" Gracie challenged. "It's hardly used."

Monique nodded agreement but looked troubled. "Ah, yes, well, their instructions are to check even the little-used rooms, like the games room and the Chapel, and clean them if they need it."

"That's it, then," Claude pronounced, sounding relieved and regretful at the same time.

"No, not necessarily," Gracie rejoined before Detective Valois could say anything.

"That is correct," the Detective offered reassuringly. "There may still be traces of whatever the mark was, on the altar, and maybe in the area around it."

"Which is why I asked for the ALS flashlight," Gracie finished. She knew marble was quite porous and soft, as stones went: she'd learned that when she'd been choosing new countertops for her kitchen renovation. Therefore, she thought it would likely still have traces of whatever the stain had been, even though the area had been cleaned with bleach, and looked spotless to the naked eye. As she spoke, she dug her iPhone out of her pocket and brought up the photo she'd taken of the stain. Wordlessly, she held the device out to the Detective, who looked at it, and grunted.

Noel Malraux came trotting back in at this juncture, face mask, Luminol and ALS flashlight in hand. Detective Valois shooed everyone back a few paces and then nodded: Malraux held the mask over his mouth and nose, and then carefully sprayed the area of the marble that Gracie had indicated.

"What is that you're using?" Monique asked, curious.

"The trade name is 'Luminol,' Detective Valois replied. "It's a mixture of aminophtalhydrazine and hydrogen peroxide," he explained. "It will not stain," he assured Monique.

"The Luminol shines blue under UV light in the presence of hydrogen peroxide, but it needs a catalyst in order to show up, like iron," Gracie put in helpfully.

Detective Valois shot her an assessing look, and nodded. "Correct, Mademoiselle. And…" he turned back to Monique. "Of course there is iron in blood."

"My goodness!" Monique exclaimed, and Gracie thought that she must not watch many crime programs on television, or she would have been familiar with the famous Luminol.

"The problem is, there are other catalysts, such as plant material and cleaning products—like bleach," the Detective went on.

Claude moved over to the light switch and turned it to off. Then Malraux turned on the ALS flashlight and aimed at at the corner of the high altar.

The angled marble as well as a portion of the side panel lit up a brilliant blue.

chapter Twenty-three

Gracie was allowed to return to class, and she did so happily, but not before she drew the Detective aside in the Chapel, and asked him the question uppermost in her mind. Claude and Monique were talking in hushed whispers near the altar; the Assistant Detective was taking measurements and photographs, and festooning the spot with yet more of the black and yellow crime scene tape. He swabbed the marble altar and stuck the samples away in evidence bags: lab tests would be able to accurately say if there was blood on the altar, even though it had been cleaned with bleach.

With what looked like grudging permission from Claude, Malraux also cut a tiny portion of the carpeting at the base of the altar, and tucked it in an evidence bag. Gracie knew this would be tested, to see if there were any blood on it, and if the blood matched Angelique's.

Out of deference to the antique carpet, they had not doused it with Luminol, which could have faded the fibers. However, given the photo of the original stain that Gracie had shown them, and the results of the Luminol test on the altar, the Detective and his Assistant felt it was likely some blood might have dripped onto the carpeting.

"That was very good investigating, Mademoiselle," Detective Valois complimented her. To his credit, he didn't sound at all upset that a civilian had found the crime scene when he had been unable to. "You are, perhaps, more familiar than most with such things, given your profession," he added with a touch of respect.

"Thank you, Detective," Gracie replied humbly. "It was just—a hunch. Perhaps now you would share something with me?" she continued, whispering. "I promise not to say a word to anyone, but—does the corner shape of the altar match the shape of the head wound you found on Angelique?" Gracie asked curiously.

"Ah—Mademoiselle…" the Detective began to prevaricate, shaking his head. "I cannot tell you details…"

"Look, I'm not stupid:" Gracie interrupted, her whisper becoming fierce. "Upstairs in Angelique's room you were looking at the <u>corner</u> of the fireplace mantel. Here, I find blood on the <u>corner</u> of the altar," Gracie rejoined somewhat heatedly. "Clearly, her head wound was caused by something with a corner, or an angle. It could have been some kind of—of— instrument, I suppose," she continued, thinking out loud. "The square edge of a shovel or something, but a corner is less common than you might think, and the fact that you seemed to be searching for evidence that would match such a wound tells me that the head wound had to have had right angles. Am I correct?" she finished, eyes blazing.

She knew she had absolutely no right to any privileged information on the case. But she'd just provided the Detective with a key piece of evidence, and the murder scene! The least he could do, she thought, was share a little information with her.

The Detective looked at her for a long minute with those kind, knowing eyes. He seemed to be deciding something, and conducting an internal debate. Then he leaned close, so close that Gracie could smell his peppermint mouthwash. "I am not the coroner," Detective Valois began, his whisper matching Gracie's. "And we will have to compare the measurements. But provisionally—provisionally, you understand—yes, Mademoiselle, it appears that the wound on Madame Rochambeau's head and the corner of this altar are—similar. "

"So Angelique—"

"Madame Rochambeau might have hit her head on this altar somehow, especially if the tests are positive for her blood."

Gracie smiled grimly. In her brain, a scenario was beginning to play out, unfurling like a flag in a lively breeze. She didn't think Angelique had tripped and fallen against the altar, then somehow managed to return—unseen—to her room and collapse and die on her bed, even if that was what most people, including the police, had presumed.

No: someone had pushed her. Perhaps intentionally, perhaps not. But they had pushed or shoved Angelique and she'd struck her head against the corner of the marble altar and—what? Been knocked unconscious. Then what had the assailant done? Probably panicked, and scooped up Angelique and carried her to her room, placing her on the bed and hoping that she would just wake up. Gracie felt that the attacker had probably never imagined the woman from Toulouse would die; he had very likely thought she would have had no more than a bruise and a bad headache.

Gracie looked around at the Chapel, and spotted the balcony at the rear. A door led from that balcony out into the first floor corridor, very close to Angelique's room. Her eyes traveled down to the main floor of the Chapel: she thought she spied a door on one side. This might lead up to the balcony. Was it unlocked? She'd have to ask Claude.

Then, quickly, Gracie turned her attention back to the Detective. He was gazing at her with something very like admiration, she thought, and she seized the moment.

"Detective Valois, did you by any chance hear from the Coroner that bruises had begun to show up on Angelique's wrists?" she whispered, her tone both deferential and collegial.

Detective Valois drew his breath in sharply. "And how would you know that, Mademoiselle?" he asked, sounding more surprised than offended. She had referred to bruising in their earlier chat in Angelique's room, but not asked directly.

"I know that perimortem bruising sometimes does not present until a day or so after death, because at death, the victim's blood flow stops," Gracie replied quietly. "I deal with this kind of thing in my line of work," she reminded him gently. His involuntary response had been as good as a 'yes.'

The Detective said nothing, but nodded his head, once: it looked as though the action strained his neck.

"So that would indicate a struggle, and support my theory of murder," Gracie murmured.

Detective Valois let out a long breath, and nodded again.

Noel Malraux approached them at this point, and Gracie nodded at the Detective with a small smile and thanked him for his help. He and his Assistant left the Chapel, then, headed for one of the salons to speak with Sophie again.

Gracie walked over to Claude, who was still talking excitedly with Monique up near the altar and the crime scene tape.

"Did you see what they did to our beautiful rug?" Claude asked Gracie with slightly exaggerated despair.

Gracie nodded. "They need to see if it's Angelique's blood," she answered simply. "Better than fading it with the peroxide in the Luminol," she reassured him.

Monique shuddered, said she had things to do, and rushed off.

"They only took a really tiny piece," Gracie comforted Claude. Together they peered over the tape barrier at the one inch square of missing carpet. "It's hardly noticeable," she added in mollifying tones.

Claude sighed. "I suppose I can patch it with a bit of something—from somewhere. That's what owning a property that is many centuries old is all about: patch a little here, shore up a little there, tighten this, glue that." He sighed again.

Gracie grinned and explained about her 300+ year old farmhouse, and the renovations she'd had done on it thus far. "Whenever I hear a noise I can't explain," she went on as Claude listened, appearing happy for the camaraderie, "I know I'll find something that's fallen or broken in a day or two," Gracie laughed. "Once, it was the inside of the chimney—the flue was made of terra cotta and had cracked in several places over the years, and once a big piece broke off and fell into the flue. I heard the noise, and went to the part of the house where I thought it had happened, but I couldn't find anything."

"You're lucky the chimney wasn't blocked," Claude remarked sagely.

Gracie nodded. "I know! It was summer time, so I wasn't using the furnace. And before I used it much that autumn, I had the furnace guy come and clean and check everything as I do each year, and he discovered the problem." She paused. "I had them take the old terra cotta liner out and put in a new stainless steel one."

"Very wise," Claude agreed.

They were walking, now, towards the back of the Chapel and the door to the ground floor hallway.

"By the way, Claude, where does that door go?" Gracie asked, pointing to the door at one side of the back of the Chapel.

"There is a small room for storage," Claude replied. "You know, things like white runners for weddings, tall candelabras, that sort of thing," he continued dismissively, and Gracie was disappointed. "And a small staircase from inside the storage room leads up to the balcony," Claude added, pointing over his head. "I am not sure why: it makes little sense to me," he added with a shake of his head.

Gracie nodded, and tried not to grin.

"Is the storage room locked?" she queried.

"You want to see it?" Claude asked, sounding both surprised and eager to show off more of his lovely property to someone who clearly had an appreciation for historic things.

"Sure!"

"No, it's not usually locked," Claude answered, twisting the antique door knob and throwing the plain wooden door wide. He flipped a switch, and a single bulb near the ceiling illuminated just what he'd described: stacks of extra kneelers, rolls of white, red, and purple runners, a few extra chairs, and several pairs of tall candelabra of varying heights.

And tucked away to the far left was a narrow metal spiral staircase, probably a modern addition from the early twentieth century, leading up to the balcony.

Gracie moved quietly over towards this, and peered up: she could just make out a faint light coming from the illuminated balcony. This meant there was no door between the balcony and the stair.

Nodding in satisfaction, she thanked Claude for the 'extra tour,' and together they left the Chapel.

chapter Twenty-four

Gracie had a lot of catching up to do to get her fenetra ready, since her investigations with the Detective had used up more than an hour of class time. However, she made quick work of the cake while the rest of the students moved on to the curried courgettes.

It helped that thoughtful Anna had made double the required amount of the apricot conserve; she surreptitiously slid a small bowl of beautifully sweet, caramelized apricot jam over to Gracie's work station under the guise of loaning her a dish cloth.

Gracie was certain that Chef Pernod was well aware of the subterfuge, but since he said nothing, neither did she. She was walking on the proverbial eggshells just now and hoping that Chef wouldn't expel her.

"Thanks, Anna, you're a life-saver!" Gracie whispered with a fast grin.

"What happened?" Anna murmured. "You were gone so long! And Roberto said he had seen a police car parked out back," she continued worriedly.

Gracie slid her eyes quickly around the room: everyone seemed quite focused, oblivious to anything going on around them.

"I called the police first thing this morning," Gracie whispered back to Anna. "And they finally showed up, and, well, we found the crime scene." She supposed it wouldn't do any harm to tell Anna that.

Anna gasped.

"I'll tell you more at lunch," Gracie promised, and bent once again to the merengue she was attempting to whip in a copper bowl.

Lunch was the usual salads and cold meats and fish, with bread. Gracie loaded up her plate and poured herself a double espresso. Then she looked around for Anna: she was seated at a table with Elspeth and Sophie.

Gracie caught Anna's eye, then motioned with her chin for the woman to follow her out of the dining room. It would be best if any discussion of the death were quiet, and certainly kept from Sophie: the police would tell her everything in due time.

However, Anna, trailed by Elspeth and Sophie, joined Gracie in the small salon. They seated themselves on one of the little sofas and on the matching, silk-stripe upholstered chairs, and began to talk while they ate.

Gracie thought she would have to be very careful what she said, and how she said it.

"Well, what a morning, eh?" Elspeth began. "It seems we're all at sixes and sevens, what with

Philippe getting chewed out by Chef Pernod for being late, and then you," she pointed at Gracie with a mustard-coated knife, "being late as well—and then getting hauled out to talk to the police!" Elspeth commented, and started in on her cold meat sandwich with satisfaction.

"Philippe was late?" Gracie queried, curious.

"Oh, yes: Chef had just finished hollering at him when you ran in, and I thought he'd start all over again," Elspeth replied happily.

"But then he smelled the bleach," Anna recalled. "That was weird: who would have used bleach to clean? We all know it's the worst thing to use in a working kitchen," she murmured.

Sophie followed the conversation, her round green eyes swinging from one woman to the next. She ate a couple of bites of salad.

"Well, anyway, then Chef started yelling about that," Elspeth said, sounding quite cheered at the memory of the vociferous Chef. "And then you got your summons," she continued in a theatrical tone. "And then poor Sophie had to go talk to them again," she finished sympathetically.

"What did the police want with you this morning?" Gracie asked Sophie gently.

"They had new evidence," the girl replied, toying with a small slice of chicken. "Which I am not supposed to talk about," she added apologetically.

Gracie supposed it was probably the location of the crime scene.

"They asked me again if I knew anyone who might have wanted to harm my mother."

"And you didn't, did you, dear?" Elspeth put in consolingly.

Gracie sighed. Nothing like putting words in someone's mouth.

But Sophie agreed. "No! That's what I'd told them before, and I told them again, today." She paused. "They told me that my mother was in very bad financial straits," she continued, low. "I knew things were tight—but I didn't know how bad they were."

"How bad?" Gracie asked before anyone could say anything reassuring: she wanted to know what Sophie knew, and what the police might have told her.

"Detective Valois said that they had run a check on my mother's finances, and that her credit cards were maxxed out, and that she'd taken out some kind of 'bridge loan' from the bank, using the flat as equity," Sophie replied calmly. "I didn't know about the loan, but I knew about the credit cards, because Mom would joke about it sometimes." Her voice, recollecting, was regretful. "I don't think she wanted me to know how—how desperate things were, or how worried she was, but I wish I had!" Sophie continued emotionally. "I could have helped: could have got a part time job or something…"

"Your mother probably wanted you to concentrate on your studies," Anna suggested reassuringly. "And you did, and you're going to a wonderful University, and you'll be a great success!"

Sophie smiled, but looked as though she was well aware it wouldn't all be that easy. "Yes. I suppose you're right. But Detective Valois told me that the bank creditors had been trying to reach Mama for weeks, because she was behind on the loan payments. And the flat hadn't sold, and I think she was—she was really getting frantic."

"Do you think she might have gone to—well— you know, one of those places that loans money at really exorbitant rates of interest?" Elspeth asked avidly.

"In the States we call them 'loan sharks,'" Gracie put in. It was an appropriate moniker.

Sophie sighed, and put her plate down. "I don't know. That wouldn't have made much sense: to get a loan to pay off another loan?" She shook her head.

"Ah, but people in tough situations do strange things to try to put it right," Anna counseled.

When Sophie mentioned the bank loan, which Gracie's search on Angelique's finances had not turned up, and then Elspeth brought up loan sharks, Gracie thought back to the man she'd seen pursuing

Angelique at the Market. Perhaps that had been one of her creditors? Could he have discovered that Angelique was here, taking the Cordon Bleu course, and travelled up to press her for payment?

That made sense. And a creditor who wanted to be paid and a woman whose finances were tapped out and who literally had no money until her flat sold could have argued. So that could explain what Gracie had seen at the Market.

But the location of Angelique's death, and presumably of another argument that could have led to her death, didn't make sense: why would someone from a bank in Toulouse, or even a loan shark, choose the Chapel as a venue for a discussion with Angelique? One of the salons would surely have been more appropriate, and both the Library and the Games Room could be shut off for privacy if needed.

"Did the police say anything else?" Gracie asked, now. She, too, put her plate on the small table in front of the sofa, having finished eating. She gestured to Sophie's salad. "You really must try to eat a bit more, Sophie," she said gently. "I know this isn't exactly pleasant conversation…"

"Oh, no, no, it's fine," Sophie replied with a small smile, and picked up her plate again. "I don't mind, you know: I want them to find out what happened, and if—if someone—hurt—Mama, I want them to catch him." She shrugged, then, as she speared a bright red tomato slice and a creamy chunk of mozzarella with her fork, and brought it to her lips. "But they don't seem to have much to go on, anyway, at least, not yet," she murmured, staring at the tomato and cheese combination as though evaluating its appeal. Then she popped it in her mouth and chewed. As the flavors hit her tongue, her eyes involuntarily widened in pleasure and she smiled despite the circumstances and the conversation.

Of course, the police had asked everyone for alibis that first day when they'd questioned them all. In the meanwhile, they had also been questioning those who had known Angelique best—like her daughter, Sophie.

Now, feeling more at ease among these women who had been her mothers fellow students and friends, Sophie told them that her step-father, Thomas Rochambeau, had been summoned to Loches from Toulouse, and questioned in connection with his former wife's death. But not only did Thomas Rochambeau have a solid alibi, Sophie related, he appeared to have had no motive whatsoever for killing Angelique: their divorce had been as amicable as such things could be, and he had appeared quite devastated at the news of her death.

Gracie knew that Thomas Rochambeau was a successful HVAC technician and businessman, running a small but profitable company in the Toulouse area: as such, he had no obvious reason to want his ex-wife dead. He even told the police, Sophie related now, that if he had known the financial troubles Angelique had been having, he would have happily helped out.

"Mama never took a penny from him in the divorce," Sophie confided.

Gracie suspected that much of what Sophie was revealing was, strictly speaking, privileged information. But she also realized that Thomas Rochambeau had likely not been Angelique's killer.

"So you saw your step father?" Gracie asked kindly.

Sophie had nodded. "Yes, at the police station." She smiled. "He's a kind man."

Sophie swallowed, took a sip from the water glass she'd brought with her, and went on. "The police have only told me pretty much what was in their news report: mother hit her head and died from the resulting subdural hematoma. They did tell me that they found white fibers under her fingernails, but the Detective said that was pretty inconclusive, since they could have been from anyone's chef's whites, even her own," Sophie went on.

That was a piece of evidence Gracie hadn't known before. Although it appeared, as Sophie had said, inconclusive, Gracie had learned from Jack to consider every piece of information, even if it seemed insignificant, because it could be important. As he said, 'you never know where the clue that unlocks the mystery will come from.'

Gracie sighed: she missed Jack, and found that she was really looking forward to talking to him later.

She turned her attention once more to the discussion between her and Sophie and her fellow students.

White fibers under Angelique's fingernails could mean that Angelique's assailant had been a fellow student. It could narrow the field of suspects, even if not by much.

Sophie blinked tears from her pretty green eyes, sighed, and ate a piece of lettuce. "The police weren't sure, initially, how it had occurred, and I think they were going on the assumption that Mama had tripped and fallen on something and hit her head."

"They were trying to find—erm—the place where it happened," Elspeth put in helpfully.

Gracie and Anna exchanged a look but said nothing.

Sophie nodded, and ate a bite of chicken. "I know. Since she was found in her room, that was the most logical place I guess," she related haltingly.

"But you said this morning they wanted to speak to you because they had found new evidence?" Elspeth urged.

Sophie nodded. "Yes. They said they have a couple of tests to run, still…"

"What kind of tests?" Elspeth broke in, and Gracie gritted her teeth.

Sophie shrugged. "I don't know. They didn't say. But they said that once they've run the tests they'll know more certainly where it happened, and whether or not it was an accident," Sophie replied.

chapter Twenty-five

Gracie spent the break before the dinner service that evening making notes in her room, and thinking. She jotted down several miscellaneous thoughts and details, things that probably had nothing to do with anything, like 'Philippe late to class,' and 'Gary liked Angelique?' and 'BLEACH.' Then she made a rough kind of outline on one of the back pages of the notebook that she'd been using to write down nuggets of Chef Pernod's wisdom.

The police had confirmed that Angelique had died from a subdural hematoma caused by a blow to the head. She knew, and the Detective had confirmed, that the blow had been caused by something with a corner.

She scribbled 'corner' and made a rough sketch.

She also knew that the Chapel's altar was very likely what had struck Angelique's head, especially if the blood tests from the stain showed a match for her blood type.

The crime scene, then, was probably the Chapel.

There was, of course, the question of the stain itself: why hadn't Angelique's attacker wiped it clean when the injury had occurred? And who had cleaned it this morning? The cleaners? Quite probably. She presumed the police would question them and find out if they'd tidied the Chapel and wiped down the altar.

She wrote, 'cleaners.'

But why hadn't the assailant cleaned the blood off on Wednesday night, when the argument with Angelique must have taken place?

Although it hadn't been really obvious, the mark had caught Gracie's eye even in the low light of the chapel, so she thought that the attacker must have noticed it as well. She could not imagine that, having seen it, the attacker would have neglected to clean the stain. But, Gracie considered, perhaps in the heat of the moment, especially if Angelique's fall had been unintentional, the assailant had panicked, and had likely not noticed the blood. Additionally, the assailant's main concern had probably been getting Angelique out of the Chapel and back to her room.

Angelique would probably have remained unconscious for a few minutes, at least, and so would have had to have been carried to her room by her assailant. This almost certainly meant the assailant had been a man, someone large enough and strong enough to accomplish this feat.

Gracie wrote 'man' and underlined it.

Gracie had discovered that Angelique could have been carried up the small metal circular staircase in the Chapel's stockroom, to the balcony, and out the first floor hallway door to her room, which was close by. Although the assailant could not have been completely sure of not being seen, since the time of death had been placed at between midnight and two a.m., the attack, or at least Angelique's fall, could have happened as much as two or three hours earlier.

By that time in the evening, nearly all the students were in their rooms, and the route used—through the stock room and out the balcony door—would have meant that the perpetrator would have risked being seen carrying Angelique for only a very short time: no more than ten or fifteen seconds, Gracie thought.

She drew a little map that showed the Chapel, the stockroom staircase, the balcony, and the upper hall with an X representing Angelique's room.

This scenario also supported Gracie's theory that the perpetrator had been someone at the Château, not a stranger like a loan shark or a banker, because it suggested that the assailant had been somewhat familiar with the layout of the Château and the Chapel in particular, if they knew about or discovered the storage room staircase to the balcony and upper hall.

What about getting into Angelique's room? She would probably have had her key with her, if she had locked her door, Gracie concluded a second after she asked herself the question. No problem there. But then she recalled having heard from someone— Elspeth, perhaps, who'd been chatting to one of the police officers guarding the Château—that Angelique's room key had been found on the dresser in her room.

So there were two questions: had Angelique's 'fall' been accidental? or intentional? And, of course, who had done it? Gracie felt the answer to the second question to some degree would devolve from the answer to the first.

She thought it highly unlikely that someone seeking to harm, injure or kill another person would choose shoving them into a handy piece of masonry as a method. It would be far more likely that someone would clunk his or her victim over the head with something heavy. Also, the location of the Chapel seemed odd to Gracie: she didn't think someone would plan to harm another person in a chapel. The basement, maybe, or on the grounds, or in a remote part of the Château, or even in Angelique's room, but not in the Chapel.

Therefore, Gracie theorized that the 'fall' had been an accident. She wrote 'accident' down in her notebook. But she didn't think Angelique had tripped and fallen when she had been alone: her unconscious body had been moved, which clearly indicated another person present. Gracie supposed that the other person could have been uninvolved with Angelique's fall, but why, then, cover it up by moving her? Why not just call Monique to bring the first aid kit and ring for an ambulance?

No, the other person had to have been involved. Perhaps she or he—probably he—had got into an argument with Angelique. The bruises on her wrists that Detective Valois had been so surprised that Gracie had thought of fit with that concept. Maybe the argument had become physical, and maybe the man had pushed or shoved Angelique, and she'd stumbled, or fallen, and hit her head on the altar corner.

That worked, Gracie thought, and drew a star next to her scribbles.

So, Angelique had been arguing with someone —the white fibers might mean it had been another student, or they could simply be from Angelique's tunic—and whoever it had been had apparently pushed Angelique in the course of the argument, and Angelique had fallen and hit her head. Alarmed, the other person had removed Angelique, carrying her up to her room and laying her on her bed, where the assailant had very likely expected that she would wake up in a few minutes or so with a blinding headache and a big bump on her scalp. Then, what?

Well, then the assailant had left the scene and returned to his or her normal routine.

Who had been at the Château Wednesday night? The front doors were locked at nine p.m. and there was an alarm system. As she had thought before, Gracie felt that the assailant was someone who belonged at the Château. Although it was possible the perpetrator had entered the Château earlier and remained hidden or unobserved until the confrontation with Angelique,   this scenario did not fit with the theory of Angelique's death being an accident. Entering and hiding in the Château and then attacking Angelique would have been a premeditated act, and the more she thought about it, the less Gracie felt that was what had happened.

Gracie sat back in her chair and gazed out her window: the vines that covered the fifteenth century tower that encompassed her room were bare at this time of year, but she could see them sturdily clambering up the masonry and around the downspout that ran the length of the tower to the ground. The sun was about to set: it was time to get moving for the dinner service, as they still had to cook the courgettes and sauté the duck.

She glanced over her notes again: so, the assailant was probably someone who belonged at the Château: one of the other students, or staff. And it was most likely a man, to have been strong enough to carry Angelique from the altar of the Chapel up to her room.

Whoever he was, he must have been even more shocked than the rest of them when Angelique had been discovered in her room, dead, Gracie thought solemnly. She was positive, if her theory were true, that Angelique's injury had been an accident, and that the other person had genuinely expected the woman to wake up with a bad headache, and perhaps accuse him of roughhousing, or even assault. But he had not expected Angelique to die. Try as she might, Gracie couldn't recall anyone reacting to the announcement of Angelique's death in a suspicious or odd manner. They had all been stunned.

So, the next question was: who among them might have argued with Angelique, and pushed her, which resulted in her hitting her head, and dying? Who might have had cause to argue with her? And about what?

The theory that it had been a creditor who had tracked Angelique down to the Château and chosen the Chapel for a confrontation had too many implausible details that made little sense for Gracie to give it much merit. So if the argument hadn't been over money, then what could it have been about? Love? Or at least, lust?

Quickly, Gracie began to list the male students in the course who might have developed an attraction to Angelique. She left out Gilles because there was no way he would ever have been able to get away from Brigitte, and she omitted Sam and Peter because they wouldn't have been interested in Angelique that way.

She wrote, 'Roberto, Jean, Henri, Philippe, Bob Kress, Gary,' realizing that she always thought of the man from Southampton by both his given and surname, as though it were one.

She looked at the list. Roberto seemed too young, frightened and overwhelmed by Chef Pernod and the daunting course to even be thinking about women or sex. He hadn't mentioned having a girlfriend or a wife, though, which could mean he was 'in the market' for female companionship. Of course, Gracie wasn't a man, and freely admitted that sometimes their motivations puzzled her. But she had never seen or heard Roberto do or say anything to indicate any special feeling or attachment towards Angelique.

Jean had displayed so little emotion that Gracie couldn't imagine him developing a crush on Angelique (or anyone else), let alone acting upon it: she would have been surprised if he had even clocked the woman's existence! Again, she didn't know if he had a 'significant other' in his life, so maybe...

Henri was a good bit older than Angelique had been, and while that didn't rule him out, Gracie felt in her gut that he wasn't the type, because he seemed so focused on the course and the food. He had never mentioned a wife or a girlfriend—or boyfriend, either.

Gracie made a little dot next to those three names. In her shorthand, developed during grad school and perfected when she worked at the Boston Globe, that meant, 'unlikely though not impossible.'

Philippe? No, he had a wife. Of course, that didn't mean he might not have looked longingly at Angelique: certainly he might have. But Gracie thought that a pre-existing relationship could be a deterrent to wayward behavior. And Gracie had never heard Philippe say anything suggestive about Angelique. On the few occasions when they had talked about their personal lives, Philippe had, in fact, seemed very much in love his wife, Zoë. He had told them proudly that she was an extremely gifted needleworker. She'd won county and national awards and had some of her work commissioned for historic sites because her technique was so perfect. She had, however, zero talent in the kitchen, Philippe had related with a smile. But since he loved cooking, this was the perfect arrangement, as he was left free to conceive all the menus and prepare all their meals.

Zoë had encouraged him to take the Cordon Bleu course because he so rarely did anything for himself.

They sounded like a devoted couple.

Gracie made a check mark by Philippe's name, indicating that he was okay.

Bob Kress, the restaurateur from Southampton who was going to open a Titanic-themed restaurant there and who had objected to Gracie being in the course because she was not professional: could he have gone after Angelique? She had never heard him mention a wife, or a girlfriend. The man had seemed married to the idea of his restaurant. He'd never said a word about anything else, not that Gracie had heard, so she put a dot next to his name, since he seemed unlikely.

Gracie wondered if Gary, the good looking, brash and ambitious sous-chef from Australia, might have been the one to get into an altercation with Angelique. Gracie had overheard him make several remarks about Angelique's attractiveness. Maybe he had made advances to Angelique, and they had been rebuffed, and he'd lost his temper? Gary did seem like the type who thought he was too good looking and clever to ever be turned down, Gracie thought.

Suddenly, she noticed the time: she'd be late! She stood and quickly adjusted the little white cap they all wore, grabbed her notebook and exited her room, still thinking.

Perhaps Gary had approached Angelique, maybe more than once, perhaps he'd made a suggestive comment, or come right out and propositioned her, or even had been physically assertive? Tried to kiss her, perhaps?

In the Chapel?

Gracie shook her head as she ran downstairs, through the dining room that was nicely set and ready for that evening's meal to be served, and down to the kitchen.

Well, the Chapel was private. Maybe Angelique had gone in there to say a quick prayer or something, and Gary had followed her? That at least made more sense than a creditor stalking Angelique and choosing the Chapel as a venue for their discussion of overdue loan payments! Gracie could imagine Gary seizing the opportunity to be alone with Angelique and paying no mind to the sanctity of the Chapel itself: he would have been focused on his desires and his intentions.

In any case, Gracie thought as she began the preparation for her courgette dish, Gary was the only fellow student she knew of who might have had any reason to get into a heated discussion or argument with Angelique. As such, that made Gary her prime suspect.

chapter Twenty-six

"Did you hear? Turns out that *was* blood on the altar," Gracie whispered to Philippe. She had debated about speaking further with him on the subject of Angelique's demise, since he had been so angry and dismissive at their last encounter. However, Gracie couldn't help wanting to gloat, just a little, that she had been right about the stain, and he had been wrong.

She had been so busy during the day with Detective Valois and then in the kitchen trying to catch up, that this was the first moment she'd really had to speak with Philippe.

The first course of that evening's dinner was ready to be served, and all the students had assembled in the corner of the dining room in front of the open door to the prep kitchen: Chef Pernod was making a speech. It was, after all, the last night of the course. They even had several bottles of a very nice champagne ready to open, to celebrate.

"Oh? Was it indeed?" Philippe replied, sounding only mildly interested. "How do you know that?"

Gracie answered, undaunted. "I called the police," she informed him.

Philippe's head snapped around and he stared at Gracie. "Foutre!" he exclaimed involuntarily under his breath.

"And even though there was no stain there when I showed them the altar, I also showed them the photo I had taken, earlier, before the cleaners wiped it off," Gracie whispered excitedly, unfazed by Philippe's vulgarity.

"The cleaners?" Philippe murmured, at sea. "What photo?"

Gracie continued, "the photo on my phone: I took it last night. I called Detective Valois this morning, but by the time he arrived, the regular Sunday morning cleaners had wiped up the spot. Still, after I showed them the photo, Detective Valois and his Assistant used Luminol and an ALS to check the altar, and that corner lit up like a Christmas tree! Only blue." She paused. "They're running tests on the surface of the altar, and they're testing the rug, too, since they think some blood might have dripped," she added, unable to resist a slightly smug tone of voice. Well, Philippe was probably not used to being wrong, or being corrected, not by a civilian, not when the matter under discussion was a police case. "I bet you anything that blood is a match for Angelique's!" she declared. "The thing I can't figure out is, what exactly happened?" Gracie asked.

Philippe fixed his gaze back on Chef Pernod, who stood near the center of the dining room, and was speaking with surprising eloquence about the achievements of all the students. Philippe cleared his throat. "But you said the cleaners had wiped the altar…" he whispered out of the corner of his mouth, not looking in Gracie's direction but pretending to be completely enthralled by what Chef Pernod was saying.

"Yes. The stain had been cleaned sometime after I showed it to you and before the police arrived. Monique said the cleaners come every Sunday morning, so bad luck there," Gracie repeated, "But the police were still able to get traces from the marble," Gracie explained. "It's quite porous. And there was more staining on the side of the altar, and probably on the rug," she added.

"The rug," repeated Philippe. "I never thought of that."

Chef Pernod's eyes, which had been roving around the room as he spoke, lit on Gracie. She gave him a big smile and a nod, and the Chef continued speaking, and looked away.

"So it looks like the Chapel is where the accident happened," Gracie whispered. "But like I said, I can't figure out how it happened, or who else was involved. I think it was an accident," she went on, dropping her whisper even more and shuffling just slightly closer to Philippe. "I think Angelique was arguing with someone."

Philippe grunted.

"Can you think of anyone who, well, who might have had a reason to get into an argument with Angelique?" Gracie asked him. She wanted to see if he had noticed Gary's interest in the dead woman, or if he at least might agree with her theory of a frustrated suitor as Angelique's assailant. She intended to tell Detective Valois of her theory, but she wanted to use Philippe as a sounding board before she did that. "Surely, your talent for that kind of thing is greater than mine," Gracie continued deferentially. "I mean, you're a Detective. Just because this isn't your case doesn't mean you might not have good insight into it."

Philippe turned and looked at Gracie then, his green eyes blank for a second. Then he blinked.

Chef Pernod had finished speaking and Claude was pouring out the champagne while Michel opened successive bottles with the characteristic muted 'pop.' Monique was daintily placing the filled flutes at each table setting, and smiling for the first time in a while.

The students had begun to move towards the warming trays where their plates of curried courgette waited.

"I must apologize for the—the way I spoke to you this morning," Philippe said unexpectedly to Gracie. "I was—I had not slept well, and I had things to do before class, and did not wish to be late…" Philippe explained with a small smile.

Gracie nodded understandingly. "That's ok."

As it turned out, she recalled, he'd been late to class anyway.

They went to get their plates and then lined up with the rest to be told which place to serve.

"So, you were saying you think someone was arguing with Angelique?" Philippe asked probingly. "Do you have a theory?" he continued, intrigued.

Gracie sighed. "I was hoping you would," she confessed. "I mean, what are the reasons people argue? Money, or love," she answered herself. "It all boils down to that, really."

Philippe nodded. Ahead of Gracie in line, he received a number from Claude, and stepped aside so Gracie could get hers.

"I don't think it was money, even though I understand things were tight for Angelique just now," Gracie continued as she, too, was told whom to serve and moved out into the dining room with Philippe. She didn't elaborate on the victim's financial difficulties because it did not seem to her to be germane to her theory.

Philippe put his plate at the designated spot and turned towards Gracie. "But it might have been money problems," he countered.

"But why talk about that in the Chapel?" Gracie returned, wrinkling her nose. "If her assailant was a creditor, he or she wouldn't have picked the Chapel for a discussion, or an argument," she continued confidently.

Philippe nodded, cautious. "Yes, I suppose that makes sense," he admitted.

Gracie put her plate down where she'd been instructed, then she and Philippe began walking towards their own tables, to begin dinner. "No. I think the location probably was just chance," Gracie continued. "But I don't think the argument was about money."

Philippe looked curious.

"So that leaves us with love—probably unrequited love, or at least affection." She looked up at Philippe, and frowned. "What do you think?"

Philippe gave a classic Gallic shrug that was almost a caricature of itself it was so perfect. "You tell me," he urged.

"I think it was someone who liked her, perhaps came on to her, but when Angelique wasn't interested, they took offense?" Gracie offered in a fast whisper. "Have you noticed that Gary was quite taken with Angelique?" she finally suggested. "What if he, well, made advances to her, and she told him to take a hike? He's got a temper, and he's quite used to women doing as he wishes, I think…" Gracie trailed off, unsure.

Everyone else was sitting at their places, and Claude and Chef Pernod were looking expectantly over at Gracie and Philippe, who were still standing.

Philippe looked suddenly very excited. "I think you may be onto something, Gracie!" he exclaimed in an enthusiastic whisper, and his eyes sparkled. "Yes, the more I consider what you theorize, the more it makes sense."

Gracie smiled.

"Have you told Detective Valois?" Philippe whispered urgently, putting his hand on the back of his chair and pulling it out.

"Well, no, not yet, I…"

"You must! Do not delay: call him—now!" he insisted, although a second later both he and Gracie had taken their seats at their two separate tables and Claude and Chef Pernod had given the signal to begin.

Heartened by Philippe's support of her hypothesis, Gracie pulled her iPhone out of a pocket, and, as everyone began to taste their champagne and courgette starter, she texted the Loches Police Department, requesting that Detective Valois contact her ASAP.

Then, relieved that the mystery of Angelique's death might be soon concluded, Gracie turned to her food.

chapter Twenty-seven

Dinner was a bittersweet success. The Toulousain dishes were delicious—everyone got 4's for grades, even Roberto. And the atmosphere was festive because of the champagne. But even though all the students were relieved at having completed the week long course—and they could now put 'Cordon Bleu trained' on their résumés— their high spirits were tempered by what had happened to Angelique, and the fact that her death was still unsolved.

The news had come earlier on Sunday that the police had re-classified the case as a homicide, but no further details had been released. Gracie, however, knew this meant that they'd got at least preliminary results back from the tests on the carpet and the swabs.

As everyone relaxed towards the end of their final meal with coffee, the delicious fenetra cake, and more champagne ('it goes with everything!' Monique had declared happily) Claude and Chef Pernod withdrew to tally the total scores. Then they returned and listed the students' rankings.

Henri Schilde and the Bernards were in a three way tie for the top spot. Behind them by one point were Jean Soules, Sam and Peter, and Anna.

Gracie gave her a hug and congratulated her.

"I really tried these last couple of days, in Angelique's honor," Anna said, a little shaky and with tears in her eyes. "Maybe it was her spirit that guided me," she added, and once again Gracie thought that Anna was quite impressionable.

Bob Kress, Elspeth, Philippe and Gracie came next, all tied and again only one point behind. Following them in last place were Gary and Roberto.

It was while everyone was starting to clean up that Gracie's iPhone buzzed in her pocket. She had just been gathering the plates and glasses from her table, so she moved quickly into the prep kitchen, set her dirty dishes down and answered her device. It took only a minute for her to explain to Detective Valois on the other end that she suspected that Gary might have been the one arguing with Angelique on Wednesday night. She kept her voice very low and made sure no one could overhear her.

The Detective seemed quite anxious to accept her theory, and told her he would act on her information immediately.

Gracie also asked the Detective about the blood stain tests and he confirmed her supposition that the preliminary results showed a match for Angelique's blood on the altar and also the carpet.

Then the Detective had to go, and Gracie didn't have a chance to ask him if he'd confirmed that the cleaners had been the ones to wipe away the stain. But really, Gracie reassured herself as she disconnected, what other explanation could there be? And it really didn't matter in the end.

"You called Detective Valois?" came Philippe's voice from the prep kitchen doorway. He had seen Gracie on her phone, and had come to find out whom she had been talking to. Most of the other students were once again down in the kitchen for a final cleanup.

"Yes. That was him," Gracie replied, indicating her phone as she tucked it back in her pocket. "He seems to think it's worth looking into," she continued, and Philippe nodded in a satisfied way.

"I must confess, Gracie, I also stepped out after the first course and made a quick call to the Detective," Philippe told her in a low voice. "I left the message that you had some new information, and that it was imperative for him to speak to you."

"Oh!" Gracie was surprised. Then she realized that Philippe, as a Detective, would probably have had some pull, more than she had at any rate, with the Loches police. "Well, that was probably a good thing, Philippe, because I've been calling Detective Valois a lot lately," she admitted. "Your influence probably made him decide to call me back so quickly," Gracie finished with a smile.

Philippe followed her as she went down to the kitchen.

"I will tell you, Philippe, I'll be happy when they get this whole mess settled," Gracie confided as she took over loading one dishwasher from Jean, who moved off to wipe down his work station.

Philippe nodded. "Of course."

"I'm staying on for a few days here, to do a bit of sightseeing," Gracie continued. She shut the dishwasher door and smiled. "It would be nice if I could do that without worrying about a homicide!" she noted in a whisper. "And I think it would be good for Sophie to have closure as soon as possible, too," she added as they both turned to go clean their work stations. A couple of other students were exchanging notes and chatting, and two more were scouring the cook tops and ovens.

Philippe coughed.

"You okay?" Gracie asked solicitously. "I bet you'll be happy to get home, and dazzle Zoë with all your new recipes!" she added on a laugh.

Philippe nodded again, and said that he would.

On Monday, everyone was told that they could leave the Château if that is what they had planned, since the police had a suspect in custody.

"But who?" everyone asked everyone else, looking around the dining room at breakfast. The only people missing were Brigitte, who had another of her migraines according to Gilles, and Gary.

"Gary?" asked Elspeth, her brows shooting up to her crinkly hairline in surprise.

Gracie bit her lip. It appeared her theory had proven correct.

Everyone seemed surprised at the resolution to the mystery of Angelique's death: they had known Gary could be brash and insensitive, but no one had pegged him for a killer. Even Gracie had to admit to herself that she'd initially thought Gary more bluster than bite. But since he'd been the only possible choice, really…

Without giving away the fact that it had been she—and Philippe, of course—who had called the Detective about Gary, Gracie suggested to her colleagues that perhaps it had been an accident, or at worst, a crime of passion.

"Maybe they got in an argument over something, and perhaps his temper got the better of him," she said vaguely of Gary.

"I thought he had an alibi," Roberto countered, his dark face in a worried frown. "He told me he'd gone to Cígoné…"

Gracie looked a question and Roberto shrugged.

"Well, I'm sure that if he does have an alibi, and if it's solid, the police will release him," she reassured Roberto.

Gary had been in Cígoné on Wednesday night? Well, she hadn't been privy to Detective Valois' investigation notes, so she didn't know if anyone had given more than an 'I was in bed sleeping' alibi. Apparently, Gary had, at least initially. Perhaps Detective Valois would test the solidity of that alibi with further questioning.

They were gathered in the small salon, where many of those who were leaving had assembled with their luggage to wait for taxis and other transport. As far as Gracie knew, she was the only one staying on at the Château, and as she had told Philippe, she wouldn't mind the peace and quiet: it had been quite an action packed week!

Fond goodbyes were being said, with promises to email and stay in touch. Best wishes were being given for success, as well. Gracie told Elspeth that she would certainly visit Edinburgh and her new restaurant once it was up and running. To her surprise, Henri Schilde extended his hand to Gracie along with a business card.

"Mademoiselle, if you ever find yourself in Belgium, please be sure to contact me: dinner 'on the house' as you say, at my restaurant in Antwerp," he told her with a funny little bow.

Gracie was too surprised to say anything, but shook his hand, smiled, and nodded happily.

Only Gracie, Roberto and the Bernards remained in the salon when suddenly a car shot through the gates of the Château and came to a screeching stop in the forecourt. They heard the sound of gravel spraying against the stone steps.

"Who on earth…?" Gracie exclaimed, startled.

Seconds later, the front doors banged open and a raging Gary came stomping into the reception foyer.

"Bleeding cops!" he shouted at no one and everyone at once. "They thought I killed poor Angelique, said we'd had a blue, and I'd shoved her and she'd hit her head," he continued, breathing hard. His Australian slang was in full force in the wake of his high emotion but from context Gracie figured out that 'blue' meant 'argument.'

By now, everyone had come from wherever they had been in the Château to the foyer to see what the noise was all about: Roberto, Gracie and Gilles Bernard stood in the petit salon's doorway while Claude, Monique and Michel stopped short at the alcove that led to the main hall.

Gary stood, mirrored sunglasses hanging by one finger and his blond streaked and spiked hair standing up more wildly than ever from his flushed face. His brows were drawn and his jaw worked.

"But you had an alibi," Roberto said, again.

"That's right, mate, I did," Gary returned, and nodded defiantly. "I told that Detective when he asked me the first time, I'd gone into Cígoné for a few beers."

Gracie saw Claude begin to say something, and then stop himself. No need to get into the middle of it now, when it was all over. The fact that the Château had a fully stocked bar and fridge with not only liquor and wine but several types of beer really didn't matter. If Gary had wanted to go out for drinks, that was his right, of course.

"And they believed you, the police?" Gilles asked, concerned.

"Why would they even suspect you?" Roberto chimed in.

Brigitte said nothing, but remained seated on the small love seat in the foyer, her head in one hand, watching everything from lowered lashes: apparently her migraine was still troubling her. Gracie was not sympathetic.

Gary shook his head. "Ah they got some cockamamie notion that I'd been cracking onto Angelique and got angry when she refused me," he answered.

"And is that what happened?" Monique asked in a voice that sounded as though she wouldn't be surprised if the answer were 'yes.'

"Nah—I mean, she was a lovely sheila, but she was, well, she was a lot older than me," Gary explained ungrammatically. "And she had a kid, and all that: responsibilities. That's not my scene. And I could tell she was the serious type, not interested in just a bit of fun, more's the pity," Gary went on.

Everyone held their breath and waited. Was Gary the killer, or not? If not, the police had been too hasty, perhaps, in allowing the rest of the people from the course to leave: perhaps the real killer was long gone by now!

"So—what was your alibi?" Gracie finally asked, feeling that somehow she and Philippe couldn't have both been wrong.

Gary replied that although he had, indeed, gone to Cígoné for a few beers, it had developed into more than that, and he'd spent the better part of the night with a local girl he'd met at the bar. He hadn't initially gone into that detail when the police had asked him his whereabouts on Wednesday night, but had, of course, given all the details now.

"I gave the police her name when they hauled me in at the crack of bleeding dawn this morning," Gary related, still looking very agitated. "It took 'em a bit to contact her, but when they did, she told them the same thing: I was with her all night. So I'm off the hook," he finished with a sour grin.

Well, that was a real pickle, Gracie thought to herself when Gary had gone upstairs to finish packing and Roberto's ride had finally come. The Bernards had also left in their sedan; Gracie noted it had tinted windows and that Gilles, of course, had been driving. She would have bet dinner at a three-starred Michelin restaurant that Brigitte would recline her seat and sleep all the way back to Rouen.

Gracie walked slowly upstairs and decided to sort out her belongings, and maybe do some laundry: Monique had offered her the use of the washer / dryer in the scullery just off the big basement kitchen, and Gracie thought that afternoon might be a good opportunity to get all her soiled clothes clean again. Additionally, she wanted to plan out where she would go in the next few days: Chenonceaux, for sure, and Amboise, where she could not only tour the magnificent Château but see DaVinci's house, Clos Lucé.

She organized her course materials and bundled all the clothes she'd worn into a laundry bag that Monique had kindly provided, and headed down towards the basement. Maybe she'd drive into Reignac for a light lunch, once she'd popped her clothes in the washing machine, she thought to herself. There had been a little café that she'd noticed, which looked quite appealing. And Monique had told her that Chedigny, just a quick drive down the A-10, was a lovely village for some sightseeing.

The only thing Gracie couldn't find in her room was the notebook she'd kept during the course. That was important: it had all the information and recipes for all the dishes they had made! She had very likely left it down in the kitchen, or maybe in the prep kitchen, she thought, the evening before. In all the excitement of the final dinner, and with the added pressure of talking to Philippe and calling Detective Valois again—which now seemed to have been for naught—she must have left the notebook behind.

Gracie slung the laundry bag over her shoulder and headed down the grand staircase.

chapter Twenty-eight

Lunch in Reignac had been quite tasty, and Chedigny was, just as Monique had promised, quaint and adorable. Gracie was charmed, and took several photos of gracious stone houses, promising gardens and narrow, cobbled streets. The sun came out as well, and on the drive back to the Château de Reignac, Gracie felt the tension of the week drain away from her.

She intended to enjoy the next few days: what wasn't to like? She was staying in a gorgeous Château in the Loire valley, a hire car at her disposal and some of the world's most beautiful and historical towns and villages around the corner! Not to mention the food. And the wine!

If only the police would solve Angelique's homicide, she frowned as she drove through the Château de Reignac's gates and parked her car. And, clearly, it was a homicide: the bruising on Angelique's wrists indicated a struggle at or very near the time of her death. While the bruises weren't conclusive, they supported the scenario of another person being with Angelique when she'd fallen. And that made more sense than the idea of her being alone in the Chapel and stumbling, hitting her head, falling and then getting up and going back to her room to lie down.

Gracie headed for the laundry room to check on her clothes. She hadn't heard from Detective Valois, and somehow she wasn't surprised. After her theory about Gary had proven to be so completely off the mark, Gracie didn't expect the Detective from Loches would have much to say to her.

One load of clothes was finished, the other nearly so. Gracie folded the dried clothes neatly, by which time the second load was dry. She folded those items and scooped everything up into her arms, using the flattened laundry bag as a base. She headed upstairs and ran into Michel in the main hallway of the ground floor.

"You are having dinner here tonight?" he confirmed with a smile.

"Yes!" Gracie agreed with a grin. "It will be such a treat to not cook!" she giggled.

Michel gave an answering smile, and said he understood completely.

"By the way, Michel, could you and Monique have a look around?" Gracie asked, then from behind her pile of freshly washed clothes. "I seem to have misplaced my notebook from the course," she admitted ruefully.

"Oh, no!" Michel looked genuinely concerned. "I'll definitely have a look and I'll ask Monique, too:

maybe she already found it and put it away for safekeeping," he added hopefully.

Gracie nodded. "I did check the prep kitchen and the main kitchen, but I didn't see it," she added glumly.

"We'll have a look around," Michel assured her. Then he said, "You might like to hear that Madamoiselle Sophie left earlier today, and took all of her mother's things," Michel added. "She said she would be staying with her step father in Toulouse until she was ready to go to University in Tours this September."

Gracie had started towards the stairway with her load, and grinned. "Oh, that's great, I'm glad for her. And for him: it's nice they have each other in a time like this, and I'm glad Sophie has someone to look out for her."

Michel said he would have a bottle of wine open for her in the grand salon about a half hour before dinner, and Gracie said she would look forward to that very much, and they both went on their way.

"Could you not contact one of the friends you made in the class, and ask if they would copy their notes?" Claude asked solicitously that evening. He had joined Gracie in the grand salon for a glass of wine, and she had told him of her missing notebook.

Michel and Monique had both reported that they had not seen it anywhere, and Gracie was convinced that either one of the other students had picked it up by mistake, or that it had been thrown in the rubbish by accident. Unfortunately, garbage collection had been that morning, so if that was what had become of it, short of pawing through a landfill, Gracie wasn't likely to see her notebook again.

"I thought of that," Gracie said. "But first I thought I'd email everyone to see if anyone had it with their own notes from the course. Maybe they would mail it back to me," she added, but she didn't sound too hopeful.

"Meanwhile, I have copies of all the recipes from the course, which Chef Pernod gave me, and I will make copies for you, so at least you will have that," Claude offered kindly.

"Oh, that would be wonderful!" Gracie replied thankfully. "I can go through them and jot down whatever I remember about making each dish," she added, and smiled. Well, it was better than nothing.

Dinner was a refreshing mélange of julienned spring vegetables in a light tomato aspic followed by gorgeous diver's scallops dusted with rice flour and sautéed in brandied butter and herbs. Monique served it with lightly wilted, sliced fresh brussels sprouts in a vinaigrette, and a timbale of couscous. Dessert was a strawberry and custard tart that Gracie thought had come from that wonderful local patisserie: not that she minded. The little bakery on one of the side roads leading out of Reignac had the most mouth watering creations she'd ever seen, and a trip there earlier in the week had prompted her to take several photos of the bakery's products, and mail them back to Tyler and Joey. With luck, Tyler would be able to recreate a couple of them!

As always, it was quite late when dinner was over, but Gracie didn't feel especially tired. She found herself wandering the ground floor until she came to the comfy library, where she sat down in one of the squashy-cushioned armchairs and began to make notes for the next day's adventure: Château Amboise and Clos Lucé.

The grandfather clock in the long ground floor corridor had just struck eleven when Gracie put her pen down, pushed aside the paper she'd been using and her iPad that she'd been consulting, and stretched, yawning. Now, she did finally feel a bit tired. She'd go back to her room and get ready for bed, and then give Jack a call. With the time difference, she'd probably catch him at home, and she could tell him all about the false alarm with Gary. Maybe he would have some comforting bit of wisdom to offer, since the thought that Angelique's assailant was as yet unidentified—and not caught— was a bit unnerving.

She stood, and left the library, turning out the light as she did.

As Gracie walked along the ground floor corridor, she thought she heard someone stepping softly behind her. She turned, and peered into the darkness. No, of course no one was there: the corridor lights here, just like in the first floor hallway, would come on automatically when they detected movement. Still…

"Claude?" Gracie called uncertainly. She knew the Château's owner generally went to bed before now, and took an antihistamine for allergies. He slept, by his own admission, very soundly and rarely woke before dawn. Monique had long since trotted down the path to her little cottage, and Michel had loped to his house a couple of streets away.

She reached the reception foyer, which was, of course, deserted. Feeling silly, Gracie tried the front door: locked, naturally, as it would be this time of night. The alarm monitor shone a steady green. All was secure, she had nothing to worry about, no one was in the corridor behind her!

Chuckling to herself, Gracie turned, and then let out a small shriek.

"Philippe! My god, you scared me half to death!" Gracie exclaimed, seeing the man, who was standing just inside the archway that led from the reception foyer to the hall that held the grand staircase. "I thought you'd gone home," she added, frowning slightly.

He <u>had</u> left: she remembered saying goodbye that morning.

Philippe smiled at her. "I heard that our friend Gary alibi'd out," he said, his tone regretful. "Pity."

Gracie nodded. "Well, yes, I suppose, in a way, but if he didn't do it, I mean, I wouldn't want him wrongly arrested and charged…" she trailed off, looking curiously at the Detective.

Philippe gave her a long look that Gracie could not interpret, and then withdrew a familiar looking object from inside his jacket.

"My notebook!" Gracie exclaimed, and moved to take it from him. "You found it!" That must be why he'd returned to the Château de Reignac: to give her notebook back to her!

Philippe snatched it out of her reach. "Yes, I found it," Philippe confirmed, but his voice sounded peculiar. He sounded bitter.

"Well, come on: let me have it," Gracie insisted, grabbing again for her property. "You have no idea how tiresome it is to have to keep searching out bits of paper…" she said with a grin, but her grin faded.

Philippe still held the notebook away from her and was now paging to the last section, the part where Gracie had scribbled down her theories about

Angelique's demise. He looked at her notes, and then looked up at Gracie, his green eyes intent.

Suddenly, Gracie realized something, and also realized that she should have noticed this long before. Philippe's green eyes were the exact color and shape as—

"Your eyes," she murmured, feeling quite cold suddenly—and it had nothing to do with the ambient temperature. "They're green. Like—like Sophie's," she whispered.

Philippe said nothing, just held her notebook, and stared at her.

"You are Sophie's—father?" Gracie questioned, knowing the answer.

Philippe did not move a muscle, he just waited for Gracie to continue.

"You knew Angelique—when she was at the Lycée!" Gracie declared, her voice strengthening as she realized how all the pieces were fitting together. "You—and Angelique…" She paused.

Philippe inclined his head ever so slightly.

"But you didn't know!" Gracie continued, suddenly figuring it all out. "You never knew. Angelique never told you, just went away to Toulouse and had the baby."

Again, Philippe gave a tiny nod.

"Until this course," Gracie went on breathlessly. "Sunday and Monday, we were all getting to know each other, everyone was showing photos around of their families and houses and pets, and saying where they were from and so on, and Angelique mentioned that she had a daughter, Sophie, who was going to University in the autumn." Gracie swallowed. "You saw the photo, and did the math once Angelique said Sophie was seventeen. You figured out that Sophie had to be your daughter."

"Yes, Mademoiselle, I did," Philippe finally answered.

He still held her notebook in his hands.

"Well, that's—I mean, that's—erm…" She didn't know quite what to say. Was it good? Or was it sad? It surely must have been a surprise. Perhaps Philippe and Angelique had argued about it, too. Gracie remembered the argument on one of the first days of the course between Henri and Gary over how to trim asparagus. When she had gone up to her room after dinner that night, Gracie had heard further arguing, and had thought it had been the two men continuing their disagreement. However, she had then heard Henri's snores emanating from his chamber. And then, she recalled, she'd decided that whatever was going on was not her business, and she'd gone to her own room.

But the raised voices had been coming from the end of the hall where Angelique's room had been. Could that have been Philippe and Angelique having one of the first of their arguments, perhaps? Had he confronted her?

"It was, for me, a bit of a shock," Philippe confessed now, sounding almost wry. "To find out, almost two decades after the fact, that the woman whom I had loved, who had left me without any explanation and never contacted me since, had borne our child—my child!"

"You must have been very upset," Gracie put in, trying to sound sympathetic. Well, she was, actually. "Did you talk to Angelique about it?" she asked gently.

Philippe's gaze narrowed. "Of course, Mademoiselle," he replied, biting off the end of each word. "More than once."

Gracie suddenly remembered the day had seen Philippe rushing down from the first floor during a break: she had mistakenly assumed from that moment on that his room was on the first floor. It hadn't been: it had been on the ground floor, next to Chef Pernod's suite. Had Philippe, in fact, been coming from Angelique's room? Had they been having another discussion, or argument?

Quite possibly. And that would explain why Angelique had looked so troubled and tired! And the night Gracie had been star gazing and someone's light had been on—that had been Angelique's room, she realized now. The woman had been sleepless over the situation.

"What did Angelique say, when you talked to her?" Gracie asked, her voice gentle.

Gracie recalled, too, overhearing Claude tell Monique that Angelique had wanted to leave the course, had come to him in a panic the very first night, but that she had decided to stay since she could not get a refund on the tuition. That had to have been her reaction when she realized Philippe was one of the students in the course! Had she, perhaps, read the list of students in the course guide they'd all received? Certainly. And then, she'd gone to Claude and asked if there were any way she could leave the course. She'd used the excuse of not having any money, but had apparently decided to stick it out because she felt the course would be so important for her, and because there were no refunds. She clearly had intended to keep her distance from Philippe, but he, of course, had had other plans.

Now, Philippe gave a scornful, short laugh and unconsciously fingered the edges of Gracie's notebook as he answered. "She said she was sorry— sorry! for keeping my daughter a secret from me. Sorry for keeping half my life hidden away. Sorry. Sorry!" he repeated, and shook his head. "But she refused to tell Sophie, even now. Refused to allow me to be a part of her life, still. Refused to even attempt to make right what she had done wrong seventeen years ago!" he exclaimed, and his voice was harsh, and anger made a vein stand out on his forehead.

"Oh, Philippe, I can't imagine how you must feel," Gracie said honestly. She remembered the birth certificate for Sophie, with no father listed, and felt that Angelique had done a thorough job of eradicating Philippe Zafran from her life, for whatever reason. She supposed no one would ever know why, now, since Angelique was dead.

Being the compassionate and rather sweet person she genuinely was, Gracie was overwhelmed by the tragedy of Philippe's situation, and took a step towards him, to give him a friendly hug. Times like these, she thought, were when everyone needed a kind touch.

He shoved her away, and Gracie stumbled in surprise.

chapter Twenty-nine

"Philippe! What're you doing?" Gracie exclaimed, recovering her balance.

She looked at him, and then frowned: he was wearing a dark grey windbreaker that somehow looked familiar. "That was <u>you</u> in the Bléré Market, running after Angelique in the flower stalls," Gracie murmured, thinking fast.

Philippe got a strange smile on his face. "Ah, yes, Mademoiselle, that was I. Once more, I was trying to talk to Angelique, make her see reason."

Gracie nodded: that made sense.

"But you know that, Mademoiselle, so do not pretend to have sympathy," Philippe advised her harshly. "I know you have figured everything out," he said, and waved the notebook at her.

"I—what?" Gracie stammered, sounding quite dull-witted.

"It is all in here, and I imagine it is just a matter of time before you tell Detective Valois your new theory. You have probably called him already, have you not? And this time it will be correct," Philippe declared.

New theory? What was he talking about, Gracie wondered, looking at his face, and then at her notebook. "What new theory?" she asked, frowning.

"Those scribbles? I was just trying to figure out who might have had a disagreement with Angelique," Gracie explained quietly: Philippe seemed quite off kilter and she didn't want to upset him even more. "That was when I came up with the idea that it might have been Gary who had argued with her," she added. "Remember? I floated that by you first, and when you seemed to think it had merit, I told the police. But I was wrong."

"Ah, yes, Mademoiselle, I do recall that, and I do remember that you were wrong," Philippe agreed almost chattily. "It would have all worked out so beautifully if Mr. Jerome had not been able to produce a verifiable alibi," he murmured regretfully, and Gracie stared at him.

She remembered the alacrity with which Philippe had supported her theory about Gary, and his encouragement about calling the police. He had even said he'd phoned them himself! Now that she really considered it, she realized that Philippe had been, in hindsight, rather too eager to latch on to the Gary theory, and very insistent that she involve the police right away.

Gracie now understood that Philippe had hoped to throw the blame for Angelique's demise on Gary.

Because it had been he who had caused Angelique's death.

Gracie began to look somewhat wildly around for an escape route: the man was crazy! For a split second, neither moved. Then Gracie, inspired or at the very least motivated by the somewhat unfamiliar emotion of fear, tossed the pen she'd been holding towards the far wall.

When Philippe involuntarily turned his head to follow the small noise it made when it hit, Gracie made a run for it.

She knew she couldn't get the front doors unlocked in time to escape Philippe's grasp, although that would have triggered the alarm, which would have helped. She also knew that, while she could probably best him in a sprint, in a long haul race she would loose. So she pivoted on one foot and raced towards the other end of the Château, towards the games room. Lights came on automatically in the hallways, and small lamps were burning in the little salon and the grand salon, but the games room was in darkness, and Gracie slid through the little door on the opposite wall as quickly as she could, and hoped that Philippe was far enough behind her not to have seen where she went. With luck, he would think she was hiding somewhere in the games room: she might gain some valuable time that way.

With hardly a pause to listen for her pursuer, Gracie ran up the narrow stone staircase that led to the concealed door in the first floor hallway: the old servants' passage. Again, without pause, she slid out that door and into the corridor, and dashed for her room, fingering her key in a pocket as she did so.

Where was Philippe? she wondered as she unlocked her door, crossed the threshold and shut the door behind her. She locked it as quickly and quietly as she could, even throwing the deadbolt. No matter: she had to get her phone, and call 112, the European Union emergency number.

She grabbed her iPhone that had been charging on the desk in her room. As she punched in 112, she heard Philippe at her doorway. He didn't bother with the niceties, just started slamming into the door with what must have been his shoulder.

Truly frightened, Gracie fled into the en suite bathroom, shutting and locking the door to it behind her: but it was an old door, dating from the eighteenth century reconstruction by Louis de Barberin. It wouldn't hold up to much pounding, though she thought that the modern outer door to her room might. And anyway, she'd thrown the deadbolt, so that should at least slow Philippe down.

The 112 Operator answered, and Gracie decided to just keep repeating, 'send the police to the Château de Reignac,' rather than try to explain just why. In truth, she wasn't quite sure herself. Philippe —logical, methodical, kind Philippe—had been responsible for Angelique's death. And more to the point, he thought Gracie had known that and had been preparing to turn him in. And now, he wanted to kill her, too, to silence her, and keep his secret.

She heard a loud screeching, twisting noise and knew that Philippe had somehow broken down the main door to her room. Oh, god, he was coming for her and that beautiful old eighteenth century door wouldn't delay him for more than a couple of minutes.

Where could she go?

Gracie's eyes flew around the bathroom.

There was only one escape route.

The bathroom window was the casement type, and it opened easily. Gracie sat on the wide windowsill and swung herself around until her legs were dangling outside, feet against the fifteenth century tower's exterior.   Now what? It was way too far to jump without incurring some kind of injury, she knew. Although she supposed a broken leg would be better than death.

In the pocket of her black blazer where she'd slipped her iPhone, she heard the 112 Operator's voice calling 'Madame? Madame?'

Then she heard Philippe at the bathroom door.

Quickly, and almost without thinking—because not only would thinking have used valuable seconds, it would have probably made her decide against the action—Gracie reached her left hand outside the window and grasped a number of grapevines that clung to the rough exterior stone of the tower. Then, before her brain could caution her not to, she pushed off with her left foot against the stones and swung, so that she was facing the tower, feet braced on the stones and both hands tugging at the vines in a sort of surreal abseiling position. She extended her right hand and, blessing of blessings, felt the cool, ridged metal of the drain pipe that ran down the side of the tower to the ground.

It was another leap of faith that brought her left hand to surround the pipe as well, and brought her feet over, one on either side of the pipe. She clung there, hanging for a moment like an overlarge bat, and then, spurred on by the distinct sound of splintering ancient wood, she shimmied her way down the pipe, grateful for the black ensemble she'd changed into for dinner that night, which might give her just enough cover in the dark.

chapter Thirty

"Tell me, Philippe, just how it happened." Detective Valois' voice was grave but kind, and he pushed a mug of black coffee towards his fellow detective, who was now his suspect.

If someone who had confessed could be called a 'suspect.'

Philippe Zafran sighed, and took a sip of the coffee: it was welcome, for it had been a very long night, and he found himself more weary than he could ever recall being. His clear green eyes that Gracie had remarked upon were bloodshot now, and indigo pouches had formed beneath each one as the hours since his encounter with Gracie had passed.

It was now three a.m.

The little red light blinked on the wall-mounted camera that recorded video and audio of the interview.

Philippe looked up at it, gave a weary half smile, and began.

"When we arrived on Sunday for the course, I of course recognized my old girlfriend from the Lycée immediately," he began, his voice calm and tinged with remorse. "Her surname was different: Rochambeau instead of LaMarche, but she looked nearly the same as she had as a girl," he went on, and his tone warmed with affection and reminiscence.

"Did you speak with her?" Detective Valois asked genially.

"Oh, yes, that very first night—or, at least, I tried to," Philippe replied carefully. "I approached her more than once, but each time she turned away, or moved away, or began speaking with someone else. It seemed clear to me that she was avoiding me," he finished, sounding sad.

Philippe related that he had merely wished to reconnect with an old flame—by his own admission, a woman he had loved very much in his youth—until he overheard Angelique telling someone about her daughter, Sophie.

"I was not surprised to learn she had a child," he told Detective Valois. "But when I overheard her say her daughter was seventeen and headed for University, I was startled," Philippe confessed.

"When was this?" Detective Valois asked.

"At lunch, the first day, Monday," Philippe replied.

"Why were you startled?" the Detective asked.

"Because seventeen years ago—or a little more than that, to be precise—I was the only man in Angelique's life. So I knew that this daughter she spoke of had to be my own flesh and blood."

The Detective made a motion with one hand to encourage Philippe to continue.

"Then that evening, after dinner, people were getting more friendly and showing photos around to people, you know, of their gardens, and pets and families. And Angelique was with some of the other students…"

"Do you remember who?"

"Mrs. Guteknecht, Mrs. Hume, and the two young men from California, Sam Lewis and Peter Fontaine."

Detective Valois nodded for Philippe to continue.

"They were all clustered around Angelique, looking at the photos on her tablet," Philippe continued. "I was curious."

"Naturally."

"So I moved quietly behind them where I could have a view of the tablet's screen, and looked at the pictures, too."

"Madame Rochambeau did not know you were there?"

Philippe shook his head. "No. I was behind everyone."

The Detective nodded. "You knew by then that Madame Rochambeau's daughter was yours?" he asked.

Philippe frowned at the memory. "I had done the math."

"And then you saw the photo?" Detective Valois pursued.

"Yes. Many were of Toulouse, and her flat and a little balcony garden she had. I was interested, of course. But then she brought up a full face shot of her daughter, Sophie." He swallowed. "While everyone else was remarking on how pretty she was, and how much she looked like Angelique, I was focused on the girl's eyes: they are the same shape and color as mine. As Angelique began to tell them, so proudly, too, as she should be, about Sophie's academic achievements, and her plans to attend the University of Tours, I noticed a couple of other small physical resemblances between her and myself."

"Such as?"

"Sophie was smiling in the photo, and I saw that she has the same slight overlap of her front teeth that I do," he answered, and bared his top teeth to illustrate his point.

Detective Valois did notice a minor crookedness of one tooth, hardly apparent unless one were looking for it. He nodded.

"Combined with Sophie's age and my past relationship with her mother, Sophie's physical appearance made me certain that she was my child," Philippe said. "And I realized that that had been the reason Angelique left so abruptly after the term at Lycée was over. I had never understood that, and her departure had hurt me very deeply. So I redoubled my efforts to speak with her, to find out for sure."

Philippe related that although he tried Monday night, all Angelique had told him was 'go away!' It was Tuesday morning, he said, when the students had all visited the Market, before he'd had a chance to approach Angelique and get a civil answer. "I finally got her away from the group, in the Market, a public place where I thought she would be unlikely to make a scene, and I asked her, why she did not wish to even say hello to me," Philippe related. "She said that finding me here, taking this course, had been the last thing she had expected, and an unpleasant shock. She told me she had nearly pulled out of the course, but since there could be no refunds, she hadn't wanted to lose the money she'd paid. But she said that she had her life arranged, now, and in no way wanted me to interfere with it."

"Mmmm…" Detective Valois made an encouraging sort of noise.

"I told her, 'fine, fine, but answer me one thing: your daughter, Sophie—is she mine?'" Philippe said quickly, reliving the encounter in his mind. "At first she tried to tell me it was no business of mine, but then, I pressed her. I mentioned Sophie's eyes, which were exactly like mine, not like hers. And I mentioned Sophie's angled tooth, again, just like mine. I told Angelique that these things could not be coincidences. And she finally admitted that yes, Sophie was my daughter."

"And how did that make you feel?" the Detective asked calmly.

"Both overjoyed and despairing. To discover I had a child, at last, when—when I had given up all hope of ever knowing that feeling, of ever having that gift, Detective...I was overjoyed."

"You and your wife have no children?" Detective Valois interjected, consulting some documents before him on the desk. "Zoë?" he asked, naming Philippe's wife.

Philippe shook his head sadly. "Alas, we discovered after several years of frustration that my poor Zoë is unable to have children," he answered, low. "It was, and still is, a heartache."

Both men took sips simultaneously from their coffee mugs, and then Philippe continued his statement. He told the Detective that while he had been overjoyed to learn of his daughter's existence, he had immediately been saddened, and angered, to think of all the years of her life he had missed. "I did not wish to miss any more," he said, thinking back. "And so I asked Angelique if I might see Sophie, speak to her, even, perhaps, without revealing who I was. But just to be somehow a part, even a tiny part, of her life. But Angelique refused. She was adamant, and she avoided being anywhere near me after that, as much as she could."

Philippe continued, explaining that he had sought Angelique out more than once, even going to her room to plead once more to be allowed to see his daughter. "I knew Angelique was in straitened circumstances," he explained. "And the right thing would have been for me to have contributed to Sophie's upbringing—had I but known of her existence. So I offered to make up for that, now."

"How would you have done that?" Detective Valois asked. He knew Zafran because they were both Detectives in neighboring departments. Their salaries were fair enough, but hardly munificent.

Philippe sighed. "I would have cashed in my pension, and given it to them," he confessed. "It would have been the least I could do, to make up for what they should have received for the past seventeen years." He sighed again. "But still, Angelique refused. She said she did not need anything from me, and neither did Sophie. I thought that if I kept at her, I could eventually wear her down," he admitted, looking sheepish.

The Detective asked if any of these conversations with the dead woman had become argumentative, and Philippe admitted that they had. "She was very angry, and also upset, because she felt this course was her big chance, and she felt that me being here was ruining it for her. She told me to just stay away, stay away! and pretend that she was no one and nothing to me. But I could not do that."

"And you were angry?" Detective Valois inquired.

Philippe nodded unhesitatingly. "Of course I was: I wanted to meet my daughter, be part of her life. It was my right. And Angelique was denying me that right."

The Detective considered for a moment how being in similar circumstances might make him feel, and decided that he understood the way Philippe must have felt.

Philippe continued, saying that on Wednesday night, after dinner had concluded and everyone had begun to retire for the evening, he had followed Angelique as she had left the group, thinking she was going to her room, and he had planned to beg one last time to see his child. Then, he related, if she had not agreed, he had planned to threaten Angelique that he would go to the authorities and begin legal proceedings to invoke his rights with regard to Sophie. "I knew that she did not wish me to interfere in her life. If she did as I asked and allowed me to see Sophie, even without telling her who I was, my 'interference' as she would see it could be kept to a minimum. But if I went to the courts and sued

Angelique, it would be much more than 'interfering' in her life," Philippe explained. "I planned to sue to have DNA testing done to prove my paternity, and then sue her for breach of parental rights, and for partial custody as well as visitation," Philippe told the Detective.

"But Sophie is seventeen," the Detective reminded his quarry. "The court would likely feel she could make her own decision with regard to custody, as she will be of majority age within a year."

Philippe nodded. "I know. I knew that the custody suit would not have succeeded, but it would have shown the court how serious I was about the matter. I knew I would win, and I knew that the visitation permitted by the court would probably be much more frequent than any visits allowed by Angelique of her own accord. And, of course, Sophie would know who I was if I sued for my rights, and that was something Angelique was completely against." He paused. "She seemed to hate me. So much. I did not—do not—understand her reasons."

"So you felt you had a good case to present that Wednesday night?" the Detective asked.

Philippe nodded, and continued. He told the Detective that after going to her room on Wednesday night, Angelique had gone to the Chapel. Philippe said he thought that perhaps Angelique needed to pray. In any case, Philippe had followed her, and they had argued once more over the same issue: Sophie.

Then, Philippe said, he had given her his ultimatum.

chapter Thirty-one

'She became more angry than ever, that I would even think of doing such a thing,' Gracie read the statement Philippe had made to the Loches police with increasing fascination. 'She said that if I tried to use any legal means to force her to let me see Sophie, she would take her away to another country, and that I would never find them.'

Gracie sat back in the padded swivel chair in Detective Valois' office and lifted her eyes from the transcription of Philippe's statement.

"This is unbelievable," she said.

Detective Valois, behind his desk that was covered with files, post it notes and lists, nodded wearily. "Read on, Mademoiselle," he encouraged Gracie. "I think, given your—ahem—encounter with the suspect last night, you have a right to know," he offered.

Gracie bent her head back to the document in her hands. She had given a brief statement the evening before, when the police had arrived at the Château and found Philippe racing down the grand staircase trying to catch up with Gracie, while she had been huddled in Monique's kitchen. She had run to Monique's cottage after her dramatic descent from her window *via* the ancient tower, and fortunately

Monique had been home, and immediately let her inside.

Apparently Philippe had thought the better of copying Gracie's precipitous exit, and had chosen to go downstairs by more normal means—the grand staircase—and had been apprehended.

This morning, Tuesday, Gracie had driven to the station in Loches to give a more complete statement. She had been quite surprised when, after she had finished, Detective Valois had invited her into his office, closed the door, and handed her the file containing Philippe's statement from a few hours before.

Now, she continued to read. Philippe had told the police that when Angelique had made her threat on Wednesday night in the Chapel in response to his ultimatum, he had at first become furious, and said that he would never let that happen. Then, he had said, he had reflected on where they were, and had decided to try a calmer approach.

'I reached out for Angelique's hand,' Philippe's statement read. 'I merely wished to reason with her. But she snatched her hand away. I grasped her wrist...'

Aha, Gracie thought to herself, that explains the bruising.

'And she stepped backwards to get away from me, and tripped on the edge of the carpet,' Philippe's statement went on. 'She lost her balance, and although I reached out to steady her, it happened in a split second: she fell, and struck her head as she fell, on the corner of the altar.'

Gracie looked up from the transcript. "So—it was an accident, wasn't it?" she asked.

Detective Valois nodded, and he passed one hand over his face as though trying to smooth out the lines there. "A tragic one, yes. To be sure, Detective Zafran is not even slightly culpable in the case of Madame Rochambeau's fall. Not the fall itself. He will, however, be charged with negligent manslaughter, failure to render aid, and other lesser charges," Detective Valois revealed. "And that is just in Madame Rochambeau's case. There will be more charges pending from his attempt to harm you," he added.

The Detective looked exhausted, Gracie thought. Well, he had probably been up most of the night! And seeing a fellow detective in such pitiable circumstances had to be emotionally draining.

"I guess I should press charges," Gracie murmured. "Although I don't really wish to: after all, Philippe is well aware of how potentially harmful his actions towards me were."

Detective Valois nodded. "Yes, he is, of course: but even if you do not wish to bring charges against him, Mademoiselle, the State will, on your behalf, because the crime of attempted homicide is a serious one."

Gracie nodded grimly and said she would fill out any paperwork needed. "And I suppose if I have to return to France to testify, well, I guess I could live with that!" she finished more happily.

Detective Valois smiled.

The rest of Philippe's statement revealed that the circumstances of the previous Wednesday night had been almost exactly as Gracie had theorized. When Angelique had fallen and hit her head, she had been knocked unconscious. Philippe had tried to rouse her, but had been unsuccessful. Philippe had panicked, and thought only of getting Angelique back to her room. 'I presumed she would awaken after a few minutes and complain perhaps of a headache and a bruise,' he had said. 'And I was certain she would accuse me of assault and have me thrown out of the course. But I did not care,' his statement had said.

Philippe had then told police he had never even thought to look for blood on the altar, because the wound on Angelique's head hadn't seemed to be bleeding that much.

Gracie realized that was likely because, although the skin had split where it had struck the marble of the altar, the main damage was not so much to the skin, as to the tissues, structures and organs beneath. It was the subdural hematoma that had caused Angelique's demise: the bleeding had mostly been inside her skull, not outside.

"Philippe told Detective Valois, that when I mentioned the stain to him, he had been unpleasantly surprised," Gracie told Jack later on Tuesday. She'd returned to the Château, her plans for the day delayed until Wednesday, and called Jack after a solicitous Monique had fixed a light lunch for her.

"I'll bet it was an unpleasant surprise," Jack repeated with a grim chuckle.

"Yeah," Gracie grinned. "So anyway, apparently Philippe went looking for cleaning supplies as soon as he could that morning. He found the bleach-based bathroom cleaner they use here at the Château and some rags in a cabinet down near the kitchen, and went back up to the Chapel, where he cleaned the marble altar off as thoroughly as he could. He knew the bleach in the cleaner would also fluoresce if anyone should test it, so the presence of blood would at least be masked."

"Yeah, but you'd think a Detective would know better," Jack opined. "I mean, anyone checking for a blood trail who comes upon a big puddle of bleach gets suspicious."

"I know," Gracie agreed. "But as Detective Valois pointed out, and as you and I both said before,

Philippe wasn't thinking clearly: not when he confronted Angelique, not when she fell, and surely not following the incident, especially once she'd been found dead."

"Did the police check with the cleaning crew, to be sure?" Jack asked.

"Yes: the cleaners told them that on Sunday they had looked into the Chapel, seen everything looking tidy, and so hadn't even gone inside," Gracie replied. "The police were here again this morning: they found the rags Philippe used in his suitcase, stained with blood and smelling of bleach. I guess he was planning to take them home and burn them if he'd got away with everything."

Jack grunted. "Why did he come after you? You were convinced Gary had been the one to argue with Angelique, and you even told Philippe!" Jack protested. Gracie had begun the call by updating him on the events of the evening before.

Gracie now explained that Philippe had told the Loches police that when she had told him she had taken a picture of the bloodstain with her iPhone, his first thought had been to somehow get her phone and delete the photo. "But as you know, my phone is usually in my pocket, so he didn't really have an opportunity to get it," she told Jack, who agreed. "Then, after we cleaned up Sunday night, Philippe noticed I'd left my notebook in the kitchen," Gracie continued. "He said he'd picked it up, intending to return it to me, but that he'd been curious as to what I'd written down about one of the recipes we'd made —I forget which one," Gracie confessed to Jack. "Anyway, as he was leafing through it to find my notes, he saw the things I'd written in the back— some of Chef Pernod's famous quotes and tips, and then found the page where I'd outlined what had happened to Angelique, and listed people I thought might have had a reason to want her dead. He told the police that when he saw his name on the list, with a check mark beside it, he had just assumed that I thought he was the murderer."

"Turns out he was," Jack noted laconically.

"Well, kinda: there really was no murder, *per se*," Gracie corrected him. "And ironically, of course, in my shorthand, what that check mark next to Philippe's name really meant was that I thought he was okay, not at all involved," she went on. "I would never have considered the possibility that it might be someone from so long ago in Angelique's past who would be involved, now," she admitted. "And of course, I didn't know about Philippe being Sophie's father until, well, until it was too late." She paused. "And I think I kinda assumed that because Philippe was a Detective, he was above suspicion," she added ruefully.

Jack chuckled aloud now. "Well, that's nice you have such a high opinion of law enforcement, Gracie, but you know as well as I do that we're all just people. If something hurts us deeply enough—and particularly if there's shock and surprise involved—we can act irrationally, just like anyone else," he explained.

"Yes, of course, you're right," Gracie agreed.

"But I thought you said Philippe had left Monday, with everyone else?" Jack asked then.

"He did," Gracie confirmed. "But he returned that evening before the alarm was set at nine o'clock, and slipped in without being seen."

"No CC-TV?"

"Nope. So, Philippe had decided to hide out in the Chapel store room of all places," Gracie related, "until he could get me on my own. He knew I was the only guest at the Château this week, and he knew Claude was way up on the top floor, and Monique and Michel leave once everything is done for the night. He saw me go into the Library after dinner, and while Claude and everyone were still milling around—Michel had his jazz music playing in the dining room, I remember, because it was loud enough that I could hear it from the Library—he sneaked out of the store room and knocked out the hallway light near the Chapel, using the music as cover."

"Handy. So with the light out, he could follow you without you seeing him, at least at first," Jack put in. Gracie had told him about the automatic lighting at the Château.

"Right." She sighed. "I should have been more suspicious of him."

"But why? Like you said, he's a police Detective, probably the last person you'd typically suspect of something like this."

"Yeah, but when he kept bugging me about calling the police to tell them that Gary might have had a motive," Gracie murmured ruefully. "I should have suspected something was up, but instead I was flattered that he thought my theory was so strong. In hindsight, of course, I can see that he was way too motivated to throw suspicion on someone other than himself."

Jack chuckled. "Well, you were caught up in the investigation and everything," he reassured her. "Hard to be objective."

"Well, maybe: but I should have realized how much Philippe and Sophie look alike!" Gracie protested.

"But why, Gracie: you had no reason to think they could be related," Jack countered. "Lots of people have green eyes and slightly crooked teeth.

Angelique had told you Sophie's father had died. You had accepted that as fact, so the possibility of her father being alive wasn't one you were even considering."

"Yes, you're right. And I have to say, Jack, I'm really grateful to you for being so supportive," she added thoughtfully. "I expected you'd be angry with me for getting myself in a sticky situation," she explained.

"Angry? No, Gracie." Jack sighed. "I get upset if I think you take unnecessary risks, but in this case, you did nothing wrong."

"But if I'd just been a little more suspicious, a little more vigilant…and more careful, not to leave that notebook behind!" Gracie insisted.

"Well, if you hadn't, Philippe probably would have got away with it. No one would have ever figured out who'd been arguing with Angelique when she fell and hit her head," Jack reassured her. "It was actually good luck, from a crime solving point of view at least, that you forgot the notebook, and that Philippe is so nosy he looked through it," he added. "I'm just glad you're okay."

Gracie could hear the smile in his voice, and sighed again, but this time happily. She had been moved, at Claude's insistence, to the loveliest room in the Château, the suite that the Bernards had vacated the day before. Monique herself had cleaned the room, and put a vase of bright mixed spring flowers on the bureau. The door to Gracie's original room had, of course, been shattered by Philippe when he had been pursuing Gracie. Oddly enough, the deadbolt had held, but the wooden door itself was in ruins.

'Good to know the hardware is reliable,' Claude had quipped when he viewed the damage. And, he had told Gracie he had plans to install security cameras, at least around the Château's exterior.

"Oh, I am, Jack: I'm fine. And I'm looking forward to finally, finally getting some sightseeing done!" she laughed.

They spoke for a few more minutes about the châteaux and villages Gracie was planning to see: Amboise, Blois and a few others.

"Sounds like you've got it all planned out, and it should be fun," Jack agreed. "So…when are you coming home?" he asked. It was the question uppermost in his mind. He knew Gracie had enjoyed the course, and would adore driving around seeing châteaux and charming picturesque towns, but he missed her. Rather a lot.

"Well, I called Tyler and Joey, and Pumpkin is doing fine, and then I called the airlines and explained that I needed to change my flight home," Gracie replied. "I'll be home Sunday night."

Jack said nothing. Originally, Gracie had intended to fly back on Thursday, but since her schedule had been interrupted by recent events, Jack supposed he couldn't begrudge her a couple of extra days. Then: "so…where are you going this afternoon? What is it, about two o'clock there?" he asked solicitously.

"Just about," Gracie replied. "I think I'll drive to Chenonceaux," she told him. "That's only about a half hour away, and it's a pretty drive along the Loire, according to Monique."

"Well, be careful, and have fun," Jack told her. "And no, the two are not mutually exclusive," he quipped as they said goodbye and disconnected the call.

Gracie went to the large double glass doors that led to the gracious stone balcony off her beautiful new suite. She opened them, stepped out, and then leaned over the balustrade and regarded the view of the small hill that was to one side of the Château, and the distant red clay colored rooftops of the village of Reignac.

She sighed.

—33—
FINIS

www.ingramcontent.com/pod-product-compliance
Lightning Source LLC
Chambersburg PA
CBHW030550260626
47157CB00006B/2259